MURDER AT THE 42ND STREET LIBRARY

ALSO BY CON LEHANE

What Goes Around Comes Around

Death at the Old Hotel

Beware the Solitary Drinker

CON LEHANE

MINOTAUR BOOKS
A THOMAS DUNNE BOOK
NEW YORK

For Librarians Everywhere

A THOMAS DUNNE BOOK FOR MINOTAUR BOOKS.
An imprint of St. Martin's Publishing Group.

www.thomasdunnebooks.com
www.minotaurbooks.com

Designed by Omar Chapa

Library of Congress Cataloging-in-Publication Data

Names: Lehane, Cornelius, author.
Title: Murder at the 42nd Street library : a mystery / Con Lehane.
Description: First edition. | New York : Minotaur Books, 2016. | "A Thomas Dunne book."
Identifiers: LCCN 2015045810| ISBN 9781250009968 (hardcover) | ISBN 9781250036872 (e-book)
Subjects: LCSH: Murder—Investigation—Fiction. | Libraries—Fiction. | BISAC: FICTION / Mystery & Detective / General. | GSAFD: Mystery fiction.
Classification: LCC PS3612.E354 M87 2016 | DDC 813/.6—dc23
LC record available at http://lccn.loc.gov/2015045810

Our books may be purchased in bulk for promotional, educational, or business use. Please contact the Macmillan Corporate and Premium Sales Department at 1-800-221-7945, extension 5442, or by e-mail at MacmillanSpecialMarkets@macmillan.com.

First Edition: April 2016

10 9 8 7 6 5 4 3 2 1

Acknowledgments

Librarians are among the most knowledgeable and helpful people in the world, generous to a fault with their time and knowledge—and underappreciated and underpaid almost everywhere. Here I want to thank the multitudes of librarians in schools, colleges, and public libraries who over the years helped me in so many ways, beginning with the kind woman who checked out my first book—about Matilda the cat—from the Greenwich, Connecticut, public library when I was in first grade.

Special thanks to Jay Barksdale, now retired, who presided over the study rooms at the 42nd Street Library and who welcomed me to the fold of the Frederick Lewis Allen room (where I wrote a good part of this book), despite my questionable credentials, and answered a ridiculous number of questions about the workings of the library. Thanks also to Carolyn Broomhead who carried on Jay's guardianship of the study rooms when he retired. She, too, answered myriad questions and took me on an eye-opening, back-of-the-house tour of the 42nd Street Library (carrels in the stacks, a carpentry workshop, who would have guessed?). Thomas Lannon, the 42nd Street Library's Acting Charles J. Liebman Curator of Manuscripts, sat down with me a number of times to talk about what curators of library special collections actually do. He did this with patience and good humor, while providing a running commentary on the history of New York City. Dr. Isaac Gewirtz, Curator of the Henry W. and Albert A. Berg Collection of English and American Literature, provided an introduction to the remarkable collection he presides over.

Lesa Holstine, Collection Development Manager at Evansville Vanderburgh Public Library in Evansville, Indiana, formerly Arizona Librarian of the Year, proprietor of *Lesa's Book Critiques* blog, as well as a book reviewer for a number of journals including *Library Journal*—and friend to mystery writers everywhere—helped me so much when I was first embarking on this endeavor. My thanks, too, to Jane Murphy of the Westport, Connecticut Public Library, who also helped immensely in the beginning stages of the book and introduced me to a bibliography of librarian detectives. Doris Ann Norris, Molly Weston, Kaye Wilkinson Barley, and many others, librarians and other mystery lovers, on the listserv DorothyL have kept me informed and entertained for more than a decade now.

My agent Alice Martell provides great advice, never fails to return calls, responds to requests in seconds, and, best of all, is ever hopeful. My editor at Thomas Dunne Books, Marcia Markland, rescued me years ago from the remainder bin at the Strand Bookstore and has stuck with me ever since. Quressa Robinson, also at Thomas Dunne Books, provided editorial suggestions for the book that were invaluable. My thanks also to everyone else at Minotaur/Thomas Dunne/St. Martins, especially copy editor David Stanford Burn, Hector DeJean and Sarah Melnyk in Minotaur's publicity department, and Talia

Sherer, Macmillan authors' fabulous link to the librarians of the world. Thanks to Tom Mann for his astute comments on the book, and a special thanks to Roan Chapin, the best first reader ever, who came to know my characters at least as well as I did and helped me see them for who they are.

Author's Note

In the spirit of the times, I've made some alterations to the iconic 42nd Street Library. For the most part, I've left reading rooms and stairways and such things—and most importantly, the stacks—where the original architects of the library put them. I did add an office, Harry's, and a reading room, the crime fiction collection, to the second floor, and moved a couple of other rooms to places I could better get at them. While the New York Public Library has world-renowned collections, including the Manuscript and Archives Division, the Henry W. and Albert A. Berg Collection of English and American Literature, and others, alas, you will look in vain for the library's crime fiction collection. It is a figment of my imagination, as are all of the characters populating these pages. Any resemblance to any person, living or dead, is coincidental.

I and the public know
What all schoolchildren learn,
Those to whom evil is done
Do evil in return

—W. H. AUDEN

Prologue

Dr. James Donnelly climbed out of a cab on Fifth Avenue in front of the marble stairway that led to the entrance of the 42nd Street Library, pulling his worn leather shoulder bag behind him. He wore a green tweed sport jacket over a green sweater-vest, brown gabardine slacks, and brown loafers; his salt-and-pepper beard was neatly trimmed and shaped. A passerby might have seen his bearing and his expression as haughty, and thought him arrogant, as he studied the building in front of him. A scholar, he felt awe in the presence of one of the world's great libraries. The haughty expression was to steel himself for what lay in front of him.

As he started up the steps between the two marble lions to the main entrance, he didn't notice the person who watched him from the curb and climbed the stairs a few seconds later. Donnelly, unaccustomed to being followed, didn't think to look behind him. Had he done so he would have recognized the person. Certainly, he would have been surprised. It's far from certain he would have been fearful, though he should have been.

After catching his breath in the rotunda, he headed up another set of marble stairs to the second floor. The person following lingered for a moment in the lobby before setting off behind him. If Donnelly heard footsteps, he paid them no attention. He knocked on the door to the office of Harry Larkin, the director of library Special Collections, and waited until he was buzzed in. He took a few steps into the room, letting the door close. Seconds later, the door beeped, clicked, and opened behind him. He turned to look. At that moment, he recognized the face that was inches from his, felt cold, hard steel pressing against his neck, and knew he was about to die and why. If he heard the explosion that ripped his throat open, shattered his jaw, and sent a bullet through his mouth into his brain, it wouldn't have been for more than a fraction of a second. The second bullet wasn't necessary.

Harry looked up as Donnelly entered. He saw the door open again, caught a fleeting glimpse of the person who came in next. He didn't notice the gun until after he heard the shots that killed Donnelly and saw the barrel turn toward him. Diving behind his desk, Harry heard the next two shots splintering the wooden desk and caroming off the marble wall. Waiting to die, he didn't see or hear anything else, not the clatter of footsteps echoing along the marble hallway toward the back staircase, not the startled cries of a group of Asian teenagers as the killer bowled through them on the way down the stairs.

The killer, not looking like anyone would imagine a killer to look, sprinted down the stairs on the 42nd Street side of the library to the ground floor and left by the side door next to Children's Center, walking calmly past the guard in his booth, turning right, ducking into the subway entrance, and boarding a Queens-bound 7 train, as if it were a waiting getaway car.

Chapter 1

The morning was chilly, damp, and gray, an April Friday morning in a Brooklyn cemetery. Early April shouldn't be so cold, but such cruel days descended on New York almost every spring. The damp, chilly air, portending rain, reminded Raymond Ambler of playing baseball as a boy on such a day, the grass recently starting to grow in green, forsythia bright yellow against the dull gray of the day, daffodils bobbing in the cold wind in the yards of row houses across the street from the parade grounds in Windsor Terrace. Your hand stung if you caught a line drive and both hands stung unmercifully if you held the bat too loosely when you hit the ball.

Ambler shivered as he waited in the chilly wind, flecked with drops of rain, for Harry Larkin, his friend and supervisor at the 42nd Street library. That Harry was late wasn't surprising. A medieval historian, former Jesuit, and absent-minded scholar, Harry wasn't noted for his promptness. He ran the library's Special Collections Division as haphazardly as the proprietor of one of the dust-covered odds-and-ends stores you once found along Broadway below 34th Street before the garment district began to gentrify. What you were looking for might be there in the store, but the proprietor was the only person with a hope of finding it.

Adele Morgan, who also worked in Special Collections, where Ambler was the curator of the collection in crime fiction, asked Harry, even though he was no longer a priest, to perform the Catholic burial service for her mother. Ambler hadn't known Adele was Catholic. He came to the funeral because in recent years she'd become his best friend.

For reasons not clear to Ambler, Adele took a liking to him the first day she arrived at the main branch of the library and hung her diploma from the School of Library and Information Science at the University of Iowa on the wall of the cubicle next to his. Since then, with the exuberance of an Iowa cheerleader and the smart-alecky cynicism of a Brooklyn roller-rink queen, she'd taken him under her wing, defending him against the not infrequent fallout from his lack of social graces, pugnacity, and proclivity to take on quixotic battles for truth and justice that no one else much cared about.

He didn't know how old her mother was when she died. He suspected still in her fifties, not much older than him. She'd died quickly after a diagnosis of lung cancer from a lifetime of smoking—Brooklyn girls of her era began smoking cigarettes in front of candy stores and on neighborhood stoops when they were around thirteen.

On the morning of the funeral, he rode in the funeral home limousine with Adele, an arrangement that caused him some embarrassment because Adele's on-again, off-again boyfriend Peter should by rights have been her escort. With no explanation, she took his arm and walked with him from the church to the car, leaving Peter standing on the sidewalk in front of the church.

Wearing a black dress, a black veil over her pale face, her lips red with a thin line of lipstick, his friend, whom he'd always thought pretty, became, in her grief, hauntingly beautiful.

"It's not that she died young, still in her prime," Adele said three days earlier when she told Ambler of her mother's death. "She never lived. She died four blocks from the house she grew up in, married young, never left the neighborhood. She went into Manhattan a half-dozen times in her life."

Adele cried in his arms after that, her head pressed against his chest, her tears dampening his shirt. He'd gone with her from the hospital back to the house where she'd lived with her mother since she was a child, except for her time away at college. She'd made him dinner, leftover chicken casserole of some sort that seemed appropriate to the modest, working-class neighborhood in South Brooklyn.

They drank wine. When neighbors called on the phone, she spoke to them briefly. The few who knocked on the door, she spoke to on the stoop. When it got late and Ambler made to leave, she asked him to stay. He slept with her nestled in his arms, both of them fully clothed. Yet at some time during the night, their mouths met. They kissed gently and went back to sleep, Adele still in his arms. When he left in the morning, neither of them mentioned the kiss or their night together.

At the cemetery, by the time Harry finally arrived, tumbling out of a taxi a few rows of gravestones from the burial plot, the chilly wind whipped droplets of rain against Ambler's face. He'd worn only his suit, no topcoat. The same wind pressed Adele's black knit dress against her thighs and carried most of Harry's words off toward Jamaica Bay. The group around the grave was small, mostly women from the neighborhood, most of them past middle age. Fewer than expected showed up because of an informal boycott by the strict-constructionist Catholics who saw the proceedings as sacrilegious because of Harry's defrocked status. Ambler found it strange that Adele seemed to have no relatives.

Harry, normally a cheerful, roly-poly sort, a veritable Friar Tuck, was this day distracted and out of sorts but didn't explain why until after the handful of folks who'd gathered after the funeral at what was now Adele's home, or stopped by carrying chafing dishes of meatballs, tuna salad, and such things, were gone—and after he'd gulped down a good-sized tumbler of brandy.

"Someone was shot in the library?"

"Killed," Harry said. "Murdered. Right in front of my eyes."

"Who?"

"A man who came to my office."

"Who shot him?"

"God, if I know . . . a crazed killer."

"Is there any other kind?" Adele asked. She was frozen to the spot, a glass in one hand, bottle in the other, about to pour Ambler a glass of wine.

"A philosophical question," said Ambler. "Does someone need to be insane to commit a murder? Perhaps. Practically speaking, insanity doesn't provide much of a murder defense."

"It wasn't really a question," said Adele.

"The killer got away?"

"It seems so." Harry looked helplessly at Ambler, seeming bewildered by what happened, drifting off into his thoughts or memory every few seconds, staring blankly into space.

"What now?" Ambler asked Adele. He was helping her wash dishes and wrap and put away leftovers after they'd poured frazzled, tipsy Harry into a car service cab and sent him off.

"I want to get out of this neighborhood as quickly as I can.

I'm terrified I'll end up like my mother." Her face was drawn, with lines at the corners of her mouth he hadn't seen before. Her voice was strained.

"Your life will be different than hers," Ambler said.

She straightened up from stuffing the last of the plastic containers of leftovers into the refrigerator and faced him. "How different, Raymond? How will it be different?" She sounded irritated, angry, but really she was sad. "Life is pretty miserable for most people, isn't it? Sad, painful, lonely—" Her eyes sought his, a rebuke; then, in seconds, the sadness returned; her lip quivered. He hesitated before walking closer to her and placing his hand on her shoulder. Leaning into him, her voice small, she said, "I'm missing so much in my life." In another few seconds, she broke away from him.

Adele was pretty, with blondish hair cut short, soft, full lips, and dimples so she looked impish when she smiled. Her prettiness seemed a kind of afterthought, as if she didn't pay much attention to it; even so, he sensed she knew she was pretty. Her sadness made her seem fragile. He didn't know what to say to comfort her. Like her voice, she seemed to have grown smaller. He wanted to take her in his arms. But he didn't think she wanted that. She did want to talk, so he let her.

"She had a house. She made a living," Adele said. Her mother had worked for the telephone company since she graduated high school. "And she had a child she raised by herself. A child was something, even if it was only me." Adele's voice held a good deal of regret. Things had gone wrong in her life. Her father left her mother and her early on. She'd had her own difficulties, an early romance that went badly. She didn't explain and he didn't ask. He sensed that what they spoke about made little difference. Talking kept her connected to someone. When he left, she'd be alone, alone in a different way than she'd ever been.

Later, on the long, jerky train ride back to Manhattan, mired in Adele's sadness, as if it were contagious, he began to think about the murder at the library. The subway car, dingy and dimly lit, with only a few other passengers, tired and bedraggled as he was, had an ominous feel, reminding him he was in the city late at night and danger wasn't far away—not as much danger as in years past, but reason to keep alert. He eyed his fellow passengers and checked the subway's doors each time they opened.

Thinking about the murder depressed him. At the same time, an unsolved, or yet to be solved, homicide piqued his interest. He'd believed since he read Camus in college that taking someone's life for any reason could not be justified. He saw no irony between this belief, a kind of pacifism, and his interest in homicide investigation. Camus's characters battled pestilence without hope but without despair. "The task is impossible," Camus said, "so let us begin."

Chapter 2

The 42nd Street Library stretches along the west side of Fifth Avenue from 42nd to 40th Street. The landmark beaux arts structure houses the humanities and social sciences collections of the New York Public Library, the largest research collection of any public library in the nation after the Library of Congress.

The collections are available to journalists, historians, and other scholars, graduate students writing dissertations, authors working on books, individuals tracing a family tree, anyone who wants read a newspaper or magazine, and many others. But the books, journals, manuscripts, maps, photographs, newspapers, baseball cards, comic books, don't circulate. The 42nd Street Library is a research library, not a circulating library. Everything stays in the library. Under such an arrangement, it has served the research needs of millions for decades.

The Rose reading room, on the third floor, is two city blocks long with rows and rows of long oak tables and chairs. The tables stretch out on either side of a small foyer and a central desk where readers turn in their call slips and pick up materials that have been retrieved by pages from the seven levels of iron and steel shelving beneath the reading room. The Rose reading room is the largest of a number of reading rooms in the building. The Manuscripts and Archives Division reading room is at the north end of the main room, the Berg Collection of English and American Literature is also on the third floor, along with the Arents Tobacco Collection and the Carl H. Pforzheimer Collection of Shelley and His Circle. Throughout the building are other smaller reading rooms housing collections of various sorts, including Ambler's tiny crime fiction collection on the second floor.

On the morning after the funeral, he got to the library early, using the 40th Street entrance, across from the black and gold American Radiator Building—once the proud home office of the eponymous manufacturing company now the Bryant Park Hotel. Two uniformed city cops stood next to the security booth with the library's guard, reminding Ambler, if he needed reminding, that a murder had taken place.

After climbing the marble stairs to the second floor, he sat at his cluttered desk, not unaware of the irony that the bookshelves on the walls around him and on another tier of shelves on a catwalk-like mezzanine above him held many of the finest detective novels ever written. It would be an hour or more before the library opened. In the meantime, he needed to call up the collection of an obscure Dallas mystery writer, Sam Hawkins, who'd written a series of police procedurals in the 1940s featuring a Texas Ranger. A graduate student working on her dissertation e-mailed the library a week earlier requesting the files. He had no idea how she'd found Hawkins or discovered his papers at the library.

The writer died in combat in Korea, leaving no heirs to claim his effects. His papers ended up in Ambler's crime fiction collection because he'd entrusted them along with his books and other worldly possessions to his agent when he went off to war. The agent later donated them to the library and the collection gathered dust in the archive stacks until Ambler found it and added it to the crime fiction collection.

He was filling out the call slips for the boxes when the door banged open and Adele burst into the room. "Have you heard?"

He looked at her blankly.

"The murdered man is Kay Donnelly's ex-husband."

"Who?"

"She's a reader working on the Nelson Yates collection."

He recalled an earnest young woman, probably in her thirties, whom you wouldn't pay much attention to until some liveliness in her eyes suggested her understated manner might be a cover for a more adventurous spirit. "I wouldn't have thought her the type to have an ex-husband."

Adele wrinkled her nose. "I'm surprised you paid so much attention to her. What type of woman does have an ex-husband, by the way? Different I suppose than the type like me who's never had a husband."

Ambler knew he'd said something wrong. He wasn't sure what.

"Actually, Kay is the only one of that crew using the Yates collection who's halfway civil. The head guy's a pompous ass, and his wife's a glamour puss who thinks she shits Baby Ruths."

Ambler lowered the papers he'd been sorting through, to scrutinize Adele as if he weren't quite sure what he'd heard.

"Sorry." She tossed her head like a pony and headed for the door. "An old Brooklyn expression."

As the morning wore on, everyone who worked in the library, it seemed, stopped by his desk, assuming—for no sensible reason—that he knew more than they did about the murder. He told them he had no idea what happened but that in most murders the victim knows the killer, so they shouldn't suspect a killer with a vendetta against the library was on the loose and would pick them off one by one. He doubted he convinced anyone. For most of the day, the snaps and clicks of office door locks echoed along the marble hallways.

The afternoon sunny and mild after the chilly drizzle of the day before, he took his lunch to the terrace behind the library overlooking Bryant Park, where he often sat before work or after lunch in nice weather. A panhandler stumbling past reminded him of the morning he first came to work at the library. On that morning in the mid eighties, you couldn't take three steps into Bryant Park before being accosted by a herd of winos looking for handouts or a parade of skinny, nervous kids whispering, "smoke." A murder wouldn't have been out of place in those days.

A freshly sodded lawn, wrought iron tables and café chairs, sculpted ivy beds, a small, cheerful merry-go-round, and fashionable Manhattanites sipping lattes from the kiosk near Sixth Avenue replaced the scraggly bushes, plastic garbage bags, beer cans, pint wine bottles, used rubbers, and sleeping winos one would have found in the park in those days. Little did he know when it began that the restoration of the park in the early nineties was a harbinger of the sanitizing and homogenizing that would turn Times Square—and soon the rest of Manhattan—into the Mall of America.

Looking up from his ham and brie sandwich—whatever happened to Swiss—he saw a truculent looking man in a well-worn trench coat, open like a sail, striding in his direction and recognized Mike Cosgrove of the NYPD homicide squad.

"Got a minute?" Cosgrove said. The detective's twenty-plus years of dead bodies and senseless killings were carved into his face, his dark eyes blazed out of deep sockets like polished black stones, his hair, now steel gray, was still in the marine crew cut he'd worn in Vietnam. He'd given up smoking some years back, substituting toothpicks, one of which danced across his lips.

"Good to see you, too, Mike." Ambler smiled. Despite their differences in almost all ways possible, he liked Mike Cosgrove. Besides being the only NYPD homicide detective who didn't go ballistic when he tried out his ideas on crime detection on cases he worked on, Mike was observant, and thoughtful—and not always so sure he was right. He pondered things. He had imagination.

They'd met a few years before when Ambler began an investigation on a whim after reading about the death of a man in Kips Bay. He was intrigued by a photo of the widow in the *Daily News* because of something peculiar in the expression of the man standing behind her. Her husband, the man who was killed, a financier, was run over by a cab on Park Avenue South on a rainy night.

The incident made the tabloids because of the size of the insurance policy he carried—five million dollars—and the fact that the policy contained a double indemnity clause. The coincidence was so glaring he began to look into the accident. He discovered the victim died of a broken neck—not unheard of in a pedestrian fatality but not that usual either. When he phoned the NYPD detective in charge of the case, he met Mike Cosgrove. They compared notes. Later, Cosgrove found the widow and the lawyer vacationing in Cancún. The rest was history.

Cosgrove's expression didn't change. He nodded in the direction of the library. "In there, when I ask a question, everyone says talk to you. They think you're in charge of the investigation."

Ambler laughed.

Cosgrove gestured with his head, this time toward the park.

"Everyone's nervous," Ambler said as they walked down the steps and onto the gravel walk that bordered the central lawn.

"They should be." Cosgrove's hard-eyed stare took in the tourists strolling through the park and the office workers hurrying along the sidewalk on 40th Street alongside the park. A blaring horn from a delivery truck stuck in traffic interrupted the steady hum of the city. "So, what happened?"

Ambler shook his head. "All I know is rumors."

"We'll get to the rumors. What do you know about the victim?"

"Almost nothing. I'm told he was the ex-husband of a reader in the library."

"A reader?"

"That's what we call our patrons. Kay Donnelly. She's doing research."

"Have you talked to her?"

"Is she a suspect?"

Cosgrove raised his eyebrows. "Is she your suspect? An ex-husband fits for a victim who brought it on himself."

Ambler shook his head. "That's not exactly my theory."

"What's she like?"

"From the little I've seen of her, she's intense, driven, aloof, like a lot of women who've worked their way up in the halls of academe. She's an assistant—or as they say in those circles a junior colleague—of Maximilian Wagner, who's writing a biography of Nelson Yates, a writer whose papers the library recently acquired."

"The victim, James Donnelly, was a writer."

Ambler shook his head. "I don't recognize the name."

"What about Maximilian Wagner, the guy you mentioned?"

Ambler stopped walking. He had a lot to say about Max Wagner, not anything to do with the murder though. "He calls himself a literary biographer. Actually, he's a scandal-mongering sensationalist posing as a scholar."

"Am I picking up distaste?"

Ambler smiled. "There you go with those powers of detection."

"This Nelson Yates is one of yours, a mystery writer?"

Ambler nodded. "Maybe the best of his generation."

"You know him?"

He'd like to say he did. A few years ago, he'd interviewed Yates at a library forum. They'd had dinner and drinks afterward, and talked well into the evening. After that, he'd emailed the writer a couple of times when one of his books came out, and Yates responded with thanks and a suggestion they get together again one day for a drink. You wouldn't call them friends. Yet Harry said that during the negotiations for his papers Yates asked if Ambler was still in charge of the crime fiction collection.

"We've met," he told Cosgrove. "Had dinner and a couple of drinks together. Having a drink with a hero . . . like you slugging down shots and beers with Dirty Harry."

Cosgrove chuckled.

Another reason he liked Cosgrove, not what you'd expect; he got the irony of things.

"How about Larkin, the ex-priest, the director of whatever it is—"

"Special Collections."

"Collections. Who'd want to kill him?"

Ambler stopped. Harry? Kill Harry? "No one. He's a saint."

Cosgrove grunted. "Saints get killed, too. That's how some of 'em got their positions. Whoever killed Donnelly took a couple of shots at the Jesuit."

Ambler considered this. Harry didn't mention it. "Maybe because he was a witness."

"Maybe. Was there some trouble with the deal for that Yates collection? Do people fight over that kind of stuff?"

Cosgrove was good, no denying it. If it was something connected to his case, he caught it. If he didn't hear it or see it, he smelled it in the air. There was competition for the Yates papers. The acquisition was unusual—an anonymous donor provided the funding, everything done quietly, not exactly secretly, but without fanfare. Since Yates would be part of the crime fiction collection, Ambler should have been involved in the acquisition. But he wasn't. At one point, there was a problem—meetings behind closed doors, Harry hurrying out of the library unexpectedly two or three times. No one told Ambler anything. Harry made clear he shouldn't ask. Then, it was over. The library had the collection. He told Cosgrove what he knew.

"Donnelly, the victim, had an interest in the Yates collection. It might not mean anything. Could be he has a current wife who wanted him killed. He might have stepped on someone's toe on the way into the library. That's a killing they had up in the Bronx last week, only at a bodega not a library."

When they started walking again, Cosgrove was quiet, but Ambler knew what was coming. "Are you going to get involved in this one, Ray?"

Now it was his turn to be quiet. Even before Cosgrove told him the killer shot at Harry, he was troubled. Surely, a killer could find a better place than the library to do his work—unless the killer was already there, hidden among the staff like the purloined letter.

"Are you telling me not to?"

"Would it do any good?" Ambler followed Cosgrove's gaze as he looked out over the newly sodded, bright green lawn at the center of the park. A small fence of thin rope, no more than a foot off the ground, girded the lawn; small signs asked folks to stay off the new grass until it established its roots. "One more thing . . . a witness said the victim was carrying a briefcase when he got to the library. We didn't find it on or near the body. Larkin says he didn't see a bag."

Ambler raised his eyebrows.

They'd circled the park twice and walked to the corner of Fifth Avenue near the library's main entrance. Cosgrove stopped and watched a man getting a shoeshine on the stand near the corner. "Maybe the friar will open up to you."

"You've lifted the ban on my butting into your investigations?"

"No. We're better at this than you are. You got lucky a couple of times and helped. You as easily could've gotten yourself or someone else dead, not to mention contaminating evidence, tipping off suspects, or finding other ways to fuck up an investigation."

"I never thought otherwise."

Their eyes held, until Cosgrove broke off with a slight smile. "Okay, my friend, what's next on the recommended reading list?"

"Try Yates."

After watching Cosgrove walk away down Fifth Avenue, Ambler stood for a moment in front of the library, taking in the grandeur of the building—the lions, Patience and Fortitude, standing guard, the marble steps, the massive bronze doors, the flow of tourists up and down the stairs. Mike didn't usually tell him any more about an investigation than he'd tell the press—things that were public. This was understood between them. He'd listen to what Ambler had to say. He might even ask Ambler what he thought of something. Ambler knew not to ask him anything beyond that about a police matter.

What he knew after talking to Mike was that the victim was a writer, had an interest in the Yates collection, and had been carrying a book bag or briefcase that disappeared. He'd also learned that the killer fired shots at Harry. Harry hadn't told him any of this. But then he hadn't asked him about the murder yet.

Near the end of the day, Ambler stopped by Harry's office, hesitating for a moment in the doorway to watch Harry, who was working at his computer and didn't hear him come in. He cleared his throat and knocked on the doorjamb.

"Jesus, Harry! After what happened I'd think you'd be more aware of someone at your door."

Harry looked up. "I was sending an e-mail."

"The police think someone tried to kill you."

"No one tried to kill me."

"Someone shot at you."

Harry swiveled his chair to face Ambler. "You don't have to tell me. I assume it was a warning not to follow."

Ambler searched Harry's face. Something was wrong; some pain in his usually mild expression made him look older and careworn. "Do you mind telling me what happened with the shooting?"

"I've told the police everything I remember."

"You might have missed something . . . something that might prevent another murder."

Harry cringed. "I don't believe that. Why would there be another murder? That's your imagination again. This isn't a detective novel."

"Why did James Donnelly come to your office?"

"I don't know." Irritation edged Harry's voice.

"Was it about the Yates papers?"

"Why do you ask that?" Here it was again, something hanging in the air unsaid. It was like he was visiting a friend with an illness neither of them wanted to talk about.

"Mike Cosgrove said Donnelly had an interest in the collection."

Harry took off his glasses and rubbed his eyes. "The killer shot Donnelly, not me."

"That's why I asked. What did the shooting have to do with the Yates collection?"

Harry didn't hide his impatience. "The person who did the shooting didn't make a speech. Asking me a lot of question won't change that. And I have work to do—and so do you."

Ambler was out of sorts when he went back to his desk. He browsed through an auction catalog, but his attention wandered. What the hell was going on with Harry? He was too guileless to get away with a cover-up—and what in God's name would he be covering up—but that's exactly what he was doing. Asked an innocuous question, he squirmed like he was getting the third degree.

Chapter 3

Ambler got to the Library Tavern that evening as cocktail hour was winding down, a more subdued and more relaxed gathering than during the week. McNulty the bartender glanced in his direction, the glance noting his arrival and suggesting he take his seat and wait until McNulty got to him, which wouldn't be long.

Brian McNulty was an old-school bartender who ruled over his establishment as if it were a fiefdom bestowed on him, rather than a job. The bar owners had given up trying to rein him in, since as curmudgeonly as he was, fully three quarters of the bar's patrons came specifically to see the bartender. Not much of a glad-hander, he earned the loyalty of the after-work crowd by his craftsmanship and by his sincere interest in those things the folks who frequented his bar wanted to tell him.

Ambler sat down. As he expected, before he was fully settled in, McNulty delivered his beer. A few minutes later, Adele came through the door. She squinted at Ambler. "What's the matter with you? Pretty soon, you'll be as grumpy as McNulty."

The bartender, not far away, shot her a mildly reproachful glance and went back to making the drinks a waitress had ordered. Finished, he sauntered over. "Did you take a number when you came in?"

"I don't want a beer. I want to try a new drink. Cognac and Coke." Adele was searching through her bag.

McNulty shook his head. "I'm not going to make that. It's a waste of Cognac."

She poked her head out of her purse. "I'm paying for it."

McNulty, both hands on the bar, bent toward her. "Drink the Cognac straight, in a snifter. With Coke have rum, if you must."

She turned to Ambler. "Is he like this to you?"

"Some days he's touchier than others."

"I'll go back to having a beer."

McNulty drew the beer and delivered it, taking a moment to lean on the bar in front of them. His hair was long enough to be considered shaggy, his expression somewhere between bored and impatient, his manner bordered on surly. What gave him away was the twinkling in those Irish blue eyes. "Doesn't she brighten up the evening?" he asked Ambler while looking at Adele, who smiled.

"What have you heard about the shooting in the library?" Ambler asked the bartender. He'd known McNulty a long time. A journeyman bartender and Equity-card carrying actor, the son of a card-carrying Communist, McNulty had had run-ins with, and at times ran with, any number of denizens of the mean streets. He'd also read half the books in Ambler's crime collection.

"I got something. Hang on a minute." He turned and walked to the service bar where two waitresses stood patiently. Neither had called him. They'd waited only a few seconds.

"He saw those servers out the back of his head," Adele said.

They sipped their beers watching McNulty.

"I had a strange conversation with Harry this afternoon," Ambler said. "I asked him about the shooting and he didn't want to talk about it. You'd think he'd be more concerned that someone shot at him."

Adele jolted up straight. "Someone shot at him?"

Ambler nodded. "Mike Cosgrove said the victim was interested in the Yates collection. Harry didn't want to talk about that either." He waited for her reaction. She'd been privy to some of the hush-hush negotiations over the Yates papers.

"That's strange." She paused. "That the man who was killed was interested in Nelson Yates is strange, not that Harry wouldn't talk about it. He's not supposed to."

"Someone didn't want the library to get the donation, right?"

"Nelson Yates didn't donate his papers. We paid for the collection." She paused, as they watched McNulty shaking a cocktail. "His wife, Mary, didn't want the papers to go to us. Someone else—I don't know who—made a fuss. Harry thought the deal might fall through. Then, we met with the donor—"

"The donor—"

Adele rolled her eyes. "Don't grill me, Sherlock." She put her hand on top of his to quiet him. "The funding came from a donor who doesn't want her name revealed."

"Do you know who the donor is? A her?"

"Anonymous, Raymond. An anonymous donor." She made a sour face. After another moment, she grabbed his forearm with both hands. "Guess what?"

He looked at her blankly.

"I'm moving to Manhattan."

"Oh?"

"I know. The rents are shocking. But I really want to live here. How about if I move in with you?"

Ambler felt a rush of panic.

She giggled. "You turned as white as a ghost." She peered into his eyes. "I'm not that bad, am I?"

"No. No. . . . No. You're not bad at all. It's . . . It's just—"

"Stop. I was kidding. I wouldn't want to live with you. You're too grouchy."

When their eyes met, something plaintive in her expression tugged at him. He'd lived alone for years. He was grumpy, and old, too; yet for a moment, the idea that Adele might come home with him and stay formed a picture in his mind, causing an unfamiliar longing for something he couldn't name.

"God, Raymond. What's wrong? You're about to have apoplexy. I said I was kidding."

He took a long swallow from his beer mug, watching her out of the corner of his eye.

"I might as well shack up with someone. I broke up with Peter, this time for good. I'm sure he's relieved. The big, handsome hunk, women fall all over him. He'll do fine." She watched Ambler, smiling, for a long moment. "I think I found an apartment in the West Fifties."

"Already?" Ambler tried to take a drink from his glass, but it was empty. He signaled to McNulty for another. "You have something to tell me?" he said when the bartender arrived with the beer.

McNulty leaned closer. "About the shooting."

"You know something about the shooting in the library?" Adele practically leaped at him.

McNulty shook his head. "This guy was in last night. He's doing something at the library, so he's been stopping in—a writer, your kind of guy. He writes detective novels. His name's Yates."

"Nelson Yates!" Adele's eyes shot open.

"He donated his papers to the library," Ambler said.

"A couple of guys at the bar were talking about the shooting.

I happened to be standing near him. He wasn't part of the conversation, drinking by himself. He said something I didn't get, so I asked him what he said. 'Chickens coming home to roost' was what he said."

"Was he drunk?" Ambler asked.

"He'd had a few. I asked him, 'The guy in the library?' He said, 'Chickens coming home to roost.'"

"What's that mean?"

McNulty looked aggrieved. "It's a saying. It means—

"I know what it means. I meant what did he mean. What chickens? Whose chickens?"

The bartender frowned. "The chickens, I believe, would be those of the deceased. Where they were coming from or why they arrived when they did, I couldn't tell you."

Adele laughed.

Ambler shot her an irritated glance and then turned it on McNulty. "Why's he telling you this?" His tone was more challenging than he meant it to be.

"People confide in their bartenders." McNulty challenged right back.

A little while later, after saying goodnight, clumsily, to Adele and putting her into a car service cab in front of the bar, Ambler walked across town the few blocks to his apartment. He'd lived on 36th Street between Second and Third avenues for more than twenty years, since the end of his marriage.

Thanks to rent stabilization, his rent was manageable. Other apartments in the building had been gutted and renovated to justify higher rents. His, on the third floor of the four-story brownstone, was much the same as when he'd moved in. But now, with Adele on his mind, he looked at it in a different way. A floor-through, the living room overlooking 36th Street, the bedroom in the back overlooking the asphalt and cement backyard of an apartment building that faced 37th Street. A hallway ran between the living room and the back of the apartment, a bathroom off the hallway, the kitchen at the end of the hallway next to the bedroom. By Manhattan standards, it was large and, yes, might easily be comfortable for two people.

Over the years since the end of his marriage to Liz, a few women had spent varying numbers of nights in the apartment with him, but no one moved in. His relationships, not that there were many, seemed to run their course in somewhere between a couple of weeks and six months, with long periods of solitariness between them. He didn't so much choose to be alone as recognize solitude as a kind of destiny.

The next afternoon, Sunday, Ambler glanced up from his computer screen to see Benny Barone open the door of the crime fiction reading room and look back over his shoulder before closing the door behind him.

"What's up?" Ambler asked.

Small and wiry, olive-complexioned, with jittery, somewhat squirrel-like, movements, Benny looked shifty, even when he wasn't tiptoeing into the room looking over his shoulder like he was on the lam. "Something weird's going on, man."

"Oh?"

"The dude I'm working with—" A knock on the entryway to the reading room froze Benny in mid-sentence.

The knock was followed by a tall, crew-cut, gray-haired man wearing a tweed jacket. He went immediately to Ambler. "I want him replaced." The man, whose head was shaped like a Rottweiler's and whose hair was the color and consistency of metal shavings, nodded toward Benny. His dark eyes were blazing.

Ambler didn't like Maximilian Wagner, the truculent reader who stood in front of him. "Benny's a good researcher, Max. I wouldn't know who to replace him with. Besides, that's Harry's job."

"That's a no?" He squared his shoulders. His thick chest heaved. "You're assigned to work with me on this kind of thing."

"I don't think so, Max."

Wagner's stance, legs apart, feet firmly planted, and demeanor, combative, were more that of a fight promoter than the literary biographer he'd made his name as, especially when he was angry, as he was now. He sputtered. "You haven't changed much have you?"

"What'd he mean by that?" Benny asked when Wagner turned on his heel and left.

"Once, in the dim, murky past, we were friends—"friends" probably isn't the right word. We knew one another."

"At Columbia?"

"At Columbia."

Benny waited. Ambler knew he wanted to ask what happened to Ambler at Columbia—something he never talked about—but knew better than to ask.

"I wouldn't mind being replaced," Benny said. "I don't like the guy."

"I understand. Max doesn't care what anyone thinks of him. That's his advantage over civilized people."

"What I came to tell you . . . " Benny lowered his voice. "Did you know he had an argument with the guy who was killed?"

"Oh?"

"I didn't hear the whole thing. The guy who got killed used to be married to Kay, Wagner's assistant."

"A love triangle?"

Benny's eyebrows shot up. "Love? . . . Kay? No. God, I hope not. She's—" He stopped. "No. It was something scholarly—plagiarism. I'm not sure. The guy was mad at Kay, too. He accused them both."

"Of what?"

He wrinkled his brow, seeming perplexed. "Something to do with the Yates biography, not a love thing."

"Did you tell the police about it?"

"I told Harry. That's why I wanted to ask you. You're friends with that detective, right? Harry said I shouldn't get involved."

"Too bad. I don't know why he'd say that. You need to tell the police." He dialed Cosgrove's number on his cell phone and handed the phone to Benny.

A while later, Ambler again looked up from his work—writing finding aids for a backlog of crime fiction collections that hadn't been processed—to see Kay Donnelly standing at the reading room door. Her face showed the strain she was under. Quite a bit younger than Wagner, her boss, probably in her mid-thirties, she was, as he'd told Cosgrove, tightly wound. Yet something in her bruised expression was appealing, a depth of understanding or possibly sympathy in her eyes, the kind of understanding that's a product of having understood some pain of your own.

"Hi," he said cheerfully. He didn't want to bring up the murder but thought it disingenuous to say nothing. He gestured toward a chair. "Sit down, Professor Donnelly. Kay, isn't it? May I call you Kay? I'm sorry about your ex-husband's death."

She frowned, making it clear she didn't want to sit down, didn't want to be called Kay, and didn't want to talk about her ex-husband's murder. Flashing a smile as sincere as a banker's handshake, she said, "Dr. Wagner doesn't understand how the Yates collection is organized. He wants you to arrange for me to go into the stacks, so I can see the entire collection."

Ambler scowled. Harry made him liaison between Wagner and the library staff, despite his objection, based on logic available only to Harry.

Kay Donnelly's rigidity—what they used to call "uptightness"—irritated him. "Sorry. Readers don't have access to the stacks, not even renowned scholars like Max."

"I'm sure exceptions have been made—" Her face was a mask.

"If they have, I didn't make them. We haven't processed the collection. No one could make sense of it. Max knows that."

He could see anger seeping around the edges of the mask. "What should I tell Dr. Wagner . . . that you won't help?"

She phrased the question carefully, a sneaky rebuke she couldn't be challenged on. He wasn't much into character analysis, but her style was that of an angry, aggrieved person who ducked out of the bushes, took her shot, and ducked back in, rather than go toe-to-toe with someone. He couldn't blame her if she spent a lot of time around Max Wagner.

"Try Harry."

After she left, he sat for a few moments wondering if he'd been chatting with a murderer. Cosgrove didn't say so, but according to the homicide book of Hoyle—she'd be at the top of the list of suspects.

"You're Mrs.—" As he was leaving for the day, Ambler thought he recognized the woman standing near the top of the main staircase in the second floor hallway.

"Not Mrs.—I'm Laura Lee McGlynn." She was pretty—glamorous, really—fashionably dressed in a beige blouse, black slacks, and dark green high-heeled shoes, a flash of color he didn't expect. She spoke with a pronounced southern accent. Dark, almost black hair framed her face and bangs brushed her forehead, her lips were red, her teeth sparkling white; her eyes danced as she held out her hand. "Doesn't Laura Lee sound better than some old Mrs. Somebody?" She laughed.

Laura Lee McGlynn came across as someone who made her living being attractive, an actress, a TV newswoman, a trophy wife. Yet her easy laughter gave her a certain charm, a kind of down-to-earth aura about her, along with the glamour.

Ambler was chatting with her, smiling more than he ordinarily did, and feeling a bit foolish because of it, when Max Wagner came chugging toward them along the second floor hallway. He kissed the woman's cheek, which she turned toward him, her expression for the briefest of moments like a child enduring an obligatory kiss from a fussy aunt.

"I see you've met my wife," Wagner said in a tone that suggested Ambler had gotten away with something.

"Just this minute."

"Max has no manners," Laura Lee said. "He only believes in—what's the term—"exchange value," I think. Social interaction has merit only if it benefits him."

Max watched his wife as she spoke before turning to face Ambler, meeting his gaze with a hard stare. A kind of systemic anger, low-level rage, simmered beneath his air of disdain, so you thought it just as well he was indifferent to you because if he wasn't he'd probably sink his teeth into your throat.

Ambler met the stare with his own steady gaze. He wasn't afraid of Max, and didn't care much what he did or thought, except to wonder where the anger came from, the anger and the drive—the kind of drive that would run you down or ruin you to get what he wanted, and the anger that must fuel it. Laura Lee had her husband's number all right. She also wore an engagement ring next to her wedding ring that had a diamond as big as a doorknob—exchange value for her? he wondered.

Max shifted his gaze to her. "I haven't told you Ray and I are old friends from grad school. He had quite a career."

"Oh?" said Laura Lee, smiling at Ambler.

The smile asked for an explanation that he didn't want to provide. "Max can tell you what happened. My academic career was derailed. How and why depends on who you ask."

"Ray was quite the man on campus: a college baseball player expected to go professional, a major political figure among the campus radicals, an up-and-coming American literature scholar. Now, here he is a librarian." He didn't need the smirk to make his point but threw it in anyway. That was Max. Overkill. One push too many. Never able to quit while he was ahead.

Ambler kept his expression placid. "Honest work, Max. Where would you be without librarians?" He turned to Laura Lee. "Max has a knack for fanciful biographies, doesn't he?"

He was tempted to ask about the argument with the murder victim but thought better of it. Like a lawyer with a hostile witness, he wanted to know the answer before he asked the question.

Laura Lee slipped out from under Max's arm as they waited in a line for the security guard at the door to check their bags. She wanted to shove him. For Max, putting his arm around her wasn't a simple gesture but a rite of ownership, showing off. He should know better than that. She wasn't something he'd won. She resisted the temptation to berate him where they stood, embarrassing him down to his toes, since he looked contrite enough now with his hands stuffed into his pockets like a truculent schoolboy.

Jim Donnelly's murder had freaked him out. She didn't get it, and he wouldn't explain. It was as if he knew who the murderer was, or if she didn't know better—or at least think she knew better—he'd killed Donnelly himself. Now he was going on about Ambler the librarian. Max wasn't normally afraid of anyone, one of the reasons she liked him. Yet the librarian made him uneasy.

"Stay away from him."

"Why?"

"He'll ask questions. He's smart. Before you know it, you'll tell him your life story. He'll start into that, digging around, tearing it apart. You'll look up and see he's pieced things together. Knows a lot more than you intended to tell him. I've seen him operate."

"Don't be an ass, Max. What do you think I'll tell him? He's going to ask me about something that happened thirty years ago?"

Max's face was a map of troubles. His nerves were eating at him. "He'll look into Jim Donnelly's murder. You can bet on it. No matter what he says. That's what he does when a murder interests him even when it doesn't happen in his backyard. He'll discover we know Donnelly and want to know more."

Laura Lee grabbed Max's arm, turning him to face her. "What do you know about that murder that you're not telling me?"

He gave her that beady-eyed stare that meant he was keeping something from her. "Nothing. I don't know anything about it. Let's hope it was a random act that has nothing to do with us."

"Why would it have something to do with us?"

"I didn't say that." Sweat beaded on his forehead. "I said don't talk to Ray Ambler. He doesn't like me. He'll try to connect us to the murder."

"What do you mean us?"

They stopped talking while the bored guard made a cursory search of Max's book bag. Suddenly, the guard stiffened and then pulled a book out of the bag. He looked inside the cover and then held it up. "You can't take this out of the library."

Max looked around guiltily. His voice low, barely above a whisper, he said, "I'm a researcher. It's from the collection I'm working on—"

The guard raised his voice. "You can't take a book out of the library."

The line grew longer and people were murmuring to one another. Laura Lee was furious. "Give him the goddamn book, you idiot!"

"Take it," Max said.

"I'm not going to take it," the guard said. "Put it back where you got it."

Max slunk out of line and headed back to the Allen Room, where he kept his research materials.

"I'm going home," Laura Lee said as she walked out through the half-open revolving door. She didn't know if Max heard her or not.

Chapter 4

As Ambler left for lunch the next afternoon, he found Benny Barone sitting on the front steps of the library, eating a hot dog from the cart across the street, watching the traffic stream down Fifth Avenue. In the distance, beyond the Empire State Building, fluffy white clouds pushed by a gentle breeze skittered across a blue sky. The warm sun hinted at summer, a perfect spring day, except not for Benny, who looked miserable. Ambler stopped when he noticed his stormy expression.

"If I see that guy on the street, I'm going to push him in front of a bus," Benny said.

Ambler sat down. Wagner wasn't someone you wanted to run afoul of. Junior faculty, department heads, even deans who crossed him wound up doing the academic equivalent of selling pencils from a cup on the street. He watched the ebb and flow of pedestrians crossing Fifth Avenue in waves each time the signal lights changed. Benny was a city kid whose Bensonhurst roots ran deep—raised among those who protected their neighborhoods, solved their problems, and settled their disputes pretty much on their own.

"Max Wagner's not worth getting in trouble over, Benny."

Benny shook his head. "Fuck him."

"Better to drop it."

"What he does ain't right, Ray." Benny glared into Ambler's eyes for emphasis. "He doesn't know how to treat people, even his own staff."

Ambler caught on. Benny was talking about Kay Donnelly, whom Max Wagner treated like a scullery maid. Benny saw behind her curt manner, severe expression, and frumpy outfits to a desirable woman lurking beneath. He'd seen them walking together in the hallway, oblivious to everyone around them, like two high-school kids with a crush on each other. Too bad she was trouble. Bad enough she worked for Wagner; having a murdered ex-husband was entirely too much trouble for a wise man to take on.

Ambler took in Benny's pointed and shiny black leather shoes, stiffly creased black dress pants, open-collar, starched and ironed Italian dress shirt, soft leather jacket. Not the way most librarians dressed. He was who he was. Presented with a bully and a damsel in distress, his choice wasn't a wise one. Yet such choices had been made for centuries. Who was Ambler to change human nature?

"Be careful." He patted Benny on the shoulder. "Max doesn't play by the rules."

Instead of grabbing a sandwich as he'd intended, Ambler kept walking down Fifth Avenue deep in thought. Walking in the city was as natural as breathing for him. Sometimes for weeks on end, he'd walk everywhere he went. Seldom did he take a cab. He might take a bus on a rainy day; you couldn't get a cab anyway. If he went some distance, he'd take the subway, although sometimes he'd walk then, too. At lunch, he walked most days, walked and observed the city around him.

On this day, he strolled downtown about twenty blocks, picked up a barbecue sandwich at one of the lunch carts at the north end of Madison Square Park, and found a bench in the park, where he sat, watching people walk by, in the shadow of the Flatiron Building, which if he remembered correctly housed the editorial offices of Nelson Yates's publisher. He wondered idly if his walk to Madison Square Park had been more intentional than random. Had the idea of Nelson Yates taken over his subconscious because his name popped up when someone talked about James Donnelly's murder?

"Raymond, come here." Adele beckoned from the doorway of the Berg Collection reading room as he headed back to his office after lunch. "Nelson Yates is in Harry's office. He's mad as a hornet about Max Wagner for some reason. Harry sent me to get you."

"Why me?" He had to wonder for a moment if his subconscious, not satisfied with leading him to the Flatiron Building, had conjured up the real-life Nelson Yates.

Adele shrugged.

Harry jumped up when Ambler came through the door. "Here he is now."

The man sitting in front of the desk was thin, emaciated, much older looking than the evening they'd spent drinking and talking not so many years ago. His long legs crossed at the knees, he bent forward in such a way as to seem permanently curled. His eyes were sunken far back in his thin face, so he looked weary—defeated and weary.

"Hello, Nelson." Ambler held out his hand. Because of the blank look he got in return, he wasn't sure the writer remembered him. "It's good to see you again."

Yates shook his hand listlessly.

"Mr. Yates is concerned that Professor Wagner has been given access to the collection before it's been cataloged. I've explained the precautions we take. Perhaps you might reassure—"

"I don't need another explanation," Yates said, not raising his voice.

Harry puffed up, as he did when he was put out. "I explained to Mr. Yates that the collection was sold to the library without restrictions."

"Harry's right, Nelson. In the deed of transfer, you give the library the right to make decisions about how the collection is used," Ambler said.

Yates held up his hand to stop Harry, who was about to say something. "I could have given my papers to Max Wagner and Whitehall University. They offered me more money than you did."

"He's a respected scholar—" Harry said.

Yates shot him a withering glance.

"He has a letter of introduction from you," Ambler said.

"Mary, my wife, tricked me."

"If you're suggesting fraudulent—"

Yates waved Harry off. "I'm not bringing my wife into this. I thought the letter of introduction was for Jim Donnelly."

Ambler shot a meaningful glance at Harry before turning to Yates. "You gave my friend McNulty the bartender the impression Donnelly's murder wasn't a surprise to you. 'Chickens coming home to roost?'"

Yates hesitated, puzzled. "Did I say that?" His eyes clouded and he seemed lost in thought. When he came back to the present, he stared at the space in front of him. Looking at him, you'd think he was unsure of himself, until his eyes caught yours and he spoke with authority as he did here. "What I said was a comment . . . musing . . . a thought that found voice. Something came out of Jim Donnelly's past. It could happen to anyone." He looked at Ambler and then at Harry. "It might well happen to me or either of you."

"Was there a problem between him and Max Wagner?"

Despite his general lethargy, the expression in Yates's eyes was shrewd. "They were rivals." Yates appraised you in a way that seemed to be seeing something about you that you'd rather he didn't, your secrets, especially the ones you were embarrassed by. "Why do you ask? Do you think Max killed him?"

"I don't know. Do you?"

"It wouldn't make for a very good plot." He laughed, a chuckle followed by a hacking cough. When he finished coughing, he reached into his pocket. "Can I smoke?"

Harry made a move like he was going to tackle him. "No! No! It's a library."

Yates put his cigarette pack back in his pocket. "I used to smoke here, years ago, in the Allen Room. Smoke and drink. Back when writers wrote on typewriters." He winked at Ambler. "We were expected to do that sort of thing."

Ambler persisted. "Was there bad blood between Max and James Donnelly?"

Yates shook his head. "I hadn't seen either of them in years. Jim Donnelly wrote me some time back. He wanted to write a literary biography, something very different from the crap Max writes. He asked for some of my writing, my notebooks, asked to read my letters. I thought the whole idea sounded pretentious."

He chuckled, followed by another fit of coughing. "When I signed the letter my wife tricked me into signing for Max Wagner, I thought it was Jim trying again. I was going to let him look through the collection."

The three men sat in silence until Ambler spoke. "He

wouldn't take it lying down, you know. Taking something from Max is like taking a bone from a pit bull."

"I know what he's like." The writer's tone changed, as if he sensed something from Ambler that he hadn't heard from Harry. "Your boss says you're a friend of his."

"We were in graduate school together. Not friends."

Yates smiled with his eyes to let Ambler know he got it. "He was my protégé. I welcomed him into my family, treated him like a son. If you know Wagner, you know he'd swindle his mother out of her widow's pension."

"I think he did," Ambler said.

The older man chuckled. "He betrayed me."

"But your wife—"

"She doesn't know. It was before her time."

"If you make that kind of charge against Max—"

"I won't. Don't let him get at my papers and keep me out of it."

"Without a reason?" Harry said.

"I gave you a reason."

"I don't see how I could do it." Worry deepened the lines in Harry's face. "Even at your request, I don't know how I would. Without a formal request from you, how would I explain? It would be impossible."

Yates stood to leave, turning to Ambler. "Maybe you can think of something."

"Maybe." Ambler was thinking of Benny's plan to push Wagner in front of a bus. He and Harry watched Nelson walk slowly through the door.

During the following week, life in the library slowly returned to normal. Ambler spent what free time he had learning more about the murder victim, James Donnelly. Meanwhile, Adele signed a lease for a small one-bedroom in an elevator building in the West Fifties, between Eighth and Ninth avenues. Hell's Kitchen, once notorious, had gentrified but retained small pieces of its history and character—rent-stabilized apartment buildings on the cross streets and a smattering of storefronts along Ninth Avenue whose tenants had long-term leases—useful stores, like hardware, dry cleaners, and bakeries that hadn't yet been turned into trendy restaurants.

"Isn't it gorgeous?" she asked Ambler. She'd persuaded the landlord to let her fix up the apartment before moving in, so she'd invited Ambler over to help paint her kitchen on Thursday, their day off together. "If you lean over and look out this window," she bent over the kitchen sink and craned her neck, "you can see the river."

Ambler was happy for her but couldn't muster much enthusiasm for her new place. It was cramped and dark, not much different from a zillion other apartments in Manhattan.

"Have you found out anything interesting about the murder victim?" she asked, after they got the drop cloth down and the painting supplies set up.

"He taught English and creative writing at a small liberal arts college—what used to be a women's college—in Westchester. He's published a couple of literary biographies; unlike the ones Max Wagner writes, his are scholarly, not celebrity bios. He and Kay Donnelly divorced a long time ago. That's all I've come up with. I haven't tried the genealogy files in the Milstein Division yet. I've been reading his books."

"Do you think they'll tell you why he was murdered?"

Ambler shrugged. "They'll tell me something. Mike Cosgrove sent detectives up to the college. Maybe they'll find he was in the white slave trade or ran a drug smuggling operation."

Adele scrutinized his face. "Was that a joke?"

He nodded and began pouring paint into a roller pan.

"I'm beginning to think your friend Max Wagner killed the guy out of pure meanness. He's a real pill. What's with him?"

"Max is self-centered. He doesn't care anything about other people."

"Except for that bimbo he's married to; he follows her like a lap dog."

"She isn't a bimbo."

Adele stopped painting and turned to stare at him.

He was surprised himself by what he'd said. He had no reason to defend Laura Lee McGlynn. "Her looks might be deceiving," he mumbled.

Adele turned back to her wall. They worked together in silence, Ambler lulled by the mindless activity of rolling paint onto the wall, while Adele shoved a stepladder about the room cutting the paint into the corners and near the ceiling with a brush. She pretended not to look at him but he could see her watching him out of the corner of her eye. She wore old, ripped jeans and a faded T-shirt that fit tightly across her chest. Her hair was wrapped in a bandana. Her face glowed—you might say she had rosy cheeks—from the exertion, he guessed, but also, despite her momentary petulance, from a kind of happiness he hadn't seen in her before.

Fortunately, she couldn't stay angry or silent for very long. "I wish Harry hadn't given Professor Big Shot access to the collection before we processed it. I don't know why he's so deferential to that ass. Now, he's letting him into the stacks. No one ever gets to work in the stacks. . . . You're dripping."

Ambler caught the drips with the roller and went back to painting the wall in front of him. Harry's kowtowing to Max Wagner bothered him, too. "Nelson deserves a biographer who tells the truth, someone better than Max."

Adele's expression softened. "The truth isn't so easy, Raymond. Harry thinks you're conspiring with Nelson Yates. Maybe that's why he's teamed up with Wagner."

They worked in silence again, until Ambler saw there were tears in Adele's eyes. He touched her shoulder and she turned to him.

"My mother's dead, Raymond. As we were burying her, someone was murdered in the library. It's so awful." He reached for her other shoulder to hold her. But before he could comfort her, she walked away from him. "I'm sorry," she said, stifling her tears. "I miss my mother."

The afternoon wore on until darkness seeped into the room where they painted. When Adele flipped on the light switch, the bare bulb in the middle of the ceiling, reflecting off the fresh paint, created a stark brightness. She stood with her hands on her hips, a spot of paint on her nose and a streak along her cheek. Ambler watched with interest as she lifted the bottom of her T-shirt as far up as her bra to see if she'd gotten paint on her torso.

He helped her wash out brushes and rollers and close up the paint cans. To get away from the fumes, they went to a small wine bar on Ninth Avenue for flatbread pizza, salad, and charcuterie, and shared a bottle of wine.

"I told you Nelson's wife didn't want him to give the collection to us." Adele put down her wineglass. "She'd been negotiating herself with a university. Whitehall."

"Where Max Wagner teaches."

Adele nodded. "Mary Yates is young, forties at most, Nelson's in his eighties; she's his third or fourth wife. I didn't like her. Nelson insisted the collection go to the NYPL, and he got his way. It's touchy, though. He's not . . . how do I say this? It's not that he's not all there. He goes in and out."

"Of where?"

"Don't be a jerk, Raymond. He forgets, loses track of what he's saying, forgets who he's talking to."

"Alzheimer's?"

"Some kind of dementia that comes with old age."

"You're afraid she'll have him declared incompetent?"

Adele cut a piece of salami into quarters. "Harry was careful about notaries and witnesses when we did the deed of transfer, so I think we're okay. And he has that woman from the Board of Trustees on his side—"

Ambler paused, the wineglass halfway to his mouth. "What woman?"

Adele pierced a small piece of the salami with her fork. "I shouldn't tell you this. A society woman donated the funds to purchase the Nelson Yates collection. This woman's pretty important, New York Upper Crust and all that. I think that caused Nelson's wife and Max Wagner to back off."

"Who is she?"

Adele shook her head. "I can't tell you. But you'd know her if you saw her. Her husband's a lawyer with one of those white glove law firms, a philanthropist. You see her picture in the *Times* at those black tie charity balls."

"I doubt it. I didn't know you kept up with high society."

"I read about British royalty, too." She smiled.

Ambler nodded, thought of nothing to say, and took a sip of wine. After a moment, he said, "I wonder why she did that."

"What?"

"Financed the acquisition."

"Funny. I didn't think about why she would. Rich people make donations. I let it go at that." Adele's eyes were round with worry, her eyelids drooping with tiredness, and for the moment, she seemed small and scared, so that Ambler felt protective of her. He looked at his glass and decided it was the wine.

• • •

The night after Raymond helped her paint her kitchen, Adele left her apartment, walking west on 52nd Street. She wanted to see if the shoeshine boy was out on Ninth Avenue again. She'd seen him the first night she was in the neighborhood visiting her new apartment, on the street at night a lot later than he should be at his age, shining the expensive loafers worn by a young guy in a business suit, who, hair mussed, tie askew, leaned against the wall of the gay bar he'd come out of. She'd taken notice of the boy because she'd seen him in the library a few days before. He was studying the Winnie-the-Pooh stuffed animal collection in the display case in the Children's Center with this absolutely rapturous look on his face. He had remarkably clear, cobalt blue eyes, almost the same color as Raymond's. When he sensed her watching him, he looked up with a half-bewildered, tentative smile. She almost laughed but caught herself when she saw the boy's embarrassed look. He seemed to be alone then, and here he was alone again, cute as a button—a street waif straight out of Dickens.

The next time, a few days later, she came upon him trudging up Ninth Avenue in front of her, shouldering his shoeshine kit, bent over as if it were filled with rocks, her heart went out to him. Thin, wearing a threadbare jacket and worn, dirty, untied high-tops, he walked like an old man. When she caught up with him, she had to stop herself from offering to help carry the shoeshine box. And when he crossed the street to head west on one of the cross streets, she followed, watching, until he turned to enter a building, one of the remaining four-story walk-up railroad flats, like her own but not yet renovated.

She thought about herself and those like her moving in and probably displacing families with kids like him. He reminded her of the children she'd worked with when she was in high school, teaching underprivileged kids to read. Actually, she'd been teaching poor kids to read since elementary school—her mother-hen complex. Her friends used to tell her she'd grow up to be the old woman who lived in a shoe. But she wasn't the old woman who lived in a shoe. She didn't have so many children she didn't know what to do. She didn't have any children at all. She didn't have anyone now since her mother died. She was alone and she wondered if this boy was an orphan, too.

He was a fixture in the neighborhood. She'd see him often, one afternoon on Tenth Avenue, wearing the uniform of the neighborhood Catholic school, another time in the evening headed down Ninth Avenue carrying a bag of groceries from the fruit market at 57th Street. He was always alone—even coming from school he wasn't part of the groups of noisy, scrambling kids who burst out onto the sidewalk when school let out—and she never saw him smile, except for that moment in the library.

For this evening, she put on a pair of old leather boots, one of the few of her mother's possessions she'd kept—the pair she used to borrow when she was young and the boots were new—and went to search out the shoeshine boy. It took more than an hour, marching down one side of Ninth Avenue as far as 42nd Street and back up the other side almost to Columbus Circle. She went by a bar where guys were outside smoking enough times to be propositioned. She was afraid if she went by it again someone would grab her and drag her inside, assuming she was playing hard to get. Finally, she saw the boy, standing in front of a different bar as though screwing up his courage to enter.

She approached him, smiling. "How much to shine these boots?"

He wrinkled his eyebrows examining the boots and then her face. His eyes were squinted closed and he spoke in a shy mumble. She had to ask him to repeat what he'd said.

"Whatever you want to pay."

"Oh," said Adele. "I have no idea what it should cost. I've never had a shoeshine."

The boy shrugged his shoulders, sinking into his jacket. He was tongue-tied, painfully shy. How did he find any customers?

"How does five dollars sound?"

The boy's face brightened and he nodded.

The only way she could think of for him to get at her boots was to lean against the wall next to the bar like she'd seen the guys doing. Now, she did feel like a streetwalker.

"What's your name?" she asked as he puttered around in his box, getting out tins of polish, brushes, and rags.

He mumbled an answer she didn't hear, but she chose not to ask him to repeat it.

She started to ask how old he was but got angry with herself for asking dumb, adult-to-kid questions a maiden aunt would ask. "You've got quite a kit there," she tried. "And you're so young to be working so hard. Did your dad teach you to shine shoes?"

In answer, he mumbled something again, so she resolved to not ask him any more questions until she got him to relax. She began by telling him she was new in the neighborhood and used to live in Brooklyn, and babbled on until he seemed to relax into his work. After a bit, she asked how long he'd been in the neighborhood.

He shrugged.

"Do you live here with your family?'

"My mom."

"Do you like living here? Do you like school?" There she was again with the Aunt Mable questions. Even though the boy hardly answered a question, she could see that he warmed to the attention.

She wanted to know more about him. There was no denying he was poor, and probably neglected if he was out on the street by himself at all hours drifting among the bars and the drunks and the nightlife. It wasn't right. She had a good mind to march the boy back to his home and confront his mother. But really, she had no right to. He was out on the street at night. That might be a violation of something, but this was New York. It took a lot more than that to get someone's attention. And he did go to the Catholic school, so that meant something. Then there were the horror stories about child protective services taking kids away from their mothers and dumping them God knows where. Butting in without knowing the whole situation, she could easily make things worse.

She tried again with his name and finally got that it was Johnny . . . no last name, though. If she could get his full name, she might find a way to check on him without causing trouble. Eventually, she got it out of him—Smith. For a moment, she suspected he made it up, said the first name that came into his head. But he wasn't evasive; he didn't seem to want to keep anything from her. He mumbled because he was shy. He smiled now, cautiously warming to her like a stray pup wary of even an act of kindness. She gave him the five dollars. She would have given him more—ten, twenty—but held herself back lest she come across as too strange and scare him away. She did tell him he'd done a great job and she had another pair of boots that needed polishing and would look for him again in a few days.

Chapter 5

The following Monday, Adele knocked on the crime fiction reading room door late in the afternoon. Ambler had spent most of the day—after updating his notebook on the James Donnelly murder—cataloging the contents of six file boxes from the collection of a 1920s mystery writer whose work had been out of print for decades. Like most of the donated collections, it was haphazardly thrown together by a family member and dumped at the library, with no one having much of an idea of what was in the boxes, much less where anything was.

"Nelson Yates is sitting in the park behind the library. He didn't know who I was."

"I'm cataloging," Ambler said, as if that would explain everything. He got up and followed her.

Behind the library, the spindly green café chairs were scattered along the slate walks among the ivy, the daffodils, and budding sycamore trees. The center lawn of the park was still roped off. Nelson Yates, an ancient, solitary figure, sat by himself on one of the café chairs alongside the open-air library. The sun had sunk behind the buildings and the breeze was chilly. He was bent over, coughing, smoking a cigarette, watching a Ping-Pong game at the tables alongside 42nd Street.

"Nelson," Ambler said. "Is everything all right?"

Yates turned his watery gray eyes on Ambler. His expression was blank. "I'm watching my son play Ping-Pong. I didn't know he could play. I never taught him."

"Don't you think it's time to get home?" Adele asked. "Your wife will be looking for you."

"Lisa?" His expression grew troubled. "Lisa left me years ago."

Adele looked confused. "Mary. Your wife's name is Mary."

He turned to watch the Ping-Pong players, silent long enough for Ambler to think he'd forgotten about them, which he had. Adele called his name.

When he turned, she asked, "Would you like us to call your wife?"

"My son will take me home when he finishes."

Ambler waited a moment. "That's not your son, Nelson. You're here at the 42nd Street library. We were talking a couple of days ago about the papers you donated to the library . . . and Max Wagner."

Yates snapped to attention. "Don't talk to me about that prick. Where is he?"

"I don't know."

"You tell him I know what he did and not to come near me again."

"What did he do?"

Yates stared at him. His expression darkened.

Ambler resisted asking another question.

"Edgar! Edgar!" Yates hollered at the group of young guys—some black, some white, some Asian—at the two Ping-Pong tables. They played aggressively, slamming the ball back and forth, but laughed a lot, shaking hands, bumping fists at the end of a game. The protocol was that the player who won kept the table and a new opponent challenged him. The person who lost stood on the sidelines for a few minutes, cheerfully chatting with the other guys and two women who showed up, and was soon back playing at the other table. The winner moved on after a bit also and eventually wound up at that other table, too.

When Yates rose and moved toward the tables, calling for Edgar, the players glanced uneasily at each other and tried to ignore him. Adele intercepted him. As she did, he seemed to notice the cold shoulder he got from the young men and hesitated.

"I'm not remembering right," he mumbled, as Adele steered him back toward the library. When Ambler came up alongside them, Nelson was at first suspicious but soon relaxed. "I'm sorry," he said. "I lost my bearings for a moment." He turned to Ambler. "Have we been drinking?"

"No," said Ambler. "Would you like a drink?"

By the time they got to the Library Tavern, Nelson was lucid. From his wariness, it was likely he didn't remember the last hour or so and was keeping a close eye on him and Adele to see what they knew about what he'd been doing.

Finding an empty bar stool near the door, they parked Adele on it, Ambler standing to one side of her, Yates the other. McNulty took their order, beers for Adele and Ambler, bourbon on ice for Yates. The bar was packed, so no time for visiting with McNulty.

"Would you like me to call your wife?" Adele asked.

Nelson took a long drink, draining his glass, his eyes clouding with his thoughts again. His expression was sullen as he ordered another bourbon. In a determined, almost angry, tone, he said, "I'd like to sit here drinking until the bar closes." He stared at his glass. When he spoke again, it was quietly. "I have memory problems. I imagine you've noticed . . . dementia. Not a good thing for a writer."

Ambler asked about his most recent book. Talking about his writing, he was more animated. Like most writers, he was more inclined to talk about the market, the consolidation of the publishing industry, the closing of too many independent bookstores, than he was in talking about his craft or evaluating his fellow writers. While he talked, he drank steadily, ordering refills while Ambler and Adele sipped their beers.

After a while, he grew melancholy. "When you get to be as old as I am, you have many regrets."

"You mentioned your son," Ambler said, aware of his own regrets.

"Son? Edgar . . . the dutiful son. Nothing wrong with him, he's a musician here in the city, plays the viola for the ballet. My daughter Emily is the regret." He motioned to McNulty. "One more of these."

McNulty looked troubled as he poured the drink.

"Is your daughter here in the city?" Adele asked

"I don't know where she is. She ran away—when she was fifteen."

"I'm so sorry," Adele said.

"I found her and brought her back. She wouldn't stay. She was lost."

Ambler remembered some of what happened with Yates's daughter. It was a tabloid scandal twenty years ago and took a toll on Nelson. He went crazy looking for her. His marriage broke up. He stopped writing, drank heavily—which he was doing right now, slugging down one bourbon on ice after another.

"I thought of something today." He turned to Ambler. "I

meant to ask Harry but I forgot. I do that a lot." The melancholy was gone, replaced by a lip-smacking kind of friendliness you might see in an old farmer who wasn't around other people all that often. "In the library, you have records and databases and such things. Someone who knew how to use those databases could track down my daughter pretty easily, I'd bet."

"Someone might," Ambler said. "Not me. I'm an archivist." He looked to Adele. She was quiet, watching.

"Emily didn't want to see me." Yates spoke to the space in front of him or to McNulty at the far end of the bar making a drink. "I wrote to her, begged her. It was a mistake." He reached out across Adele and clasped Ambler's arm. "I want the letters back." The grip on Ambler's forearm was surprisingly strong.

So that was it—the scandal. Nelson didn't want what happened with his daughter to be rehashed in his biography, or at least he wanted control over how it was handled. Max Wagner, on the other hand, would be salivating over it. Nelson released his grip. You could see the wisdom in his expression—too smart to try to outsmart someone who'd already come up with the answer.

He stared into space again before he spoke. "If Max realizes Emily has the letters, he'll try to get them from her."

"Why would she give them to him?"

Nelson waved off the question. "She was quite taken with him when she was a young girl. I don't know what she'd think now."

Ambler said he'd see what he could find out about the missing girl and was about to ask about James Donnelly when Nelson lowered his head until it was inches above his rocks glass, like a junky nodding off. In the short time they'd been in the bar, he'd had five or six drinks, and they'd hit him quickly. He was drunk.

With Adele's help, he piled the aging writer into a cab, and they headed for 78th Street between Columbus and Amsterdam. The ride was uneventful, except when Nelson revived and insisted the cab stop at a liquor store on Amsterdam before they reached his street. Ambler had misgivings, but Nelson insisted, so he got his way and the cab stopped. At 78th Street, after asking the cab driver to wait, Adele and Ambler walked him up the stoop of the brownstone building and waited while he fumbled for his keys.

Just as he got the key in the lock, the door opened and a trim, pretty, but sour-faced woman opened the door. She looked to be thirty years younger than Yates.

"Good evening, Mary," Yates said gallantly. "I'd like you to meet—"

"Oh my God," she said, her hand going to cover her mouth. "Good God," she shrieked. "You haven't let him drink, have you?" She stared at them, one hand covering her mouth, the other holding the edge of the door.

Ambler and Adele stared back at her until Adele broke the silence. "Obviously, he's been drinking. We helped him get home. We're not his keepers."

"He's not supposed to drink. His condition—"

"Don't talk about me like I'm a child," Yates said. "And don't be discourteous to my friends." For the moment, he seemed to have regained sobriety, his diction precise, though he wobbled and swayed, unsteady on his feet.

"Look at yourself. You're—" Mary Yates couldn't find the words. Her mouth moved but nothing came out, her face twisted into a mask of disgust.

"You're no fucking prize yourself," Yates said. "You sound like a shrew."

Engrossed in their battle, they ignored Adele and Ambler, who watched and listened for a moment before turning back to the waiting cab. Man and wife continued to argue in the doorway as the cab pulled away.

The following morning, Ambler stopped by the reference desk in the catalog room, where Benny Barone was working that day. He told Benny about Emily Yates, asked him to do any searches he could think of, and gave him a phone number for Nelson Yates.

"What I know about her is she ran away from home when she was teenager."

"Doesn't everybody?" Benny had gotten in with a neighborhood gang of hoodlum apprentices during his rebellious youth and at one point ran away from home. His father, a Brooklyn longshoreman, stood down the gang and brought him home.

"Runaways don't always fare so well," Ambler said.

"Don't I know it? Too often, no one wants to find them. Was it sex?"

Ambler was puzzled.

"The reason she ran away."

"Why sex?"

"Kids who run away usually do it for a good reason—lots of times it's sex or violence." Benny, as payback for his own experience, did volunteer work at a runaway center near the Port Authority for as long as Ambler could remember.

Ambler told him the little he knew about Emily Yates's disappearance.

"The desk is too busy for me to do it now. I'll do it later when I'm supposed to be doing research for the ogre."

The message came as a memo in an envelope, an ominous sign in itself in the age of instant, impersonal, e-mail notification. And the news was as bad as he thought it would be—worse. He held the memo in his hand, rereading it for the fourth or fifth time, when Adele knocked on the reading room door. Without meaning to, he snarled at her.

"Good God, Raymond! What's wrong?" She shrank back. "Did I do something?"

"Not you. . . ." He took a deep breath. "They're shutting me down."

"Shutting you down?" She surveyed the tiny room, taking in the book-lined walls, the small balcony, two cluttered library tables, unoccupied at the moment, the truth dawning on her. "No! They're not—"

"They certainly are." He handed her the memo.

She read it through and then read it again. "They can't do this. They simply can't." Tears welled up in her eyes. "I knew it. I knew when they closed the Slavic reading room it was the beginning. Everything's changing so fast. What's a library without books?"

"Harry didn't even tell me. Just this." He waved the memo.

"Well, you're not going to sit there and let them do it, are you?" Adele threw back her shoulders—a stance Joan of Arc would be proud of.

"They're going to send the books to a warehouse in Princeton. Princeton, a hundred miles away."

"We'll see about that," said Adele.

She stormed out, leaving Ambler sitting among his books and papers.

The collection had its origins in the early nineties when a New York City collector, a former mystery editor and bookstore owner, donated his first editions and extensive Rex Stout collection, as well as a small endowment to support future collecting. Ambler talked Harry into letting him take charge of the collection.

Over time, he acquired a few things here and there—a college professor's library of American hard-boiled and noir first editions, a collection of early twentieth-century American Golden

Age whodunits from a retired nurse from Long Island, a couple of other collections of first editions. Later, with Harry's help, he expanded the archival part of the collection, acquiring papers and manuscripts from well-known and not-so-well-known working mystery writers, the estates of once well-known writers who'd died in obscurity, letters, manuscripts, and notebooks at auctions. Now, his literary sinecure was coming undone.

He'd fight back, like Adele said, though the effort had a Spotted Elk at Wounded Knee feel to it. Whatever the social or economic dynamics that brought about this age of expediency in which no one cared about the things he cared about, they were running at full throttle, hell-bent on destroying the library as he'd known it—not actually tearing it down to the ground brick by brick, but literally and figuratively ripping its guts out.

He should have learned by now that as you progress through life things you thought would be there forever won't be—not even you. Not just the library, Manhattan had been transformed over the half century he'd known it from a place of neighborhoods with the characteristics of a small town—bakery, butcher, drugstore, bar—into a megalopolis-like shopping mall of chain restaurants, chain coffee shops, national brand boutiques. Pockets of the old New York remained—his Murray Hill walk-up apartment building for one—but not much was left. And now the library would change as so much else had changed.

That afternoon, Harry Larkin stopped him on the second floor landing above the lobby. "There's been an altercation. Benny Barone—"

"Someone attacked Benny?"

"Quite the opposite—he assaulted Maximilian Wagner. Professor Wagner says Benny punched him. From what I understand, he grabbed him by the throat. I'm hoping she meant shirt collar rather than putting his hands around his neck."

"Who's she?"

"Mrs. Wagner."

"Laura Lee?"

Harry raised his eyebrows.

Ambler shrugged.

"She played down the incident. What she said was, 'Maximilian got his feathers ruffled.' But he wasn't laughing."

"What's Benny say?"

"He's not saying anything. He wants Adele in the room if I question him."

"Adele?"

"She's his union steward."

"The police?"

"Not yet. We'll see."

When Ambler got to his desk, two readers were waiting for materials and the page had brought the wrong boxes to another reader. He was too busy to think about anything else until Adele showed up.

"Benny wants to talk to you," she said.

Ambler found Benny in the hallway.

"Harry sent me home."

"Suspended you?"

Benny shrugged. "I guess. Can we walk?"

They walked down Fifth Avenue. Ambler watched Benny's shiny Italian leather shoes strike rhythmically against the sidewalk.

"I grabbed him by the collar, shoved him against the desk, and slapped him." Wagner had come upon Benny and Kay Donnelly heads bent together in the microform reading room on the first floor. "He embarrassed her. His wife was with him. I told him to leave it alone. He kept at Kay, so I grabbed him and told him to shut up. He laughed, so I slapped him. I wasn't going to. But he had this mocking expression on his puss, so I slapped it off."

Ambler nodded. He'd wanted to knock Wagner's smug expression off his face any number of times.

"You've been in trouble with the library, Ray, and you got out of it."

"I didn't slug a reader."

"Not slug. I slapped him. Do you think the shithead can get me fired?

"Did he grab you, punch at you?"

Benny shook his head. "Nope. Just that smug superior expression."

"Well, you've got the union."

"Anything you can do? You know the guy."

Ambler was quiet. He thought about Max's wife, Laura Lee. "I'll see."

Chapter 6

Kay Donnelly walked back to her room at The Webster Apartments on 34th Street after getting off the crosstown bus at Ninth Avenue. The women's residence wasn't a place she liked very much—the room reminded her of being in college. Max found it for her, the only decent place she could afford on what she was getting paid for the Yates project.

He would have paid her more if he weren't scared of Laura Lee. He'd have liked her to have her own apartment for their now infrequent assignations. Laura Lee kept the books and controlled the money. The apartment in the nunnery was her way of showing she wasn't fooled. If Max had half a brain, he'd know his wife had known for some time about his occasional walk on the wild side and couldn't care less about it.

On the other hand, Laura Lee was brilliant at letting Kay know she was onto Max's indiscretions. It was as if she could speak in another language in front of him, getting her thoughts across to Kay while he was oblivious to what she said. Laura Lee was a miserable bitch, more ruthless and selfish than Max—but too good an actress, too charming and coquettish, for most people, especially men, to catch on to her.

But what could she do? Her career was tied up with Max's projects. If she was to get tenure at Whitehall, it would have to be through him, and it would have to be pretty soon. The clock was running.

In retrospect, she probably shouldn't have taken up with Benny. He was too close to home, and Max too jealous and insecure. Now, Benny was in big trouble for fighting with him. Still, he was cute, a rough-around-the-edges guy, innocent at the same time; taking him to bed, she felt like she was corrupting him. The hotel room probably cost him half a week's pay.

His chivalry was endearing and he was handsome—in a primitive, manly way you didn't come across often in the academic world. Strangely, it was the same rough-around-the-edges appeal Max had when she first met him. Max changed and the appeal, if not the brashness, wore off over the years. She didn't know how she felt about him anymore, only that she was bound to him in so many ways that no matter how hard she tried she couldn't pull away. It was her fault Benny was in this mess. The poor guy didn't know Max would have any reason to be jealous. She'd have to hope that when Max calmed down, she might get him to drop the whole thing.

The thing with Benny was fun. The archaic, relic residence hall she stayed in didn't allow women to have men in their rooms. Benny lived in Brooklyn with his parents. So, at her age, they were slinking around like teenagers, trying to find a place to have sex. He took her one afternoon to an out-of-the-way office in the bowels of the library, where they necked and petted and she sucked him off. She was afraid to take off her clothes because someone discovering them would be too damn silly and mortifying—Max would have a fit, and Laura Lee would never let her forget it.

The police detective who questioned her asked so many questions about Max she thought he might be a suspect in James's murder. He had motive enough to kill him, for reasons the police didn't know about and were unlikely to find out about. The detective asked about Benny, too. This worried her. What did he have to do with James? If Benny were going to kill anyone, it would be Max. She was half-convinced he would, too, if she asked him to, or even if she didn't, if he thought Max would harm her. It was fun to have a man smitten with her.

Max ridiculed Benny; probably he reminded Max of where he himself had come from. How Max could be so smart about literature, yet so dumb about himself—and Laura Lee, too, for that matter—was beyond her.

She wasn't surprised the detective asked her if she knew where Max was at the time of the murder. Then, he asked where she was. Why would he ask that? She got so flustered, she couldn't think of what to say. How could he possibly suspect her?

Not long after leaving Benny, Ambler saw Laura Lee McGlynn walking up the main stairway, so he followed and caught up with her at the top of the stairs on the third floor. She was as glamorous and fashionable as the first time he saw her, her smile as bright. He led her to one of the stone benches in the rotunda outside the catalog room.

"It was nothing . . . a little roughing up," she said lightly. "You know what Max is like. He deserved it."

"Why do you think I know what he's like?"

Laura Lee smiled, more of an easy, carefree laugh. "You made an impression on him when you were in graduate school."

"He told you about that? We didn't like one another."

"With Max, that's making an impression."

Ambler laughed.

"He's been telling me about you. He said you were treated unfairly. He knew you didn't do what they said. You weren't a plagiarist." Her expression when her eyes narrowed with concern was as appealing and even more intense than when she smiled. "I'd like to know what happened if you'd like to tell me. You paid a price for your radical activities—"

Ambler laughed again. "It was a long time ago."

"Someday, when you know me better, you'll want to tell me." Her tone was soothing, reassuring. "I'm a good listener." She shifted her position on the bench, moving closer to him, her eyes searching his. "Well, I can't flatter myself that you stopped me because you couldn't pass up an opportunity to chat." She didn't actually bat her eyelashes, but it seemed so. "I suppose you'd like me to ask Max not to press charges against your friend?"

"I would."

Her expression went sour in front of a fake laugh. "Kay Donnelly is as subtle as a streetwalker. It's her fault."

"I'm sure with her ex-husband's death—"

Laura Lee grimaced. "They'd been divorced for some time. She treated him badly before the divorce, during it, and long after. She's not beside herself with grief."

Her cynicism, something in her tone, suggested she might be more forthcoming than he thought. He took a chance. "How well did you know James Donnelly?"

"Max and I hadn't been in contact with him for years. Kay, as far as I know, hadn't had anything to do with him for years either. Why do you ask?"

He could say, "Because Wagner and James Donnelly had an argument the day before he was murdered." And he might have if she hadn't just lied. "No reason. Just wondering. I suppose the police asked you about him."

She stiffened. Her manner became chilly. "Yes. They did. James Donnelly was a difficult man. I'm not surprised he made enemies."

"Oh? Were he and Max enemies?"

She hesitated, blinking rapidly, before looking directly at him. "He wasn't important enough for Max to care one way or another about him "

Ambler held her gaze.

A charming smile replaced the frown. "When Max cools off, I'll speak to him about your friend."

Max Wagner wasn't happy. The Nelson Yates biography was treading water, the narrative boring—Yates did this; Yates did that. The spectacular was missing, the shocking twist that would expose Yates as the exact opposite of the man his hero-worshipping fans thought he was. The thing was he knew the shocking revelation, yet he couldn't use it. He didn't have proof.

He needed the letters Nelson had written to Emily. She hated her father, so if he could find her, he might persuade her to sell him the letters. That sort of thing worked with estranged family members before.

"That's a stupid plan," Laura Lee said. "She hates your guts. Why would she give you anything, even for money?"

"She hated Jim Donnelly, too, and she talked to him."

"Says your little groupie?"

Here it was again, another hint that Laura Lee knew about him and Kay. Yet she'd never said anything, or even asked, only the snide remark.

"Perhaps you should talk to Emily. It might not be so good for me to see her."

"A lot of good that would do. The little slut was fucking my husband. You think she'd talk to me?"

"She knew you were going to leave him."

"How'd she know that, pillow talk with you?" Laura Lee's laugh was contemptuous. "Both of you fucking a fourteen-year-old—"

Max expression was aggrieved. "That was before you . . . before—"

Laura Lee rolled her eyes. "Stop whining. It drives me crazy."

They were eating dinner, delivered from a local Italian restaurant, sitting across from each other at the small dining table in the short-term apartment on West 85th Street Wagner had rented for the three months he planned to spend with Yates's papers.

"By the way, your librarian friend wants me to persuade you to forget that incident with Kay's new boyfriend."

He fought back a rush of anger before he said something stupid. Laura Lee was trying to goad him into saying something about Kay. What did he care what Kay did? He shouldn't have let it get to him, yet she was hanging all over that punk right in front of him. Thinking about them, he got angry all over again. "Why should I?"

"So you don't look like jealous idiot," she said, not looking at him. "He also asked about you and Donnelly."

He stopped eating. "Why? What did he want?"

"I'll find out when I talk to him again." When she looked at Max now, her smile was mocking.

He put down his knife and fork. "He's no fool, you know."

"Neither am I."

Wagner cleaned up the dishes after dinner, throwing out the leftovers. He finished the wine by himself, while Laura Lee went to bed to read, staring out the window at the wall of the building next door. He didn't like Ambler questioning her. She thought she'd outwit him as she did everyone, underestimating him. It would do no good telling her that or not to talk to Ambler. She'd do the exact opposite.

"'Chickens coming home to roost' . . . what the hell does that mean?" Mike Cosgrove thundered. Ambler heard street noises, the sounds of the city, horns, the diesel whine of buses starting up from the curb, the thump and clang of trucks on the potholed street, behind his voice on the phone. The detective was irritated by the traffic.

"Well, it actually doesn't have much to do with chickens—"

"I know what it means! What am I supposed to make of it?"

"You asked me to call if I came across anything. Nelson Yates characterized James Donnelly's murder as 'chickens coming home to roost.' He said Donnelly and Max were rivals and didn't like one another. You've got that and the argument between Donnelly and Max Wagner. Seems like it might add up to something. You take it from there."

Cosgrove absorbed the new information without comment, so Ambler couldn't tell if he'd questioned Max about the argument yet.

"One more thing." He told the detective about Yates's missing daughter. "I'm wondering if you'd run a check on her. Someone in the library was supposed to but he got sidetracked."

"What's the girl got to do with this?"

"Nelson asked me to try to find her."

"It's not my territory." Cosgrove didn't let himself get sidetracked during a murder investigation. Usually, he disappeared from everyday life, barely ate or slept, fixated on the case like a bloodhound, keeping his nose to the trail while it was still warm.

"No. It's a favor."

"We'll see. . . ." Cosgrove paused but didn't hang up. After a minute, he said, "Let me ask you something. The room where the murder took place, who can get into it?"

"Not the general public, not tourists. It has a key card entry. Readers need to be approved to get the access card."

"Staff?"

"Some staff. Not everyone. Why?"

"I want to narrow the pool of suspects."

"To those with access to the second-floor archives reading room?"

"It's not a hundred percent. Someone could have gotten a card. It's still worth checking."

"That's your job, right?"

"You could give me a rundown on those who have access."

"Everyone using the Yates collection."

"I'm more interested in library employees."

"Why?"

"That's not something I can tell you."

Ambler told Cosgrove he'd see what he could find out. He held onto the phone deep in thought for a moment after Cosgrove disconnected. "More interested in library employees?" That meant something. Mike didn't speak carelessly; everything he said during an investigation was calculated, had a specific purpose. He had his sights on someone in the library. He didn't need Ambler to find out who had an access card to the reading room that housed Harry's office; he could get a list from the library administration. He wanted Ambler to know he had a suspect.

Late Wednesday morning, before lunch, Ambler decided to confront Harry. "I need to talk to you." Ambler closed Harry Larkin's office door behind him. The collections director was on the phone. He waved Ambler to a seat, shushing him at the same time.

"I see," Harry said, his head bobbling. "I understand." When he hung up, he turned to Ambler. "Nelson Yates is on a bender and missing. That was his wife."

"Missing?"

"They had an argument yesterday, so she left. When she returned late this morning, he was gone." He lowered his eyebrows and squinted at Ambler. "Two people from the library brought him home drunk Monday night—a man and woman. She thinks he might come here to the library to see you—something about his daughter."

"If she knows where he's going, he's not missing."

"He has dementia. She doesn't know what he'll do. What's this about his daughter?"

Ambler told Harry about the missing daughter. "Yesterday, before his run-in with Max Wagner, I asked Benny to search some databases and see if she comes up."

Harry frowned. "I'm not going to talk about Benny. It's a union matter now; I'd get my head handed to me. You should stay out of it, too, as you should stay out of this business between Max Wagner and Nelson Yates. I told Mrs. Yates about our conversation with Nelson. She said Nelson isn't competent. She has his power of attorney and can make the decisions about the collection."

"We both talked to Nelson. He was perfectly lucid. And she's—" He started to say Nelson's wife had been conspiring with Max, but realized he wasn't supposed to know and would betray Adele's confidence if he said anything.

Harry waited for him to finish. When he didn't, he said, "Let them work it out. I swear the Yates collection is cursed."

"Why didn't you want Benny to tell the police Max Wagner had an argument with James Donnelly before he was murdered?"

Harry frowned. "I'm sure Max told the police about the argument . . . if there was one. The murder is a police matter, not an intellectual exercise for you. You have more important things to concern yourself with."

Something ominous in Harry's tone stopped Ambler cold. "You mean the reading room closing?"

Harry's tone softened. "It's out of my hands. You need to persuade the president and the trustees that the crime fiction collection benefits the library, show that it's well-used, and used by important people, that it inspires donations and benefactors—"

"Important people, Harry?"

Harry's cheeks turned bright red; he averted his gaze. "That's not what I mean. You know what—" He looked at his watch. "I've got a meeting. Please, if Nelson Yates contacts you, call his wife." He wrote down a phone number and handed it to Ambler. "I'm late." He brushed past Ambler but paused at the office doorway. "I'll do what I can on the reading room. I know what it means to you."

When he was gone, Ambler stood in front of his desk thinking about what his supervisor had said. Was it a promise or a threat?

Still mad at Harry, Ambler had lunch at O'Casey's on 41st Street, so he could have a pint of Guinness with his hamburger, think, and cool off. He felt better after the stout and was walking back to the library, in the middle of the block between the library at Fifth Avenue and Madison Avenue on 41st Street, when Benny stepped out of a doorway. He looked stricken.

"The cops came to my house."

"About the assault?"

"What assault?"

"Max—"

"That wasn't an assault." He glared at Ambler. "I knew they were coming because Kay told me they would. When they called up from the front door, I left by the back stairs. They're going to arrest her, too."

"Did she take off also?"

"No. She got a lawyer after they questioned her about the murder. She knew something was wrong. The police told the lawyer they might arrest her and me."

"Why would they arrest you?"

"They think I helped her kill the guy."

"Did you?"

Benny's eyes went wide. "Do you think I did?"

Ambler looked into his friend's eyes. "If you tell me you didn't, I'll believe you."

"Why do I got to tell you? Wouldn't you know?"

Ambler sighed. "No. People who commit murders often don't know they're capable of murder until it happens."

"I don't know the guy; I never had anything to do with him. Why would I kill him?"

"What about Kay Donnelly?"

Benny's expression clouded. "She wouldn't do something like that."

Ambler rolled his eyes. "We just went through this, Benny. She isn't the type to kill someone doesn't cut it. Do you know for sure, know where she was at the time of the murder? Was she with you?"

Benny froze. After a few seconds, he narrowed his eyes and looked at Ambler suspiciously. "Why would you say that? Why would she be with me?"

Ambler smiled. It was good to know his friend was a lousy liar. After a moment, he said, "A friend of McNulty's is a criminal lawyer, who for some reason owes him favors."

Ambler put his arm around the shoulder of the frightened younger man and steered him around a couple of corners to the Library Tavern. He ordered a beer for himself and a brandy for Benny, who wasn't much of a drinker but could certainly use something at the moment.

When McNulty got a break, Ambler explained the situation.

McNulty gave Benny the lawyer's contact information. "He's gonna quote you a big number," McNulty said. "He likes to think of himself as high-priced. You tell him I sent you and to see me about the bill. He'll curse a lot, but he'll do it."

Ambler left Benny outside the bar on the corner calling the lawyer on his cell phone.

When he got back to his desk, he called Mike Cosgrove. "You've scared my friend Benny half to death," he said as soon as he heard "Cosgrove" at the other end of the line.

"That's not something I can talk to you about."

"He's a suspect? You're going to arrest him?"

"You're not hearing what I said?" It took a few seconds for Ambler to understand that his friend was embarrassed because he couldn't talk openly and angry because he was embarrassed.

"I know. You have a job to do. Maybe it's not even you. Still, let me tell you this. I don't know about the Donnelly woman. But I can tell you for sure Benny isn't a guy who comes up on someone from behind. If you spent—"

"Ray, please. I can't talk about this. But I do have some information on the girl you asked about."

Ten minutes later, Ambler got off the phone and sat staring in front of him. What Cosgrove told him about Emily Yates hit close to home.

Chapter 7

Nelson Yates needed a drink. Maybe he shouldn't have started again. But he had, so there it was. Right now, he needed to get the cobwebs out, after that only enough to stay even. The empty pint bottle on the kitchen counter must have been from last night—too bad last night was missing. In the refrigerator, he found a container of yogurt and forced down about half of the contents, remembering he needed to eat; too often, when he was drinking, he didn't. One break was that Mary wasn't home. He wouldn't have to explain. More to the point, he wouldn't have to argue. A morning without argument, without complaints and disapproval, what more could you ask for? He picked up the paper outside the door—and then stopped.

The last thing he remembered was going down to the library and speaking with Harry Larkin and later talking to the two librarians in the bar. He thought that was yesterday. When he looked at the front page of the *Times,* he realized he'd gone to the library the day before yesterday. It wasn't only last night; he was missing an entire day.

The Rock of Cashel was two blocks down Broadway. He hadn't been in since he'd stopped drinking, however long ago that was, unless he was in yesterday. He didn't recognize the man behind the bar, nor did the guy recognize him, which was fine. The bartender didn't bat an eye when he ordered a double bourbon. Why would he? At 11:30 in the morning, everyone was there for an eye-opener.

Yates took a healthy slug of the drink. The day before yesterday, the two librarians found him in the park behind the library after another memory lapse. They were okay, though. He liked Ambler, the crime collection guy. The woman—what was her name? Amy? Annette? No. Adele—was with Harry Larkin when he signed the deed of gift for his papers. She reminded him of Emily, somehow gentle and strong at the same time. He wondered if she reminded Harry of Emily, too, and almost asked but Harry was decidedly uninterested in the past.

He finished the drink and ordered a beer when the bartender raised his eyebrows to ask if he'd like another. He nursed beers and thought things over well into the afternoon. He didn't want to get drunk. He had things to do. It was the memory stuff—the disorientation, the lapses—that worried him, forgetting where he was, not remembering where he lived, mixing the present up with the past. He needed to find Emily before the memory thing got worse.

As soon as he stepped through the saloon door and the sunlight and spring breeze hit him, he had a moment of panic. He was disoriented, not sure where he was, where he meant to go. Standing on the sidewalk in front of the bar, he had a déjà vu moment seeing himself as if from a window a couple of stories overhead. He was on Ninth Avenue, where he lived in a cold-water flat and drank at a bar on the corner of 49th Street. He lived alone. It was soon after Lisa left him. He was on his way back to his apartment after eating lunch at the bar. But that couldn't be it. . . . No. He'd lived on Ninth Avenue years ago. What he was remembering happened now, happened yesterday. He'd come out of an apartment, and he was disoriented, as he was now.

He shook himself. His memory was running away from him again. Was he on Ninth Avenue yesterday? Was that what he remembered? But what was he doing there? Did he get a phone call? Did he remember a phone call? Everything was a jumble. Trying to bring himself back to the moment, he conjured up a method he'd developed to fight off his forgetfulness, a kind of cognitive game he played with himself: What street did he live on? Who was he married to? Where had he been last?

A couple of things started to come back. He was on Ninth Avenue yesterday, yet he had no idea why. Last night, he was drunk when he got home. He could only come up with bits and pieces, pictures, scenes, like remembering a dream, Mary screaming at him. She left. That was it. In a storm of tears, she ran out of the apartment.

That was too bad. What he did, who he was, wasn't her fault. He didn't know why she thought she was responsible for him. She probably went to her sister's in Forest Hills. Maybe she'd stay there this time—one more marriage down the drain. He didn't remember how many wives he'd had. Most of them went through a lot worse than Mary had to deal with. Some even liked him; he drove them away, too. And there was Lisa, who saw into his soul and loved him anyway. Even she didn't stay.

More of what happened yesterday came back. There'd been a phone call, he remembered, though not whom it was from or what it was about. Later, he'd been in a bar, more than one bar; something ugly happened at the door. Was he pushed out, knocked down on the sidewalk? He felt his face for bruises but didn't find anything, though he found a welt on the back of his head. Then came the argument with Mary. Some things came back. But not Ninth Avenue. What was he doing on Ninth Avenue? He hadn't had a reason to go there in thirty years.

After he'd walked down Broadway a couple of blocks, he began to gain control again. This latest scare, though, meant he needed to trust someone with what he knew, in case the time came when his memory didn't come back at all. It was ironic that the source of his writing—his memory reworked into stories—the faculty that sustained him, made him a writer, gave meaning to his life, in the end was betraying him. He couldn't imagine telling someone. He wasn't sure he could. After a couple of more blocks, he thought about Ambler. Something about the man appealed to him, a sense he got that the librarian had suffered himself and would not be quick to judge.

At the Library Tavern, Yates found McNulty the bartender and left a message for Ambler to meet him in Bryant Park when he left work that evening. The bartender wasn't as chatty as usual, so after a couple of beers, he went to sit in Bryant Park where he watched a group of boys and girls who came out of the library and were waiting for a school bus to take them home. They wore Catholic school uniforms and playfully chased and tussled with one other across the lawn, the preteen girls with their uniform skirts swishing against their slim thighs.

When a group of girls flopped down on the grass, laughing and squealing, he walked over and sat where he could see them better. One of the girls, small and blonde, her legs folded in front of her Indian-style, her skirt bunched in her lap, noticed him watching and smiled. Talking animatedly with her friends, she bounced about, shifting her position, stretching out her slim legs, carelessly lifting her skirt, holding it suspended over her bare thighs for a few seconds before letting it drape back over her legs, oblivious to Yates, whose gaze was glued to her thighs.

A second later, two loud pops echoed off the buildings on either side of Bryant Park and Nelson Yates pitched forward off the café chair he was sitting in, falling face forward onto the lawn, dead with two bullet holes in the back of his head.

The young girl who'd smiled at him screamed.

"What's up?" Adele asked Ambler when he showed up at her modular office behind the main reference desk.

He shifted himself uncomfortably. "I found out something disturbing about Nelson's daughter, something Mike Cosgrove told me a little while ago. Right before she ran away, she'd been with a married man who died under suspicious circumstances."

Adele spun her chair to face him. "What does suspicious circumstances mean?" Her voice rose. "She's an escaped murderer?"

He gestured with his hands to quiet her. "No. She disappeared before the police could talk to her. They thought her father was hiding her. He wouldn't talk to the police either."

"So, you think Nelson Yates killed the man for being with his daughter? Nelson Yates is a murderer? You think *he* killed James Donnelly?"

Ambler flapped his arms like a flustered rooster, turning his head this way and that, looking behind him and over the top of her cubicle at whoever was behind her, trying to get her to lower her voice. "I don't think any of those things; for God's sake, quiet down." He spoke barely above a whisper. "The man Emily Yates was with died from a fall. It seems it was a hiking accident. But there's some mystery about it. The police investigating the case never actually talked to Nelson's daughter."

"I'll see if I can find out more about it." Adele swung her chair around to attack her computer.

After closing the reading room shortly before 6:00, Ambler, as he did most evenings, walked over to the Library Tavern for a beer on his way home, and was told by McNulty that Nelson Yates was waiting for him in Bryant Park.

The world seemed to wear heavily on the bartender. "I've seen too many drunks in my life."

"Yates?"

McNulty nodded. "My guess is he was on the wagon and took a tumble. He's on a bender."

"Great. Dementia and a bender. His wife is looking for him," he told McNulty as he left. "I suppose I'll have to try to get him home again."

Ambler saw the police cars on 42nd Street before he crossed Fifth Avenue in the streetlight-lit twilight. Police action near the park wasn't so unusual, yet he sensed this would be different. Picking up his pace, he reached the scene as an unmarked police car pulled up to the curb and his friend Mike Cosgrove hauled himself out.

"What happened?" Ambler asked.

"You don't know?" the detective raised his eyebrows. "Right here in your backyard? . . . I thought you'd have the first one solved by now. And here we have another."

"I don't know what happened."

"Someone murdered someone." Cosgrove's tone was heavy. "Happens more often than you'd expect in a supposedly sane world. What brings you out here if you don't know what happened?"

Cosgrove had him there. The truth was he didn't expect to find a random killing. He expected that when he was told who the victim was, it would mean something to him. Sure enough, a few minutes later, when Cosgrove gave instructions to a couple of detectives and rejoined him, Ambler had his answer.

"Nelson Yates."

The strange thing, he wasn't surprised. He should be shocked, but he wasn't.

Cosgrove gaze bored into him. "More chickens came home to roost, Ray. Why'd someone kill him?"

Ambler shook his head. He spoke slowly, not sure even he was speaking to Cosgrove. "You'd have to think whoever killed James Donnelly did this."

"Maybe. . . . That's a supposition, based on what? What you see is not always what you get."

"You think the murders aren't connected?"

Cosgrove was stone-faced. "I don't think anything. Any facts you got, I'd be happy to take a look at." He looked at the murder scene, taking everything in for a moment. "We'll want a statement."

Ambler stared blankly.

"Ray?"

He came out of his trance. "I will. I will, but not now." He sat down on a wobbly chair on the terrace behind the library.

Cosgrove gestured with his head toward a detective who was questioning two young girls in Catholic school uniforms, huddled together clutching one another, their faces white with fear. "Ed Ford will talk to you when he's finished with the witnesses. I suspect as usual no one will have seen the shooting. How it happens, on a crowded street, someone pulls a gun, fires off three or four rounds, and no one sees it, is beyond me."

"Okay," Ambler said absently. He watched the activity in front of him: clusters of uniformed police officers, EMS medics, the crew from the medical examiner's office wheeling the gurney with the black body bag. Cosgrove was right. He shouldn't jump to conclusions. It could be a random shooting, or someone from Yates's past with a grudge, payback for skipping out on a loan shark, mistaken identity, any one of a dozen explanations. Yet this was the second murder at the library in a week. Who was he kidding?

Detective Ford introduced himself to Ambler and stood in front of him, closer to him than Ambler would have liked. Ford was younger than Cosgrove, not as jaded, aggressive in a peculiarly cheerful New York way that suggested he'd be happy to be your friend or kick your ass: take your pick.

Ambler told the detective what he knew about Yates and his connection to the library, including what he'd already told Mike, that Nelson wanted to keep Max Wagner away from the collection, that there had been an argument between James Donnelly and Max Wagner, and about Yates's "chickens coming home to roost" comment.

"He knew something about the other murder?" The detective raised his eyebrows.

Ambler didn't bother to answer. If it was up to him, he'd want to question Max Wagner and Kay Donnelly. Whatever this guy was thinking, it wasn't Ambler's business to tell him whom he should talk to. "Cosgrove knows where to find me if he wants anything else." He stood.

"Why didn't you report it?"

What was this guy's problem. "I told Mike."

"But you kept some things to yourself, right?"

So that was it. The guy had an opinion of Ambler, knew his reputation. He was fighting windmills. "I'm not in competition with you, Detective Ford."

"You told me everything?" His tone implied that Ambler hadn't.

"Everything I remember. If I think of anything, I'll call Mike."

"You can call me, too." Ford shoved his business card into Ambler's chest and stood in front of him, wide stance, braced, knees slightly bent, arms at the ready, as if he waited for Ambler to make a move so he could smack him. Ambler turned from him cautiously, surprised by the hostility in someone whom he'd spoken to for less than ten minutes. Ford's stance was insulting—demeaning—in its suggestion that he would take Ambler on if Ambler had the balls to stand up to him.

Walking away from the hotshot cop felt like backing down from a fight when he was a kid. He hoped Ford and Benny didn't cross paths.

"God, it's terrible," Adele said. She sat with Ambler on the front steps of the library watching the flow of pedestrians crossing Fifth Avenue and 41st Street. It was a cool evening; the police and everyone else who gather at a murder scene were gone. A hot dog vendor on the uptown corner of 41st Street was lowering his yellow and blue Sabrett umbrella and packing up his stainless steel rolling restaurant. "Why would someone murder Nelson?" The combination of anger and grief did something to Adele's face, gave her a kind of seriousness and depth that hadn't been there before, a deeper acquaintance with sorrow, a depth of sympathy.

"He left a message with McNulty for me to meet him in the park. He wanted to tell me something. If events were to follow a certain archetypal pattern, it would be that he was about to tell me who murdered James Donnelly, so the murderer killed him to keep him from talking."

Adele's eyes widened. "Who was that?"

"Who?"

Adele wasn't buying it. "You think something. You have someone in mind. And I bet I know who it is. Why won't you tell me?"

Ambler watched the hot dog vendor wheel his cart slowly north on Fifth Avenue. Somewhere around 45th Street, he'd head west toward Twelfth Avenue and the storage garage.

"Let's see what the police come up with."

The next morning, Ambler noticed more uniformed security in the library, in the public areas on all three floors, as well as at least two library special investigators he recognized, and a couple of crew-cut, bull-headed, thick-shouldered, linebacker types from the NYPD trying to look inconspicuous, as well as a couple of Cosgrove's fellow workers going office to office, desk to desk, asking questions.

He found Adele seated at her desk at a computer.

"I don't know what this means now that Nelson is dead. I started out looking for Emily Yates and ran into Maximilian Wagner. I'll tell you at lunch when I've finished."

They picked up lunch at the Chipotle on 42nd Street and found a table under the budding sycamores on the 42nd Street side of the park. When he realized where he was—not far from the spot where Nelson Yates was murdered—he wished they'd gone somewhere else. Since Adele hadn't been at the murder scene, where they sat didn't have the same effect on her, so he didn't say anything, instead sat with his back toward the murder scene.

She put a printout on top of her burrito bowl. "In the mid-eighties, Nelson Yates was a visiting professor at Hudson Highlands University in Rockledge." She consulted her notes. "At the same time, Max Wagner was an assistant professor of English there, as was James Donnelly. Kay Donnelly was an English graduate student—"

"That's—"

"Wait. Laura Lee McGlynn, also an English graduate student, was married to another professor, Arthur Woods." Adele paused to catch her breath. "Arthur Woods was the man Emily Yates was with . . . the suspicious death."

Her words outpaced her breath, so she paused. Leaning close to Ambler, she spoke just above a whisper. "Harry Larkin was the college chaplain." She searched his face, worry creasing her own. "Now, two of those people are dead—three, counting the man Emily Yates was with. What does it mean, Raymond?"

He didn't know. "The temptation is to think that discovering people lied or didn't tell us the whole truth about the past means more than it actually means—"

Adele's eyes sprung open, alarm giving way to incredulity. "Of course, it means something."

"You found out what folks tried to keep hidden. You'd like to think that tells us something about the murders. It might or it might not."

Adele sputtered. "You're such a pompous ass. I've read Sherlock Holmes, too."

"Wait." He couldn't hold back a smile.

Adele was having none of it. "'You've been in fucking Afghanistan, I perceive'— Don't give me that crap." She stopped to take a breath and noticed his smile, so she smiled, too. "I'll bet you this turns out to mean something . . . to mean a lot."

"It may," said Ambler.

Mike Cosgrove stopped at the Woodside branch of the Queens Library on Skillman Avenue on his way home and picked up the three books by Nelson Yates on the shelf in the mystery section.

The librarian who checked out the books—the library card he'd signed up for when his daughter was little was still good—knew about Nelson Yates's death. "I really liked his books," she said. "He wrote about real, everyday people. You felt sorry for everyone, even the murderer in the end." She lowered her voice. "And now, he's murdered, killed in broad daylight in the middle of Manhattan. Would you believe that?"

Cosgrove shook his head.

"Did you know about the shooting? Is that why you decided to read him?"

"Something like that," the detective said.

Chapter 8

Laura Lee McGlynn began her day with a two-mile run in Riverside Park, uptown to where the path wound away from the river near 109th Street, turning around under the stone bridge that held up the Henry Hudson Parkway, and trotting back to 90th Street. She picked up coffee and a bagel from The Bagel Basket on Amsterdam, took a shower, and dressed for the day, choosing a springlike, blue and white polka-dot dress from the closet. Flirtatious and demure with its full skirt and halter neck, it would appeal to the librarian, who could be either straight-laced or lecherous; she couldn't tell which.

She hailed a cab on Broadway. Max had told her the night before that Nelson had been murdered. How bizarre was that? Once her new friend Mr. Ambler figured out the connections, he was going to ask about Arthur's death. She made a call from her cell phone while the cab was stuck in traffic in Columbus Circle.

"Hi Gorgeous," Dominic said. "Change your mind about the weekend in Vegas?"

"Sorry, Gorgeous yourself. You know I'd love to go. The timing is bad, not enough notice to come up with a believable reason for the trip. I called you for a different reason. A lot has happened, including murder. I don't suppose you know anything about that."

"Who was murdered?"

She told him. "It wasn't you, was it?"

"Why would it be me?"

"I don't suppose you'd tell me if it was. People will be digging around in the past. They've already started. More than that, Max is desperately trying to find your—and everyone else's—former sweetheart. He's thinking about a private detective."

A long silence at the other end of the line. "Bodies don't stay buried. I told you that when we first met."

Laura Lee's tone went jagged with irritation. "You have looks and muscles; I don't expect you to have brains, too. This wouldn't be such a problem if you hadn't taken up with little Miss Emily when you should have turned around and gone about your business. I want to make sure neither Max, nor the police, nor an inquisitive librarian finds her. Do you know where she is?"

"I'm not saying."

"Don't be an ass."

"I can get your message to her. I told her I wouldn't tell any of you where she was and I won't."

"No message. Just make sure she doesn't get found. What's she doing these days? Is she a hooker?"

Dominic's voice became a growl. "You don't have any reason to criticize her. She never asked you for anything, and she could have."

The cab crossed 42nd Street, heading toward the curb in front of the library. "I've got to go, honey. Sorry I insulted your sex kitten."

"I told you—"

She snapped the phone closed.

Ambler met Laura Lee in the rotunda outside the Rose reading room after lunch. Knowing what Adele uncovered about her and Max's connections to Donnelly and Nelson in the past, he had a lot to ask her.

With her flouncy polka-dot dress and light blue trench coat, her big smile and sparkling white teeth, she brought the spring day with her into the library. Sitting down on a marble bench beneath a mural-like oil painting of Moses carrying the Ten Commandments down from the mountain, she patted a spot beside her.

"Isn't it shocking that Nelson was murdered?" He found her expression puzzling, not sad, but something else, like excitement.

"Sad, indeed," said Ambler. "You knew him quite well, I guess."

"Not well. Max did. They were close at one time." It seemed like a candid answer, matching Adele's research and what Nelson had told him. He didn't know how to take her candor either. Had he expected her to lie?

"You were his student?"

"I was Max's student. Max was Nelson's colleague, his protégé. Nelson was an acclaimed writer . . . and charismatic. We were young and in awe of him."

He was again surprised by her candor. "Something happened between him and Max—"

"You'd have to ask Max." Her eyes met Ambler's and held, with a kind of smug superiority that suggested she knew more than he did and pitied him his innocence. She smiled at him. "You liked Nelson, didn't you?"

"You didn't like him?"

"He's gone. Free of his tormented life—" For a moment, she looked puzzled.

Ambler caught the reaction. "Tormented life?"

"You know. Given what was happening with his mind, his memory. Max will write his biography. He'll be immortalized." She looked hopeful, the expression of the student she used to be, not sure the answer she gave was the right one.

"He didn't want Max to write his biography."

Laura Lee paused for a beat or two. "Nelson was senile. Who knows what he was thinking from one moment to the next?"

"Do you know what came between them?"

She shook her head. "Max never talked about it?"

"No."

"You never asked?"

"No."

"Why?"

"I wasn't interested."

Ambler turned away from her to watch the clusters of tourists chattering together and taking pictures in the rotunda. Something about the tourists with cameras struck a chord. When he turned to face her again, she was dismissive.

"Max is seething over the fight with your impulsive friend, so I've hesitated to bring it up." She paused to meet his gaze and smile beguilingly. "With everything that's happened, I don't know what to think. I understand the police want to question your friend. Kay has hired a lawyer." She took on a melodramatic look of surprise. "Max may have been right after all." Innuendo dripped from her pretty lips. She caught the look of irritation he couldn't smother and laughed easily. "There. There. Raymond."

"Ray," Ambler said. He didn't like her calling him Raymond. Adele called him that; no one else did.

"Raymond suits you. Things will sort themselves out, Raymond."

This wasn't a good time to bring it up, but she irritated him. "I'd like to ask you about your first husband."

For the first time, she was flustered. "My first husband died." Her eyes had a kind of wildness in them. Like every other expression, it was becoming on her. "This is painful to talk about—" Her expression crumbled. "Why would you ask me?"

"As a matter of fact, I asked because I was interested in Emily Yates."

Antsy, no longer so self-possessed, she said, "That's bizarre. I guess you've discovered she was with him when he died. She shouldn't have been—I won't go into the sordid details."

"How did he die?"

"It was accidental—scandalous, stupid, but accidental. High on pot, showing off for a teenage tramp, he flipped himself over a wall."

"Did you know Emily Yates?"

"Why would you ask about her? She disappeared years ago. What does she or Arthur's death have to do with Nelson's death?" Her expression hardened. "I don't like being cross-examined." She assumed the cold, haughty attitude attractive, charming women switch to when they don't want to be bothered. "Are you playing detective, Mr. Ambler? Too much time with your mystery novels?"

"She has a point," McNulty the bartender told Ambler after hearing about his conversation with Laura Lee. "The guy was losing his grip."

"She said I spent too much time with detective novels. Maybe she's right. A man hints that he knows about a murder and then is murdered before he can tell me what he knows. It's straight out of Agatha Christie."

"She wasn't so bad," McNulty said. "Maybe you should look to her books for advice."

"Maybe." He thought about Ross Macdonald and how the sins of the past shape the present. If chickens came home to roost for Donnelly, it was likely some came home to roost for Yates also. Laura Lee was wrong. He wasn't spending too much time with his mystery collection; he wasn't spending enough time with it.

At lunch at Szechuan Gourmet on 39th Street, Adele told Ambler she'd found a good deal of press coverage of Arthur Woods's death and Emily Yates's disappearance. "There were straight news stories and gossipy, scandal sheet stories about Nelson and his wife, Lisa Dolloway, Emily's mother, a poet. You should read her poems; eroticism. They made me blush. The press blamed Nelson and her and their privileged, bohemian lifestyle for what happened to Emily."

"I'm sure it will all be in Max Wagner's book. He's probably using the same databases you're using."

"You'd think if he was going to vilify Nelson Yates, Yates would have killed him, rather than the other way around."

"Who said Max killed Nelson?"

"Isn't that what you think?"

Ambler fiddled with his chopsticks. "We know what we know. What's more important at the moment is what we don't know, and that's quite a bit. Do I need to enumerate?"

"We don't know for sure who killed Nelson and James Donnelly or why."

"Right. We don't even know if the same person committed both murders—"

"It has to be."

Ambler shook his head. "What we know for a fact is they've both been murdered. We know how, where, and when. We don't know who or why."

After lunch, on the way back to the library, Adele told him about the shoeshine boy, Johnny Smith.

"His name sounds made up."

"I thought so, too. But I can't see the boy lying to me. He has no reason to. He wants to be friends."

Ambler let Adele talk. She was smart enough to know the city was full of sad stories and neglected children—far too many to take under your wing. The city hardened you to things like that—neglected children, homeless mothers, suffering humanity. "A happy man only feels so because the unhappy bear their burden in silence," Chekov wrote. There was a time when he cried over lost kittens and dying birds, when he took in strays. Do all kids feel that kind of empathy with suffering—the neglected and abused ones?

Adele wanted to check for a record of child neglect or abuse, family problems, police calls, anything where the authorities got involved.

"I don't think you'll get very far. Official files on child neglect aren't public, nothing to do with children is. I guess if there's an arrest of an adult, there's a record of that."

"Could your friend Mike Cosgrove ask someone to do an informal check?"

Ambler hoisted his shoulder bag and agreed to ask without believing it would do any good.

"Why the bag of books?"

"I've been rereading Ross Macdonald. I'm up to *The Zebra-Striped Hearse*. He's looking for a missing girl."

"If you can tear yourself away, I want you to come for dinner tonight. But you need to go home first and get a pair of shoes."

Ambler called Adele before leaving his apartment that evening. "Can I bring anything?"

"Only a pair of shoes that needs polishing."

He laughed. But brought the shoes, along with a bottle of Chianti, since Adele was making spaghetti and meatballs.

After dinner, she suggested a walk. "Bring your shoes."

"How could I not?" He looked at his feet.

She looked, too. "I thought you brought another pair."

They found Johnny Smith in front of his building, waiting.

"We have another pair of shoes tonight, Johnny," Adele said.

The boy couldn't disguise his glee, though he looked ready to burst with embarrassment. Hard to believe his mother would let him be out on the street at night, shoeshine or no shoeshine. Except Ambler remembered with profound regret the times Liz was drunk or high and his own son wandered the alphabet streets of the East Village at all hours.

"Let's go where it's warmer," Ambler said, and took them to the ice-cream store on Ninth Avenue.

"You like baseball?" Amber asked the kid.

The boy, who wore a Yankee cap, nodded.

"You know who Mariano Rivera is?"

The boy's expression was pleased, smug, like a kid at school when he knows the answer. "He's the best closer."

"How about Albert Rodriguez?"

The boy stopped slurping his milkshake. "Alex." He spoke distinctly.

"You don't know Albert Rodriguez?"

"Alex," the boy said. "It's Alex Rodriguez."

"Albert!"

"Alex. It's A-Rod. Alex Rodriguez."

Ambler laughed. "How about Delwood Jeter?"

"It's Derek!!" the boy shouted happily.

"Derwood?"

"Derek," said the boy, laughing. "Derek Jeter."

Adele watched them. "How did you do that?" She was starry-eyed.

For a few more minutes, Ambler and the boy talked about the Yankees and the new season, the Red Sox, and the closing of Yankee Stadium. The boy's face glowed.

"You've never been to Yankee Stadium?"

The boy shook his head. If he felt sorry for himself, he gave no sign of it. It was as if he felt no right to it, no more reason for him to go there than to go to Paris or the moon. He wasn't a kid a dad took to the ballpark, so he had no expectation of it. As neglectful a father as Ambler had been, at least he took his son to the ballpark. John loved baseball. He'd learned to keep score when he was even younger than this fellow here.

"Where do you work?" Johnny asked Ambler.

"At the library."

"On Tenth Avenue?"

"No. The big library downtown on 42nd Street. Have you ever been there?"

"I've been there," he said brightly. "My mom took me."

On the walk back, the boy remembered he hadn't shined Ambler's shoes. "I'll do it now," he said, stopping and putting his kit on the sidewalk.

"When we get to your building," Ambler said.

Johnny reluctantly picked up his kit. His posture gave Ambler the sense that he wanted to argue yet restrained himself—a yes sir, no sir kid. Was he brought up with good manners or was he dominated, afraid to disagree? Something in the boy's subdued manner suggested the latter.

The answer wasn't long coming. A few doors from Johnny's apartment building, Ambler felt more than saw the boy stiffen beside him. Coming toward them was a man, maybe in his thirties or early forties, good-sized, in good shape, wearing what looked to Ambler like designer jeans and a sleek black leather jacket, the kind of outfit tough guys, if not wise guys, wear. He walked with a swagger and his expression was calm but hard.

"What are you doin'?" he said to Johnny, ignoring Ambler and Adele. "Your mother's lookin' for you." The man raised his arm, so the boy cringed. "Get your ass upstairs." He reached to grab the boy's arm, but Ambler's arm shot out and brushed the man's hand away.

Startled, the guy stared at Ambler for a few seconds and then swung, making a fist, stepping forward, and swinging from the hip. Ambler sank into a bent-knee posture, raised his arm, warding off the punch and rolling his hips, all in one motion, so that the punch slid by his face. The man stumbled but righted himself. Putting up his hands, he assumed a boxer's stance, something between a sneer and a smile on his face. He jabbed at Ambler a couple of times to no effect, charged at him swinging both fists, one after the other, again without landing a punch. Ambler swayed from side to side, turning at the waist, shifting his weight, as each of the punches came at him. The man faked a punch, and then kicked viciously toward Ambler's groin. Ambler swiveled, bent, and brushed it away.

Winded, the man tried a few more punches to no avail, finally charging at Ambler, arms open, shoulder down, to tackle him. Ambler avoided the charge. This time, he turned farther than he had previously, pushing the man as he turned and sending him sprawling into a parked car.

Leaning against the car, bent at the waist, taking deep breaths, the man appraised Ambler. Adele stood to the side, the boy in front of her, her arms draped over him protectively. Ambler, breathing heavily himself, watched the man next to the car.

"A standoff," the man said, not an exact description of their situation. He had the hardened, chiseled face of someone both brutal and afraid—a kind of reckless cockiness in his expression that would be appealing to women attracted to bad boys but might hide the intrinsic fear of a bully. Despite this edginess, the fight-or-flee instinct so close to the surface, he took their altercation lightly, as if he were amused by it.

"You're pretty good." His smile was fake, his interest sincere. "What is that, some kind of karate?" Not waiting for an answer, he said. "It's cool but it don't make you a tough guy. You could get whacked. That fancy footwork don't help with that." He let this sink in before repeating himself. "Don't think you're a tough guy." He straightened up and dusted himself off, smoothing his jacket.

"I don't," said Ambler. "I didn't want you to manhandle the boy."

"You're strangers. How do I know what you're up to? You don't have no business with the kid. I could have you arrested."

Ambler spoke quietly to Johnny. "Would you go up and get your mother? I'd rather explain things to her."

The boy froze, rooted to the sidewalk, his eyes wild, his glance swinging from the man to Ambler. Finally, he leaned his head back and looked up helplessly at Adele.

"What do you want to happen, Johnny?" Her voice was gentle.

The man took a step toward them, holding his hands open in front of him in a placating gesture. "Look. Maybe there's a misunderstanding. My name's Dominic. I'm a friend of Johnny's mother. He knows I wouldn't hurt him, right Johnny?"

When the boy didn't answer, anger flashed in the man's eyes. "Don't fuck around, Johnny. You know goddamn well—"

"Can I go upstairs?" he asked.

Ambler's heart ached. This was the kid's home. This was his life. He couldn't protect the boy. Probably, he'd made things worse for the kid.

"The boy was shining shoes. We bought him an ice cream." In a sense, the guy was right. He and Adele were strangers. City kids like Johnny shouldn't talk to strangers, much less go somewhere with them. This was the orthodoxy, the lowest common denominator, the *Daily News* take on it. Yet despite the orthodoxy, the kid would do better with him and Adele than he would with this guy and his mother. "We were bringing him home. I'm sure his mother was worried that he's out this late. It wasn't his fault. I'd like a chance to explain to her, so—"

Dominic interrupted. "Let the kid go upstairs. She won't bother him. That's his problem; she don't bother him about anything. He does whatever the hell he wants." He paused. "I was leavin' anyway, if that's what you're worried about. I'm not going to kick his ass." He laughed. "Go ahead, Johnny." The boy started to walk toward his apartment building.

"It's his scam, you know," the man said. "Standin' on the street with his shoeshine box lookin' pathetic." He laughed. "I taught the fuckin' kid to shine shoes. I practically made him a millionaire." He tousled the boy's head as he walked past. "You goddamn con artist."

Johnny turned his sad eyes on Adele and Ambler and trudged toward his building. Ambler realized he hadn't had the shoeshine.

Chapter 9

"I don't get it," said Emily. "I just took you there. I'm not taking you to Midtown again. You got your own goddamn library right here on Tenth Avenue."

"Because they're nice. They'd show me around. You don't need to go."

Emily had to squint one eye closed to see her son clearly. "I said no and don't you dare try going down there by yourself."

What Johnny saw was his mother in her usual morning condition, hungover, irritated, half-awake, flapping about the messy apartment in flip-flops, in her underwear and a T-shirt, her hair ratty and disheveled, last night's makeup smeared and ground into her face.

"I'm telling you Johnny. You go there; that's it. I'm calling child services. You're an uncontrollable child. They'll take you away." The more she talked, the angrier she got. He'd heard the threat enough times for it to have lost most of its terror. Even he knew he wasn't the uncontrollable one. Littering the living room, besides half-empty Chinese take-out boxes, sandwich wrappers, and food-encrusted dishes, were two empty vodka fifths, beer bottles; on the floor near the couch, the shoes and socks of the man still asleep in the bedroom. She'd be the one in trouble, he knew, if anyone from child services came.

The time his teacher asked him was everything okay at home because he'd come to school so many days wearing the same clothes, he told her his mom was sick, but his aunt had come and would stay until his mom got better, so everything would be okay. He knew if he told the teacher the problem was his mom got her hands on a bunch of cocaine and wouldn't be home much until it was gone, the teacher would call child services and he would be taken away. He didn't want that, not to be taken away by strangers, not for children's services to get him.

"You hear me, Johnny. Stay away from there. Stay away from those librarian people. They'll cause us trouble. Believe me." Her voice was calmer, and her eyes glistened with something like tears. When she quieted like this, the times when the drinking wore off, when she wasn't hungover, or wasted in the aftermath of a coke bender, she looked at him the way no one else ever did.

When she looked at him like that, he understood he could trust her more than anyone else in the world. Not the teachers nor the social workers, nor anyone else cared as much about him as she did. No matter how he hated what she did; no matter the pains in his stomach or aches in his chest when she stumbled up the stairs with some new guy pawing at her; no matter how nasty she was to him or that she forgot to make him breakfast or wasn't home at dinner time; no matter how deeply he hated her for the pain he felt without understanding; no matter that he knew she was wrong and that his life wasn't as it was supposed to be; even if he knew she cheated him out of the things a child is supposed to have, he knew she loved him differently than anyone else would or could, and because of that he needed her desperately and was terrified something would happen to her, yet knew instinctively that something would happen to her, that something bad would happen to her. He knew with the certainty of instinct that his mother was on an inexorable path of self-destruction.

She went to the kitchen, found her purse, and rummaged through it. When she finished, she knelt down in front of him. "Things will be better soon, Johnny. I had a really bad week. But things are getting better. Sam's going to find me places to sing. That's what he does. He's a promoter. Here." She handed him a five-dollar bill. "Get breakfast at the Greek's on the way to school."

"I don't need money. I got money." He didn't know how to say the rest of what he felt, so he looked into her eyes, hoping she would see it in his.

She nodded. "You're a good boy. . . . Tell you what," she said, standing. "I'll pick you up after school and take you to the library."

"The one downtown?" His eyes brightened.

Her face twisted with anger. "Not the goddamn one downtown. I told you not there. Forget about downtown. Stay away from those people. They don't want you there. They don't care about you. You're an oddity to them, a kid to feel sorry for. We don't need them feeling sorry for us. You don't need other people taking care of you. . . . I take care of you!" she screamed.

He could feel tears forming in his eyes, and he hated that. His mother wailed and cried all the time. He didn't want to be like her. He didn't ever want to be like her. She calmed herself right away. Because of his tears, he knew. He was mortified.

"I'm sorry I yelled, Johnny. I didn't mean to. You know how I feel about people who think they're better than us. You're not a poor little kid. You don't need them. You come from an important family."

She'd said that before, whatever it meant. As far as he knew, he had no family but her. The only other constant in his life besides her was Dominic. Unlike the man in the bedroom who might be around for a day or a week and disappear forever, Dominic would show up for a week, and disappear again for months or years. But he'd always come back. He had since Johnny was little. But, even when he was little, it was as if he wasn't there. Every now and then, his mom and Dominic would go somewhere, usually the Italian place on Ninth Avenue for dinner, and his mom would make Dominic take him along. Sometimes she left Dominic to watch him, but all they did was watch TV. The only one thing Dominic had done was get him the shoeshine kit and teach him to shine shoes. He'd done that himself as a kid was what Dominic told him.

She kissed him in the doorway as he was leaving and hugged him for a long time. He didn't like feeling her almost naked body against him and hated the sour smell of her mouth and the sweaty stink of her body. She let go of him finally, saying, "I'll pick you up after school." He nodded, but he knew she wouldn't.

"Two dead authors," said Cosgrove. "Maybe it's literary criticism."

Ambler rolled his eyes. Cosgrove was treating him to dinner at a small French restaurant on Lexington Avenue in the Thirties that he wanted to try. A self-taught epicure, Cosgrove liked to explore the city's off-the-beaten-track brasseries and bistros.

"We've done a lot of background, a lot of interviews. Nothing connects the victims to each other in the last twenty years." Cosgrove eyed him carefully. "The stuff you gave me was good. Once upon a time, Yates was the teacher. Donnelly, your friend Wagner, and the two women, Wagner's wife and Donnelly's ex-wife, Kay, were either teachers or students. But it was one year; despite all the upheaval—death, divorce, runaway kid—that was it. They parted company."

"And Arthur Woods?"

Cosgrove nodded. "I've wondered about that, too. The guy went over a cliff. The autopsy found THC. The thinking was he was horsing around and fell. Until I come up with something better, I'll say that one isn't connected. What do you think of a vendetta against the library?"

"Neither of the victims worked at the library."

"It's still a black eye, puts everyone on edge, makes it an unsafe place to be." He paused and stared into Ambler's eyes for a long moment. "By the way, you didn't mention your boss—the saint—was part of that long-ago college scene. Maybe you didn't know?"

Ambler averted his gaze. "I didn't think it was relevant."

"He told you?"

Ambler didn't like how this was going. He examined a painting on the far wall trying to avoid Cosgrove's hard stare. "He probably didn't think it was relevant either." He knew how lame he sounded, but he pushed through. "There's a point to your buying me dinner," he said. "I hoped you'd come to see you were barking up the wrong tree with Benny Barone."

Cosgrove shook his head. "You know better than that. I never said Barone was a suspect, and I'm not saying now he isn't."

Ambler put down his fork and placed his napkin on top of his plate. "I hope you have an expense account for this."

"Yeh, right." Cosgrove poured the last of the wine into both of their glasses. "In homicide, we entertain a lot—expense-account lunches with suspects, a corporate box at the Garden for when we take out hit men and serial killers." Folding his napkin, he put it on the table in front of him. "The duck was cooked perfectly, crisp but not dry, the sauce a touch sweet for my money. How was your sole?"

"Good," said Ambler, who had no way of judging.

Cosgrove searched Ambler's face for a moment. "So what's

the connection between Donnelly and Yates? You think it's something that happened back then that's working itself out now, right? That's one of your patented theories."

Ambler didn't hesitate. "It's a possibility. Max Wagner's a connection—not only in the past. Max and Donnelly may have been writing competing biographies of Nelson Yates. I told you about the argument they had, or Benny did, possibly about plagiarism. That's an accusation not lightly made in academic circles."

Cosgrove eyed Ambler with his practiced police interrogator stare. "No offense, professor. It doesn't seem to me anyone cares enough about this literary crap to kill someone over it."

Ambler took a deep breath. Even so, his tone was sharp. "Not a professor. I'm a librarian. You asked. Take it for what it's worth."

Cosgrove shifted his gaze. Ambler regretted his reaction, which surprised and embarrassed his friend; no reason for Cosgrove to know the professor comment was insulting. Lots of water under the bridge. After a moment, Cosgrove said. "Let me try again. Back to the library, Larkin's a strange duck—"

"Why?" Something in Cosgrove's tone put him on alert.

Cosgrove snorted. "Because he acts like that, like you just did. Like he's covering something up."

Ambler remembered something. "Tourists. Tourists have cameras. Someone—"

Cosgrove nodded. "We thought of that. A group of Japanese college students, most of them had cameras. There's diplomacy involved. We're working through the State Department." His manner softened. "I know you don't like what I'm asking. Think of it this way. We need to do more than catch the killer. We need to eliminate as a suspect anyone who had access to the room and might have had a reason to kill either of them. If we don't have an ironclad case, if we miss something, once we do have the killer, a good defense lawyer will ask why we didn't investigate

Jack the Ripper or Marty the Mugger or Kate the Killer, all with motive and opportunity to kill the victim. And if we didn't investigate him or her, how do we know the aforementioned Jack or Marty or Kate isn't the murderer, rather than the accused?"

What Cosgrove said was true but not the whole story. Ambler waited.

Cosgrove took out his notebook. They went back and forth about Harry for another twenty minutes. Harry was hiding something; they both knew that. Where they differed was on what it meant, and whether he had a right to keep things to himself.

"If he knew who the killer was, he'd tell you."

Cosgrove raised his eyebrows, opened his eyes wider, his expression suggesting patience. "I've put off bringing him in for a lot of reasons, one of them isn't that I don't think he has anything more to tell us."

Chapter 10

After a couple of espressos and when enough time had passed for the wine to wear off, Cosgrove began the drive home to Queens. At that time of night, through the Midtown Tunnel, he'd be home in twenty minutes, with luck. As always, the case was foremost in his mind. This one could get away if he didn't get a break soon. Too little evidence, no witnesses, everyone holding his cards close to the vest. Not that it was the first case where everyone had something to hide and lied. Scholars and librarians, a murder in the hood, a body in the library, the response was the same. No one gave up anything easily.

Ray was protecting his boss, understandable enough, also protecting the Italian kid who was getting it on with the ex-wife of the first victim. If he were honest with himself, despite the suspicions he laid out for Ray, he didn't have a suspect. The first murder looked like vengeance—another "Somebody Done Somebody Wrong Song." The ex-wife, with the Italian kid to pull the trigger, was a good bet, certainly not the only one. The victim could have done any number of people wrong. The shooter was efficient. The shock of brains and blood spurting out of the guy's head, spattering the floor and walls, would've caused most people to jerk the gun, put the next bullet in the ceiling, the wall, the floor. You had to be pretty cold to stay on target. A pro would stay on target—and maybe someone filled with hate. He didn't see that in the kid Benny. But you never know.

He wasn't mad at Ray for stonewalling him. Ray wasn't a cop. What he knew about crime and investigation—and for someone not a cop, he knew a lot—he didn't know crime the way a cop did. Ray felt sorry for everyone. When he saw the fear and the lying and the regret once the suspect was nailed, he felt sorry for the person. A cop couldn't do his job if you felt sorry for all the poor miserable bastards you had to lock up. You called them scum and garbage and assholes and you thought about what they did and who they did it to, rather than what went wrong in their miserable lives to make them what they were.

Cosgrove didn't like the train of thought he was on. The black hats and white hats were taking on shades of gray. He was thinking about the Yates book he'd been reading. It wasn't that you had illusions about the killer. It was that at the end you didn't have a sense of someone or something triumphing, certainly not good over evil. He was almost finished with the book now—he'd finish it tonight—and realized the anxious, hopeful feeling that welled up as he turned into his street was the anticipation of getting back to the book.

He found a parking space not far from the house and walked the short distance, not conscious of how alert he was to his surroundings. After dinner with a friend, on a quiet street in Queens's safest neighborhood, territory as familiar as his living room, he was like a rabbit in the field, senses heightened, ears alert to any sound, eyes sweeping the street in front of him, behind him, between parked cars, amongst the shrubbery, in the shadows of trees. He wasn't afraid, yet he believed with his entire being that danger was around him.

The house was dark, so he hoped Denise was home, and, as usual, he hoped Sarah was asleep. Ray hadn't asked about her. A couple of years now he stopped bringing Sarah along to dinner with Ray. He didn't take her to department social events anymore either. He'd lugged her out of too many of them. Cops' wives got tipsy at parties, often plastered. For too many of them, becoming a drunk or getting a divorce were options one and two. Trouble with wives and trouble with kids. It could happen to any cop—there but for the grace of God.

The thing with Sarah was he should never have married her, and because he did, marrying her when he loved someone else, what she became was his fault. After two or three times at dinner with Ray when she got shitfaced, he didn't bring her anymore. The first time he didn't bring her Ray asked, and he never did again.

Ray's ex-wife was a drunk, too. He didn't talk about her either. What they did talk about was their kids. Years ago, Ray came to him when his son John hit the wall. He'd often regretted not helping more. At the time, he didn't know the librarian well and didn't know what to make of him and his son. The boy was raised by his mother. That got him some sympathy. But Ray, as desperate as he was, seemed distant, acting out of guilt maybe, not the love you'd expect from a parent. He learned later, when he knew Ray better, that he'd been wrong on this. Ray was distant and aloof. That was how he was. It didn't mean he didn't love his son. There was nothing he wouldn't have done for the boy. He was crushed when he was sent to prison.

More recently, he talked to Ray when he worried himself sick about Denise. Thirteen years old, she came home drunk. He didn't know what to do with her. Hadn't she seen what happened to her mother? He was cursed, payback for the wrongs he'd done. Inside, Cosgrove found everyone home and asleep. What amazing peace that brought him.

Saturday morning, Harry barged into the tiny reading room, rousting Ambler from his work. "You've created a real firestorm." His eyes were blazing. "The president's office called me. He wants to answer an opinion article in the *Times* yesterday by some detective novelist blasting the library for closing the crime fiction reading room."

"That was—"

"I don't care who it was. The president is furious." He lowered his voice. "I have to draft the rebuttal."

"That's ridiculous."

"I have to. If the president asks me to do something, I do it. It's my job." Harry clasped his hands together in front of his formidable midsection. "You have to realize your reading room is only a small part, a tiny part, of a grander plan—hundreds of millions of dollars are at stake. You need to tone things down."

Ambler stared at him. "Jesus Christ, Harry, you told me I had to do something to try to keep the reading room open."

"Not that! I wasn't expecting a public fight, protests and such. We don't want the whole city up in arms criticizing the library. I meant things like a well-reasoned letter to the president."

Ambler stood. "I don't care about the new library plan. It's stupid, a corporate cabal. Bankers, Wall Street lawyers, real estate developers, what do they know about scholarship and research? They'll turn the library into an amusement park—"

"I'm not going to stand for this, Ray." Harry tried to come across as defiant, but he looked crestfallen. Poor Harry was more inclined to sit in the field and smell the flowers like Ferdinand than take on the corporate powers and the library president—or deal with murders in his library.

• • •

After his encounter with Harry, Ambler called Benny to ask him to arrange a meeting with Kay Donnelly.

"Why do you think I could do that?" Benny asked.

Ambler chuckled. Benny was the only one who thought his secret romance with Kay Donnelly was secret. "You risked your job to stand up for her. You're joined together as murder suspects. I'm sure she'd listen to you if you told her she should talk to me."

That evening, Ambler intercepted Kay as she was leaving the library. She stood impatiently in line while the guard checked bags at the Fifth Avenue door, her game face on, no smile, a forbidding expression.

"Benny said you wanted to talk to me. What?"

He walked with her down Fifth Avenue to 34th Street, where she'd catch the Crosstown Select Bus to her residence hall.

"Nelson said your ex-husband was writing a book. He'd contacted Nelson about his papers. Did you know that? Did Max know?"

She faced him. Her eyes met his. She wasn't evasive. She was scared. "It's difficult for me to talk about Max. You need to ask him what he knows and doesn't know about James." They walked in silence for a moment. After some time, she said, "I'm in a difficult position. I need Max. My academic career depends on his support—"

Ambler nodded. "I understand. Perhaps you could tell me about your ex-husband."

She searched his face for a moment. "I don't know about his life in recent years. He was angry over our divorce at first—not because he missed me or loved me. He simply couldn't accept that I'd dare to leave him. He had a superior, whiny way of bossing me around." She paused to regroup her thoughts. "James thought he was smarter than everyone else. Maybe he was. The last I knew he was teaching at a women's college: an inexhaustible supply of privileged, oversexed brats looking up to him as the sensitive poetic interpreter of life and literature. That's what he wanted from life.

"I was a romantic. I fell in love too easily, was impressed by men I thought more accomplished and smarter than I was. In my imagination, I made James into the dashing, suffering, poetic genius I wanted a man to be. We drank wine and he'd recite poetry. He wrote poems. I thought then they were for me. Later, I realized the poems were always about him. It was idiotic of me to marry him. He married me because I wouldn't sleep with him if he didn't." After a short time, she realized he didn't really want to be married or have kids. He was the center of his own universe. Everything and everyone else played a supporting role.

"He sounds like Max."

"He was like Max. They competed . . . for everything." Her expression, embarrassed and defiant, was suggestive on the one hand and daring him to ask what "everything" included on the other. He chose not to ask.

"There are things about Max you're not willing to tell me."

"That's right."

Ambler waited.

She sighed. "Max is hard to understand and harder to like. For reasons of his own, he's supported me in my career. It's more difficult than you might think for a woman at elite universities, even now. I owe him a lot."

"To protect him at all cost?"

She shook her head. "Max is ambitious, ruthless, and unforgiving of anyone who crosses him. He's not a murderer."

"You know that for sure? You were with him?"

She shook her head and looked away, splashes of red erupting on her cheeks. "Are you finished?" Her expression was stern, unsmiling. "Benny said I can trust you to keep what I've said to yourself."

"I will, Mrs. Donnelly. Let me know when you're ready to talk about Max."

"Call me Kay." She got into another line of people, this time to get on the bus.

Adele knew Harry was in trouble. Looking into the pasts of people you know and trust and even love can be a shattering experience. What she discovered about Harry, she didn't want to tell anyone. She didn't want it to be true and tried to put him out of her thoughts. What was the term? He was "collateral damage." It was Emily she was interested in. Each day now, she stole some time to pore through the Yates collection—more than a hundred boxes of papers, photos, journals, notebooks, letters, index cards, bar napkins with handwriting on them, Christmas cards, God knows what else—looking for whatever she could find on his daughter.

Raymond wasn't so interested in Emily. He cared about the murders. Of course, he would. As much as he presented himself as a simple librarian living quietly among his books and papers, he thought of himself as a reincarnation of Sherlock Holmes—or lately, Lew Archer.

She'd found newspaper accounts of Arthur Woods's death. He and Emily Yates were in an area local lore called a lover's leap. The girl was in shock, hysterical, when she flagged down a car. She didn't remember what happened. Her parents rescued her. Lawyers and psychiatrists got involved. She was tucked away in a psychiatric hospital. She ran away from there. She kept running away. Could it be because Arthur Woods was murdered and she knew who the killer was? That would be a reason to run away and stay hidden.

The precocious child of famous writers, Emily grew up in a world of culture and books, college towns and university campuses, while Adele, the daughter of a cigarette-smoking, meat-

and-potatoes cooking single mom navigated between row-house stoops, candy stores, cement sidewalks, and asphalt parks. Yet Adele's life had gone more or less the way lives are supposed to go—except for that not having a family thing—and Emily's went awry before she was anywhere near grown up.

Nelson Yates suffered a nervous breakdown after his daughter ran away. They'd been very close when she was young. The photos of them together—not many of them because Nelson didn't like to be photographed—seemed to contain much happiness and love. He took her on book tours with him, traveled to Europe with her. She was his favorite companion. Her mother was in and out of hospitals suffering from depression when Emily was a child. For long periods of time, Nelson and Emily only had each other.

After a while, Adele felt she knew more about the Yates family than she wanted to. She felt like a voyeur, yet it wasn't so much her doing. Yates and Emily's mother, Lisa Dolloway, paraded their life out in public—the romantic part as well as the fighting and bickering. It was kind of embarrassing to read about it. People should keep some things to themselves. All that intensity and passion in the end turned to poison anyway. Their marriage fell apart after Emily ran away. It was sad. It wouldn't be so great to have such passion in your life. How exhausting it must be. At the same time, she wondered if she might not be jealous. It was awful also to live a life without passion.

Lisa Dolloway disappeared after her marriage ended. Unlike Emily, she wasn't hiding from anyone, had no reason to hide her identity, yet Adele couldn't find any trace of her once she left Nelson. You'd think she'd be easy to find, yet it was as if she'd disappeared off the face of the earth.

When Raymond told her about Nelson's funeral, she wondered if Lisa Dolloway would attend. She did love him once, and it seemed he never got over her. It wasn't to be a funeral exactly.

The body had been cremated. His publisher and his wife were holding a memorial service on April 29. They chose the date because it was the week the Mystery Writers of America held its annual Edgar Allan Poe banquet and many of his fellow writers would be in town.

"Homicide cops like to go to the victims' funerals," Raymond told her. "Most everyone who might know something about the murder comes together and, for some reason, the ritual makes them want to talk about what happened. Often, the killer shows up."

"Maybe," said Adele. "I doubt anyone will throw himself on the casket and confess. Have you been reading Perry Mason? Are you going?"

"I'd want to pay my respects."

Chapter 11

The next day was the third Sunday of the month, so Ambler, after his tai chi practice, walked up Third Avenue and across 42nd Street to Grand Central where he boarded a Hudson Line train for the hour-and-a-half-long ride to Beacon. The train car he rode in was old and worn, rickety almost. At that hour of the morning on Sunday, going north, up the Hudson, away from the city, most of the riders were on a mission similar to his. Black and Latina women, many of them with kids, some older, more matronly; many of them he'd seen often enough to nod hello to and receive a small indication of recognition.

He took a cab from the station at Beacon to the Shawangunk Correctional Facility, waited through the interminable processing in the anteroom, signed in as a visitor to John Lennon Parker—his mother's last name, though Ambler's name was on the boy's birth certificate.

When John came into the visiting room, his gaze sweeping the area, his face expressionless, he reminded Ambler of the boy's mother. He resembled Liz in many ways, a man's version of her haunting beauty, slight of build, an almost fearful gentleness about him. He didn't strike you as someone who should be in a prison, certainly not someone in prison for murder.

Ambler, feeling terrible unease as he did each time he came to the prison, sat uncomfortably at a chrome and Formica table that reminded him of a school lunchroom. His son sat down opposite him. Ambler's heart ached so he could scarcely breathe. Conversation was strained as usual, with the boy showing a smug, cynical expression, as his father labored to converse. His expression said to Ambler, as he was sure the boy meant it to, it's your fault I'm here. Whatever guilt you feel, you deserve. Over the years he'd been coming to see John in prison, little had changed. During one of his early visits, he'd made the mistake of criticizing Liz. Whatever her faults, John would hear none of it from Ambler. The boy's anger at his father—hatred, possibly—wasn't unexpected. It was better than indifference. He'd left the boy and his mother, left the boy when he was too young to defend himself with a mother incapable of making her own way through the world, much less of raising a child.

"I put a few dollars in your account," Ambler said.

John nodded. He lit a cigarette.

"Any problems? Anything I can do?"

"Nothing I can't handle, Pop." He said this flippantly to remind Ambler he had dues to pay. He knew that; yet he was hopeful. If his son really didn't want him there, he could take him off the visitor list. Instead, the boy worked out his anger on his father, and why shouldn't he?

After Ambler's attempts at conversation, punctuated by John's nonresponses and long periods of silence, the boy spoke without looking at his father. "I got something maybe you can take care of."

Ambler nodded.

"Look in on Mom. I'm not sure what's going on with her."

Ambler hesitated. "I haven't seen or spoken to your mother since the trial, John. I don't know where she is. I don't think she'd want to see me."

John's brow wrinkled; his expression softened, so that he resembled himself as a boy, the slim wisp of a boy, with dark hair that belied his blue eyes, an unconvincing tough-guy sneer, and a shy, in-spite-of-himself smile. "I don't know where she is, either. She hasn't been up. My letters come back."

Ambler stayed another two hours. This time, he'd remembered to bring pocketfuls of change for the vending machines. As the visit wore on, John's hostility wore down as well. He whispered a couple of times to Ambler, once pointing out one of the more notorious inmates—a cop killer from the Bronx who'd taken on half the city's police force in a standoff. The boy told Ambler brief anecdotes about other inmates, fights in the yard, a lockdown in the cellblock. Twice, he nodded to fellow inmates—both white guys you'd cross the street to avoid if you saw coming your way—and told Ambler how things worked in the prison.

"Gus and Wills got my back; I got theirs. That's how it is in here—only one or two guys you can trust."

Ambler cringed. John wasn't tough—far from it. He'd been a drinker, a pot smoker, a musician living the nightlife, not a gangbanger or drug dealer, not in the criminal life. He'd killed a man he shared an apartment with in a fight fueled by alcohol and cocaine—with the gun the other man pulled on him. That was John's story. Though the police, the prosecutor, and the judge didn't believe him, Ambler did. He was stunned when John was found guilty of murder rather than involuntary manslaughter. The look of hate John directed at him when the judge announced the verdict burned a hole through his heart.

On the way back to the city on the train after the visit,

thoughts of John kept Ambler's eyes moist with tears. Most of the folks he'd ridden up with were on the train going back, everyone worn out from the day, somber, hardly anyone speaking or looking at anyone else; even the kids were subdued. Many eyes, like his, glistened with tears.

He'd told John he'd look for his mother, so, the nighttime being the right time, even on a Sunday night, to look for Liz, he set out for the lower depths of Manhattan. What was it Lenny Bruce said? "There is nothing sadder than an aging hipster"—even worse, an aging flower child. Since he'd met her—a fifteen-year-old runaway—Liz had been a denizen of the East Village and its environs. The first night they spent together was in a Lower East Side tenement apartment with a sloping wooden floor and a bathtub in the kitchen. He'd find her if he walked the streets of lower Manhattan long enough. John knew that, too. Throughout his teen years, the boy had dragged his mother out of bars and shooting galleries, getting her home, making sure she ate, getting her to the hospital when she couldn't take any more.

This night, Ambler found his former wife in a narrow, noisy, crowded bar on Ludlow Street, a block below Houston Street, the music loud and out of the past, maybe Led Zeppelin, psychedelic posters on the walls, leather-vested, tattooed bartenders, the customers drinking frantically or already drunk, the drunks either angry or despondent, glaring at Ambler as he came in, as if he were the source of their misfortune. He'd been told he'd find Liz in this dive by a woman he met at a slightly more upscale gin mill in the East Village—at least you didn't smell the urinals from the doorway—who, for God knows what reason, remembered him with Liz thirty years before. The woman—three sheets to the wind herself—shook her head and told him Liz was down on her luck and the bar where he'd find her one step above skid row. "It's the kind of joint where you don't want to sit on the chairs, if you know what I mean."

Liz was drunk—angry and despondent both.

"John is worried about you."

She focused her bleary eyes on Ambler. "Poor son of a bitch. Ain't he got enough to worry about?"

Searching for Liz through old haunts in the East Village brought back memories, so he'd almost come to expect that when he found her she'd be the Liz he'd loved so long ago. On an East Village street, he passed a thin girl with black hair, big eyes, red lips, and alabaster skin, a dead ringer for Liz when she was young. So taken was Ambler by the resemblance, he stopped and stared and almost spoke to the girl.

Liz wasn't ready to talk about John, but with prodding and the price of a couple of drinks he got her to focus by talking about his latest visit—John had put on some weight, most of it muscle. She nodded, her eyes still locked on his. Seeing into the past? Seeing into the future, for all he knew. When he stopped talking, and she sat with her head slightly bent, staring into the space in front of her, he caught a glimpse of her faded beauty. Her prettiness had always been plaintive. Nothing about her said good-time girl. Instead, she sucked your heart right out of you with vulnerability and sadness. What struck Ambler was that it was still there, the plaintive beauty.

"Tell John I'm okay, that I'm doin' good." When she turned to face Ambler there were tears in her eyes. "Or tell him the truth. I don't want him to see me like this. I never did."

"He doesn't blame you."

"He don't have to," said Liz, clinging to her glass of amber liquid like it was a life preserver.

Mike Cosgrove began his workweek reading the medical examiner's report on James Donnelly for the third time. Nothing in it led anywhere. The man had two bullet wounds to the head. The angle of the first one suggested he'd turned his head before he was shot so the bullet entered under his chin, its trajectory upward, through his mouth into his brain. He turned to his left and was shot on that side. The ME said the gun was in the shooter's left hand. If the same held true for Yates—he was shot on the left side of his head—it would reinforce the connection between the murders, and they'd know the shooter was left-handed.

Everything pointed to the murders being connected, except something concrete—not a single piece of concrete anything. The only witness to the first murder was Friar Tuck, the library director. If he could describe the assailant, they'd have something to show the girls in the park who witnessed the Yates murder but who were too traumatized by it to recall anything. If he had a picture or even a composite to show them, it might jar something loose. He didn't trust the friar, despite Ambler's thoughts on the subject. He'd been waiting to reinterview him until they finished running a check on him. But he was thinking he might not wait any longer.

Although he wouldn't say so, Ray had latched on to the case, not surprising since everything happened right under his nose. But there was the problem of him protecting his friends, holding back information he thought the police wouldn't understand. Before you know it, you've altered the landscape, like driving a bulldozer through the crime scene. He couldn't tell him to butt out. There you go. That's the problem with cops having friends. You make allowances for them, and soon you're not doing your job right. The way priests take vows; that's how it should be with cops. You wanna join the force, you take a vow of friendlessness.

He called across the squad room to his partner and told him he was headed to the library to reinterview Harry Larkin. Ford's job was to put together the days in the life of James Donnelly.

He called ahead to make an appointment, so Larkin was waiting for him in his office, a nervous wreck, his paw clammy when they shook hands, sweat beading on his forehead, his eyelashes fluttering a mile a minute. Cosgrove had suspects break down and confess who didn't look as anxiety-ridden as this guy did. What the hell was he worried about? He couldn't have shot Donnelly, gotten behind the desk, and shot at himself.

"Mr. Larkin, I know this is a disruption to your work, and I apologize for that. I don't want you to think I'm questioning you again because I didn't believe you the first time around. That's not the case. In reinterviewing people, even if we ask the same questions, we sometimes find the answers are different. People mention something they didn't think of the first time, or they remember something differently, or they provide fuller answers when the pressure isn't so intense, and in the case of a murder, that pressure can be pretty heavy. So we understand each other?"

Harry nodded the entire time Cosgrove spoke, not taking his eyes off his face, about as relaxed as if someone were holding a gun on him.

"Do you recall the sequence of events? For instance, how long were you in your office before Donnelly arrived?"

"Not long, less than an hour."

"How long after Donnelly came through the door did the gunman come through?"

"Right away."

"Wouldn't someone either knock or need an access card to open the door?"

"Yes."

"Did the person knock?"

"No."

"Use an access card?"

Larkin took some time answering. "I suppose. It's possible

he came in before the door completely closed behind Mr. Donnelly, or the door didn't click shut."

"You said 'he.' The killer was a man?"

Harry's eyelashes stopped fluttering. "I assumed it was a man. I don't know."

"What was the assailant wearing?"

"I don't think I saw. Dark clothing. A hat."

"What was Donnelly wearing?"

Larkin didn't remember. "A tie, I think."

"Anything else?" Cosgrove smiled.

Larkin didn't get the joke. "A jacket, not a suit. He had a beard. He didn't have a hat."

"You said he'd been in a day or two before. What did he want?"

"I think I told you. He wanted access to one of our collections that wasn't open to the public yet."

"What collection was that?"

"The Yates collection."

Cosgrove went methodically through the rest of his questions. After the initial interview, he'd written Larkin's answers as best he remembered in the murder book. He'd compare those answers to the ones he got today. Really, he wasn't looking for contradictions. Witness observations weren't reliable. He wanted to open the guy up. Larkin had to have seen more than he said he did. He could have repressed it. He could be holding out. Sometimes, being in a different frame of mind changed what someone remembered seeing. It could also be he was afraid—told to keep his mouth shut or he'd be next. That kind of threat happened with drug killings and gang killings. He didn't see it in a library killing, though he could be wrong. Library killings didn't have much of a track record.

"It's likely Mr. Donnelly saw the shooter's face. Did he say anything, utter a sound, like surprise or recognition?"

"Not that I recall." Larkin never took his eyes off him.

Long before he got to the end of his questioning, Cosgrove knew he wouldn't get anything. He considered getting tough, but held back because he thought the guy was too smart to fall for any tricks he could think of at the moment. Still, he couldn't let go. He sat and looked at the man expectantly, watching him squirm.

After a few minutes, Harry spoke, his voice cracking. "Is there anything else you want, sir?"

What the hell? Something in the guy's manner reminded him of what Ray said about him—a former priest, an ethical person. "You used to be a priest—"

"Yes?" Harry leaned forward.

Cosgrove sat back. "I'm curious. I'm a . . . I was . . . I am a Catholic. Not a very good one, I guess. I was wondering—"

"Why I left the priesthood?" He seemed to take an interest in the question. "I'm still a Catholic, "catholic" with a small *c*. I found myself at odds with the institutionalized church. Your ambivalence about being a Catholic, I suspect, comes from difficulties with the institutionalized church, too, rather than with the fundamentals of belief."

"That's a little deep for me." Cosgrove cleared his throat. "Philosophical differences, that's it, not anything else?'

"What do you mean anything else?"

Cosgrove's answer was a hard glare. "I'm going to level with you. I'm not going to threaten you or try to trick you—"

"Is that what you normally do?"

Cosgrove hesitated. "As a matter of fact, it's what I do a lot of the time. The point is I'm not doing it here." He felt the heat at the back of his neck and heard his voice rising, so he took a breath. "The truth is you know more than you're saying. I want to know what you're holding back."

Harry waited a long moment. "I knew Nelson Yates and James Donnelly years ago. I was a priest at the time."

"You didn't want to tell us about that?"

"I didn't see what it had to do with what happened. I was a college chaplain. Anything I learned in that role would be confidential."

"You're telling me if someone confessed a murder, you're not going to tell me?"

"Officer—I'm sorry I don't know how to address you—I don't hear confessions anymore. I haven't in years, so the question is moot."

"Call me Mike. Maybe someone told you something that would be helpful. What if I arrest you for withholding evidence?" He drilled Harry with an iron glare.

"I still wouldn't talk about it. However, no one confessed a murder to me . . . Mike."

"I'm not saying that. You know something."

"What do I know?"

"I don't know."

"How do you know I know it?"

"That's why you're not under arrest . . . Harry."

It was another fruitless interview. That was okay. You had to do a bushel of those to get to the ones that did produce something. Cosgrove sat on a bench at the bottom of the staircase above the entrance rotunda and watched the crowds entering and leaving the building, a constant flow. When you ran out of leads, you needed to be careful of wishful thinking, differentiate what you actually knew from something you wished you knew. He took out his pad and began a new list: what he knew for sure; whom he needed to interview again.

"It's a lunchtime talk at the library," Ambler said. "I'm not competing with your book." Max had found out Ambler was planning a talk on Nelson Yates and complained to Harry.

"The book won't be finished for a couple of years. What you're doing is sensationalism, using the poor man's death for your own purposes."

"Which are?"

Max Wagner's beady eyes got beadier; his jaw jutted out farther. "I don't know . . . to disrupt my biography project."

"How about I want to find out who killed Nelson?"

Max's eyes were squinted almost closed. "The police will take care of that. Don't tell me you think you're going to solve the crime."

"I'm not going to tell you anything. But I would like to ask you something."

"Don't think you're going to interrogate me like you've done with everyone else." He folded his arms across his chest.

"Was James Donnelly writing a biography of Nelson?"

"How would I know?"

"Nelson might have told you or Donnelly might have told you himself. The question is did you know?"

Wagner laughed. He might have meant to sound contemptuous but it came out a nervous cackle. "Nice try. I said I won't be interrogated."

"Let's try something else. Do you and Mary Yates still have a deal or did that fall through when Nelson died?"

Max began gathering up papers from desk he was working at and stuffing them into file folders, putting the folders into the archive box on the table in front of him. "I don't know what you're talking about. More to the point, you don't know what you're talking about. I'm busy. I've had enough of this. Tell Harry—"

"Nelson didn't want you to write his biography."

Wagner paused. Where he was at first shoving fistfuls of papers into the file in front of him, he now opened the file, rearranged and straightened the papers he'd shoved into it. "That's ridiculous. Nelson was senile. If he said that, he forgot he did two minutes later."

"He seemed pretty sure to me. He said you'd defame him."

Wagner frowned. "You don't know what you're talking about. If Nelson was worried about what I'd write, he wasn't worried about untruth." His voice rose. "It's the truth he was afraid of. The book's going to be a blockbuster, shocking, compelling. But it won't be the story Nelson Yates would have told."

Chapter 12

"It's stress," Maximilian Wagner told Laura Lee after an awkward lovemaking session. She got furious when he didn't stay around long enough for her to finish what he'd started.

"Stress, my ass." Laura Lee pushed his hand from her shoulder and turned her back to him.

"I've got a lot on my mind, sweetheart. Ray Ambler grilled me for a half hour today. He thinks I killed Jim Donnelly and Nelson."

"Did you?"

"That's not funny. He keeps digging around, one thing leads to another, and you don't know what he comes up with."

"Maybe he'll find Emily Yates."

"That would be something. Somebody better find her soon."

"Hiring a private detective is a waste of money. Nelson already did that, remember?"

"They have more sophisticated tools now."

"You can do the book without her. Make something up. Isn't that what you usually do?"

He sat up in a rage, and grabbed for her hair, but caught himself, her hair bunched in his hand, before he yanked it. "You bitch—"

Laura Lee rolled over and sat up, shoving her face close to his, the sheet falling away, her breasts brushing his arm. She leaned toward him, her teeth snapping. "Your gangster upbringing is showing." She pulled back the sheet and lowered her face to his lap. Sighing, he lay back.

In a moment, he was rock hard and she mounted him. He gritted his teeth, clenching his toes, steeling himself, afraid to come until she did. When she did finally, in wave after wave, at the top of one of the waves, she reared back and slapped him hard in the face. In a moment, she shuddered to a stop, fell on top of him, and pressed her mouth hard against his before rolling off him. He shook off the slap and cleared his head. She'd hit him right at the peak of his climax.

Later, after Laura Lee smoked a cigarette, a habit she refused to give up, he paced as best he could around the small bedroom. "I'm on edge," he said, sitting on the bed beside her. "I have this feeling of dread. I think about the murders. . . . I don't know what I think."

"You're afraid you're next." Laura Lee smiled.

Adele noticed the young woman before she saw Johnny walking beside her. She was pretty in a completely natural way, little or no makeup, her hair pulled back in a ponytail, wearing a faded lightweight leather jacket and worn, tight-fitting jeans. Her face was pale, little color in her cheeks so the skin was an unworldly white, and she was thin, alarmingly thin. It was late afternoon, overcast, and cool enough for a jacket. Adele followed them for a block getting up her nerve. Finally, she approached the woman as she waited to cross Ninth Avenue.

"Hello," she said brightly. "I'm sorry to bother you. I've met your son. He's shined my shoes. I wanted to introduce myself. He's a wonderful boy."

Johnny looked up at her with an amazed expression of expectation. Whether he expected wondrous things or unmitigated disaster was unclear. The woman's face showed surprise, more than surprise; she stared at Adele incredulously and spoke not a word.

"Hello, Johnny," Adele said. "I'll need some shoes shined again soon."

He stared at her, speechless also.

When the light changed, mother and son crossed the street, leaving Adele on the corner watching them. After a few seconds, when the walk light was blinking red, she charged across the street. When she reached them on the other side, the woman turned to face her.

"I don't want you around my child," she said. "I don't know what you want from him. He has all the mother he needs."

Adele's stomach sank. Johnny's mother couldn't have hurt her more if she'd shoved a knife into her chest. Fighting for breath, she stammered. The woman watched without sympathy.

"He was on the street, alone, at night," she said finally. "I only wanted to watch out for him." She needed to speak carefully, if she wasn't going to alienate the boy's mother. "I didn't know what his situation was." She looked at Johnny and back at his mother. "I'm glad to see he's well cared for. He's such a good boy. I'm sure you're proud of him." Watching her eyes, Adele could see her waver. "You can never go wrong praising a child to a mother," Raymond told her once. "He's so self-sufficient, too. How old is he?"

"Eight," she said. When the hardness left her eyes, replaced by a softer expression, she seemed sad, more than sad, really, she seemed wounded and vulnerable from the wound. It was almost too much to hope for, but she began talking. "You're the woman from the library, aren't you?" Not waiting for an answer, she said. "I worked there once, on 42nd Street, at the main library—"

"Are you a librarian?" Adele's eagerness got out in front of her. The brightness left the woman's face. She shouldn't have said it.

"No, nothing like that, it was a low-level job, a library clerk. Waitressing paid better."

"Probably pays better than a librarian, too."

Johnny's mother smiled. "I'm a singer. Waitressing pays the bills."

"Oh, wow. I've always wished I could be a singer, but I can't carry a tune. I'm hopeless."

Johnny's mother smiled again, though her expression soon grew wistful. She looked past Adele down Ninth Avenue. Most of the buildings in that block were three or four story with shabby facades that belied their true worth to the developers encroaching with high-rise luxury buildings from the north and the south. She turned and looked west toward the river somewhere in the distance. "You live in the neighborhood?"

Adele said she did.

"Maybe we'll get together for coffee. My name's Emily."

"I'm Adele." She watched them walk away. Johnny hadn't said a word.

Dominic was mad at Johnny's mom for something; that was for sure. He wouldn't say what. All the same, she knew what he was mad about and kept telling him it was none of his business. When she told him about meeting the lady from the library, he got mad all over again.

"You should know better than that."

This time, Mom didn't yell. Her voice was quiet. "It's funny.

I wasn't going to talk to her. I told her to leave Johnny alone and walked away. Then after she crossed the street after us, something in her face got to me. She was nice. She likes Johnny. She was nice to me. I mean she was interested in me. No one's ever interested in me."

"If you know what's good for you, you'll leave her alone." He smashed out his cigarette in the ashtray and stood up. Dominic had a way of standing over you that was meant to scare people. It certainly scared Johnny. He towered over you and leaned toward you, closer than you'd want him to be. "Laura Lee told me Max wants to hire a private detective to find you. Now you tell someone from the library your name. Why don't you go sit in his lap?"

"I only told her my first name."

Mom wasn't afraid of Dominic. She laughed at him most of the time when he yelled at her like that. She didn't care what anyone did to her. She'd dare someone to hit her—and some of the men did—but she went nuts if anyone touched him . . . right for the carving knife or the baseball bat. When something like that happened, Johnny was more afraid of what she'd do than he was of what anyone might do to him. That's how she was. Mom would watch out for him no matter what. Now, she met Miss Adele from the library and she liked her. He knew better than to ask about it. He'd just hope and maybe they'd be friends.

"I trust everything is going well with your work, despite the turmoil," Harry said to his uninvited guest, forcing a smile. He didn't like that Max Wagner found his way to his apartment. The studio on the top floor of a brownstone on a quiet tree-lined street off Eighth Avenue in Chelsea was his refuge, his retreat, and had been for twenty years. It wasn't that he was antisocial. It was that he needed space that was his alone. Maybe it was the years of communal life as a Jesuit.

He never invited people from work, preferring to meet them at a neighborhood restaurant or café, and had only twice in the years he lived there had an overnight visitor and each time regretted it. His present partner understood. They slept together when they traveled; at home, each man lived in his own apartment and slept at night in his own bed. Max's visit was a violation of his privacy. This, of course, would mean nothing to Max. His needs, everyone knew, came first.

"I'm sorry I don't have anything to offer you." Harry looked around his own apartment, as if he were a stranger in it. A couch, a bed, two wooden folding chairs at the glass dining room table no more than a couple of feet from the couch, that was it. At the moment, his laptop computer rested on the table. He offered Max a seat on the couch, hoping he'd refuse and say what he had to say while standing up, and leave. Instead, Max chose one of the wooden chairs, so Harry sat on the couch.

"This must be important to bring you out in the evening . . . and to my apartment." Harry waited. Max seemed to have left his bluster behind.

"I needed to speak with you privately. Ray Ambler thinks he's investigating these murders."

Harry shrugged. "That's what he does."

"Don't you think he's going to be looking into the past also? Aren't you worried about that?"

"I try not to worry about things I have no control over."

"You're his boss. You could tell him to stop."

"I don't see that doing any good. Why would he stop?"

"Never mind." Max waved off the question. "It can't be helped, in any event." He scrutinized Harry. "The police, I imagine, have spoken to you?"

"More than once. A detective, Mike something, seems to think I know more about the killings than I do."

Max leaned forward. "Cosgrove. He's the one who's questioned me. He makes you feel like he knows you're guilty. What have you told him?"

"I told him what I saw."

"What did you tell him about us . . . about the past?"

Harry hesitated. "I don't know what you mean."

"Stop pussyfooting around, Harry—or Father Larkin. What a joke. You throw the whole fucking thing over and jump ship with everyone's confidences in your tote bag."

"I'm not sure I know what you're saying."

"Yes you do. A lot happened during that time; some of it, none of us are proud of." Wagner's expression was a mixture of contempt and ridicule. "We were young and stupid. You sprinkled pixie dust on Nelson, and we followed him like a herd of lemmings. We told you everything and asked forgiveness."

Harry put his hands to his face, fingers against his cheeks, jaw resting on his palms. He gazed into Max Wagner's eyes.

Wagner started to say something until Harry's unwavering expression caused him to pause. "Look, all I want is to be sure. You know—"

"I'm sure this is difficult for you. But you needn't have bothered. I'm no more at liberty to talk about what I heard in the confessional now than I was then."

"Yes." Wagner shifted his weight awkwardly on the small chair. He waited a moment and stood, looked around the small apartment as if he'd misplaced his hat. "I imagine there's much about that time you don't want bandied about either."

Harry watched him, seated in the same position, his chin resting on his palms, his fingers against his cheeks, his eyes trained on Wagner.

"Well, I'll be going then. Sorry to have bothered you at home. I should have known . . ." He headed toward the apartment door, stopped, and turned to face Harry. "It's those murders. I have this feeling of dread. You don't think? . . . I mean Jim Donnelly and then Nelson. You don't think—"

Harry's expression didn't waver. "I'm not who you should be speaking with about this, Professor Wagner."

"I only wanted—"

"Let me put this another way. You're not in a confessional. I'm not your spiritual advisor now. Do you understand?"

Wagner nodded, murmured a quick thank-you, and left. Harry sat on the couch staring into the empty space in front of him while a flood of painful memories cascaded through him. When he'd endured them for as long as he could, he rose, got down on his knees, leaned his arms on the couch he'd been sitting on, and prayed.

Chapter 13

Nelson Yates's memorial service took place in the Earl Hall auditorium at Columbia University, where Yates once taught creative writing. The auditorium, with high ceilings, tall windows, white walls, might be called plain. Stately in its simplicity, it was a fitting venue for Nelson's farewell. More than a hundred, possibly two hundred, mourners paid their respects. Adele and Ambler sat together, she wearing the black dress she wore to her mother's funeral, he his black suit.

Harry came alone, looking priestly in his black suit. Benny Barone, wearing a decidedly unpriestly, tight fitting black satin suit, accompanied Kay Donnelly, also dressed in black. Mike Cosgrove and another detective sat in the back row. Ambler spotted Max Wagner and Laura Lee arriving late and pointed them out to Adele.

"That's a cocktail dress," Adele whispered, "not a dress for a funeral." He smiled, feeling her breath brush his ear. Her wool dress hugged her body, the hem slipping along her slim thigh as she crossed her legs. "It's not a party." She turned to face

Ambler and noticing him looking at her legs, pulled the hem of her dress down closer to her knee. He looked up at the speaker.

After nearly an hour of remembrances, mostly from Yates's fellow writers, there was a short eulogy from his son, who spoke well of his father despite his having had little presence in his life. The young man's mother, Nelson's first wife, sat with him but didn't speak. Mary Yates, his last wife, did speak. She said Nelson tried to do good in the world. The last years were difficult, she said, but he spoke often of his friends and his editors, those he taught with, and his students. He was always glad when he heard from a former student. And of course he was always happy to hear from his readers. She seemed nervous, avoiding eye contact with the audience. Strangely, she spoke dispassionately, as if disconnected from what she was saying, and longer than she should have, seeming unable to find a way to end—and because of her obvious difficulty finding an ending, putting everyone in the audience on edge. Finally, she just stopped, turned an exasperated expression on the assembled mourners, and strode from the podium.

Yates's longtime editor spoke last. He spoke softly and had an unassuming manner, though he'd risen to the executive level of what was once a small, family-like publishing company and was now part of a mammoth entertainment conglomerate. His eulogy, tinged with bitterness for the author, seemed appropriate given Yates's years of neglect by the literary world followed by his violent death. The service ended on a somber note, fitting for a writer whose work was characterized by bleakness.

"I guess you wouldn't expect a service like this to be cheerful," Adele said, taking Ambler's arm as they followed the crowd down the steps of St. Paul's Chapel. "This was dismal."

When they reached the esplanade in front of Low Library, Adele tightened her grip on his arm, pulling him to a stop as she watched a line of people walking away from them toward Broadway. "I think that's Johnny's mother."

Ambler glanced around him. "Who?"

"Did you see that young woman?"

"Which one?"

"Dark hair. Pretty. She was wearing jeans."

Ambler strained to look across the plaza in the middle of the campus but couldn't pick anyone out of the crowd. Everyone wore jeans. "How do you know Johnny's mother?"

"I met her on the street the other day when she was with Johnny."

"Why would she—"

"I'm going to try to catch her." Adele headed down the stone steps.

In her tight dress and high heels, she got off to a slow and wobbly start, and the descent was tricky. As she reached the brick walk at the bottom of the steps, she broke into something of an awkward trot but stopped when she came upon a woman also standing on the walk looking toward the iron gates at Broadway. She shook hands and spoke with the woman for a few seconds. When the woman began walking away, Adele looked wistfully after her before turning and heading back to join Ambler.

"That was Mrs. Young," she said.

"Who's she?"

"From the library board of trustees. She donated the funding—" Adele slapped her hand across her mouth. "Oops . . ." Her eyes pleaded with him. "Please don't tell anyone."

"You didn't actually tell me."

"Please?"

"You have my word."

"Oh my God, I'm an idiot. She's such a nice woman, too. There were tears in her eyes."

"I wonder why she came to the service."

"She said someone from the Board of Trustees should attend because the library houses his papers."

"Why the tears?"

"I didn't ask her, Raymond. For God's sake, a man died. It's a funeral. People who have hearts cry at funerals."

"You didn't."

"I did, too. You didn't notice."

At the small reception following the service in the foyer of Dodge Hall, they ran into Mike Cosgrove. He stood a bit inside and a few steps away from the door, watching everyone come in.

"Let me know if you see anyone from the library I should know about," he said.

"Everyone I've seen from the library you already know," Ambler said.

Kay Donnelly hustled in with Benny in tow, trying to avoid eye contact with the detective and meeting Ambler's gaze instead. He tried to look sympathetic. She looked scared. Benny glanced about the room, ready for anyone who wanted to take him on.

"Who are we looking for?" Adele asked. Neither man answered right away, so she nudged Ambler. He shrugged his shoulders.

Cosgrove shot her an irritated glance. "We're looking for a murderer."

"The only person from the library you don't know is a woman from the Board of Trustees," Ambler said. "She didn't come to the reception."

"Oh?" Cosgrove took out his notebook. "Her name?"

Before Ambler could answer, Adele elbowed him. "I don't think you should tell him. She doesn't have anything to do with what happened."

Cosgrove cleared his throat. "Miss Morgan—"

"Miss Morgan, is it? My name's Adele. I've met you before. No need for formality here."

Cosgrove took a step back. His eyes met hers. "The more information we have, the more likely we figure out what happened. This person came to the memorial service; maybe it means something; maybe it doesn't."

Adele looked to Ambler. He nodded.

"Mrs. Lisa Young."

Cosgrove wrote it down.

What at first seemed like a murmur of crowd noises became the unmistakable sound of an altercation on the far side of the room. Ambler turned to see a hysterical Mary Yates leaning into Kay Donnelly; she'd boxed her into a corner, and was upbraiding her, like an irate manager to an umpire. Just as Ambler looked toward the commotion, Benny Barone stepped between the two women. As he tried to steer Kay Donnelly away from her tormentor, Mary Yates reached around Benny, and slapped her in the face. Kay Donnelly stopped in shock for a split second before shoving Benny in the chest and lashing out with a right cross toward the Yates widow. She saw it coming and leaned back out of the way. At that moment, Max Wagner joined the fray, stepping in front of Mary Yates and putting both hands on her shoulders. She crumbled into his arms, sobbing against his chest. Benny put his arm around Kay and walked her toward the door.

As he watched the drama unfold, Ambler noticed Laura Lee watching also, with a strangely smug expression, as if someone had gotten his or her comeuppance—and if he were pressed to say who it was she thought got this comeuppance, he'd have to say, given whom she was looking at, it was her husband.

Mike Cosgrove liked to know something about witnesses before he interviewed them. In the case of

Mrs. Young, the first bit of information he came across gave him pause. Her husband, Edward, was a partner in a Wall Street law firm.

"What that means," he told Ambler over a beer at the Library Tavern late in the afternoon the day after Nelson Yates's funeral, "is that she'll ask her husband, and he'll tell her not to talk to me, or if she does, he'll want to be with her."

"So you want me to question her?"

"Not question. Talk; an informal conversation; get to know one another."

"Why would she get to know me? I'm a librarian. She's a socialite."

"You have Nelson Yates in common. She was at the funeral."

"I could talk to her about the plan to close the crime fiction reading room, I guess. If she likes Nelson Yates, she might want it to stay open." He knew he should tell Cosgrove about her anonymous donation that enabled the library to purchase the Yates collection. He couldn't because he'd promised Adele he wouldn't. "Anything else?"

"That's enough."

"Have you thought about the spat between Nelson's grieving widow and Donnelly's widow?"

"I thought about it. I told you funerals are always good for something. I talked to Mrs. Yates. I'm not telling you what she told me. I'll talk to the other combatant."

"Kay Donnelly is one direction. I'd be more interested in Max Wagner."

"You always seem to be." Cosgrove stood, waving to McNulty for the check.

"I'll get the check," Ambler said.

Ambler was waiting in the hallway outside the Wertheim Study, around 7:45 on the evening he spoke to

Cosgrove. Kay Donnelly came along lugging a heavy book bag. She stared at him like he'd popped out of a box.

"Sorry to bother you, Kay."

"I know what this is about, and I don't want to talk to you. I don't have to. Someone's waiting for me."

"Benny? He's waiting for us at a bar down the street."

"He can keep waiting. I'm going home." Her angry tone was contradicted by the expression in her eyes, which suggested innocence and vulnerability you wouldn't expect in a woman her age. He felt an urge to put his arms around her and hug her.

He spoke softly. "You've been through a lot, haven't you?"

She stiffened. "Why should you care what I go through?"

"To be honest, I want to find out who killed your ex-husband and Nelson Yates. Finding out might help you. It might not."

She shifted her heavy bag from one shoulder to the other. By her stance and a kind of smirk, she made clear she was too busy to deal with such a silly idea. "Why should it help me or not help me?" There was a kind of wildness in her expression, not panic but something seeking release, a desire to let go.

"You want to trust me. I can see it in your eyes. What have you got to lose?"

"A lot. As I told you before, my career." Her gaze shifted to look beyond him and the color drained from her face.

He turned to see Laura Lee walking toward them. The scowl on her face changed quickly to her brilliant smile.

"Well, well, my favorite librarian. What do we have here, a tryst? You both look so guilty." Her eyes locked on Ambler's, flirtatious and challenging at once. Beside him, he could feel Kay Donnelly's embarrassment and rage.

"I've invited Kay to have a drink with me. You're welcome to join us."

"Oh no, three's a crowd."

"It's not like that, Laura Lee." There was a kind of tired impatience in Kay Donnelly's tone.

"No. No. I'd be in the way. Besides when I talk to Raymond, I want him all to myself." She turned up her smile for Ambler and flashed it toward Kay. "Be careful what you say to him, dear."

Kay scowled back but didn't say anything.

On the short walk to the Library Tavern, Kay said, "I wish that hadn't happened." She seemed less on guard with him, having come to some decision during the standoff with Laura Lee. "I'd rather she hadn't seen me talking to you. That back there was a warning shot."

Benny was waiting for them in a booth. There was something cute in their greeting, talking to each other with their eyes, trying not to let on how electric the moment was. She sat next to him and they squeezed closer to one another than they needed to.

"I'm curious about Mary Yates," Ambler said.

She swung her hand in front of her face, as if she were swatting him away. "I bet you are. That performance at the memorial service? She's crazy. Living with Nelson will do that to you. He drove all of his wives crazy with jealousy."

"She was jealous of you?"

She glanced at Benny. "She had no reason to be."

Ambler caught the tension between her and Benny and saw the danger in pursuing the question. "I really wanted to ask what the story is with her and Max."

Kay nodded, a slight movement of her eyes thanking him. "I told you it's difficult for me to talk about Max. As for Mary, he sought her out, befriended her. You'd be surprised how charming he can be when he wants something. He wanted to do the book, the biography. He knew Nelson wouldn't like it. He also knew Nelson was beginning to have memory problems and was difficult for Mary to deal with, so Max became the sympathetic ear.

To put it bluntly, he wormed his way into her confidence, so he could get Nelson's papers." She laughed. "He flipped when Nelson gave the papers to you."

"Was there anything romantic between them?"

She shook her head. "She wanted Nelson's money when he died, which she thought would be soon, or at least he'd be declared incompetent soon. Max had money through his university library's endowment for Nelson's papers—more money than your library offered. Their relationship was mercenary."

"Nelson said James Donnelly wanted his papers, too. They'd been in contact. Did you know that? Did Max know?"

She glanced uneasily at Benny before looking at Ambler again. "You need to ask Max."

"Can I ask you what the argument was about?"

Kay looked confused. "What argument?"

"Benny overheard an argument Max had with your ex-husband shortly before he was killed."

"What are you talking about?" She whipped around to face Benny. "What did you tell him?"

Benny shrank from her.

"Donnelly confronted you and Max about something," Ambler said. He turned to Benny who looked puzzled. "Benny?"

"They were in the hallway outside the Wertheim Study. You—"

Her face was a study in frustration. "God, Benny, why would you talk about something you know nothing about?"

"All I said—" He stared at her, the communing spirits ducking for cover.

Ambler watched Kay Donnelly curiously.

She snatched her hand from Benny's, clambered out of the booth, and dashed out of the bar. A moment later, Benny followed her.

• • •

Adele often walked home after work since moving into the city. After years of the long, tiring train ride to Sheepshead Bay, it was such a pleasure, especially in early spring when the evenings were long. Sometimes she walked across 42nd Street to Ninth Avenue and uptown on Ninth. Lately, she'd walk over to Tenth Avenue and come back to Ninth on 49th Street, hanging out for a bit by Johnny's apartment in case he or his mother happened to come out.

Other nights she might walk up Fifth and pick a street to walk across—47th Street, through the diamond district—or 44th past the Algonquin Hotel, or 46th Street, through Restaurant Row. She'd pick a street and find something different, often older, well-cared-for apartment buildings she wished she could afford to live in. The walks gave her time to think, to get the day's work out of her mind and adjust to the time she wasn't working.

She ate at home and mostly read at night. There wasn't time to read everything during working hours, so she often carried a few catalogs and advanced reading copies from publishers. Bringing work home didn't bother her. She didn't like to go out much and hadn't dated since she broke up with her boyfriend after her mother's death. It wasn't that she was lonely—she liked being alone. And it wasn't that she missed Peter—she didn't. They never had much in common. She'd stayed with him out of habit and because no one else came along.

After her mother's funeral, she thought something would happen with Raymond. At the time, she was sure of it. Being with him felt right. She'd thought that before, though, that everything felt right, that something would happen with Raymond, and it didn't. She knew he wanted to. She'd catch him looking at her sometimes, his expression unguarded. She could see longing there and sadness. Whatever went wrong for him in the past went wrong really badly. He was like someone afraid of the water or afraid of dogs—his was a phobia about being close.

These days, too, she thought about the shoeshine boy Johnny. Since she'd come across him, she felt something entirely different than she'd ever felt before—this idea that she might be needed, desperately needed, by someone. She'd always wanted a child. Now, in the midst of the murders at the library, her mother's death, the end of a long relationship, and Raymond's indifference, she'd found something in life she cared passionately about. She wanted to make sure Johnny was cared for. She had no idea how to do that. But she knew he needed her—not to replace his mother but maybe to help her. It was obvious her life and her son were too much for her to handle.

On this evening as she walked up Tenth Avenue and back across 49th Street in the gathering darkness, she realized her life was changing. She knew now that something was missing in her life—someone, really—a person who needed her and whom she needed. Since the evening she'd spent with Raymond and Johnny, when he'd gotten along so well with the boy and then stood his ground against a guy not much better than a street thug, protecting them both, she'd thought of Raymond Ambler, mild-mannered librarian, as her white knight. As foolish as it made her feel, she was now head over heels in love with him and biding her time—waiting for the right moment, the right place, the right lipstick, the right dress—until she made her move.

Mom was in one of her strange moods. When he was younger, she got like that sometimes but the times were far apart. Now, it was more often. What would happen is she'd stop drinking. First, she'd bang around the house, cleaning up everything, throwing stuff out; one time she painted the living room; another time, she came home with two guys carrying a rug and they ripped out the old one and put in a new one. When she wasn't cleaning or fixing things, she'd yell at him about everything, and when she wasn't yelling, she'd sit and stare out the window—all day long, she'd stare out the window. She'd be there sitting by the window, a blank look on her face, when he went to bed, and she'd be there when he woke up in the morning. Except for yelling at him to pick up his clothes or to take a big basket of clothes to the Laundromat, she wouldn't talk to him at all. She wouldn't cook and she didn't eat.

The first time, when he was real little, she took him to the country and they watched an old man and a woman who wasn't so old but seemed like she was his wife. They sat in a car outside a small house in the woods. When the man and woman who lived there went somewhere, they followed them in Dominic's car. This took up a whole day. No one talked. He and Dominic went for walks in the woods while his mom watched the house. Dominic didn't like that so much. He complained about bugs, got mud on his shoes, and ripped his pants on some bushes that had thorns. Dominic never talked to him anyway, so spending time with him wasn't like he imagined going hiking or fishing or something should be. Dominic was a guy your mother knew and who put up with you, not anything like a dad would be.

When they got home that time, she sat and stared out the window most of the next day; then, she took everything out of the closets and threw some things away and put everything else back into the closets again. That night she went out to the bars and met a guy. She started drinking and everything was back to normal.

There were other times. They'd go somewhere and watch someone. Once it was in a ritzy part of the city and there were so many people going in and out of buildings or walking down the street or sitting in a sidewalk café he didn't know who she was watching—or much care. That one didn't take so long.

A couple of times, they went to a place with buildings and lawns and older kids walking around wearing backpacks. He thought they were probably college kids. Both times, they went without Dominic. She went to the office of a man with a beard who wore a tie and jacket and who was solemn and serious. He had someone—a different girl each time—take him for a soda at a place with tables and chairs, like a school cafeteria only better, where the older kids with backpacks hung out. His mom never told him where they were or why, and he didn't ask.

Each time, he'd know a trip was coming up because she stopped drinking and went into one of those moods, like she was in a trance. Each time, she'd come out of it, start drinking, and go back to normal. When the moods started up again not long ago, he expected another trip. This time, no trip; everything else was the same, but no trip—and she was angrier than she'd been in the past and when she wasn't angry, she was like a zombie.

The good thing was that Miss Adele came by the apartment last Saturday and talked his mom into all three of them going to the zoo. He'd never been and it was much better than he expected. They rode on a train through a jungle in the Bronx. You could look out the window and see elephants, tigers, rhinos. They visited the lions and saw the new baby cubs. It was one of the best times he ever had, and his mother seemed different. She was on him a lot, telling him to stop running and to keep quiet. She got mad at him and Miss Adele joking around. But something was going on with her. She was quiet and thinking a lot.

"Harry told me Max Wagner was okay with my lunch-hour talk on Nelson," Ambler told Adele, when she pulled up a chair next to his at the glistening oak library table in the center of the crime collection reading room. "He must have concluded no one would pay any attention to an obscure librarian."

"Not so obscure. He doesn't know you have a following." Adele turned her chair to face him. "I told you I took Johnny and his mother to the zoo. He was thrilled. I wouldn't be surprised if he became a veterinarian when he grows up. He knew all about the animals. He knew the names of the lion cubs."

Adele was totally smitten, so much so it was worrisome. She might be headed for a lot of heartache. He knew too well what became of the children of unreliable mothers. His son's wrecked life was ample warning of what happened to kids left to their own devices when they were too young to handle it.

"What was his mother like?"

Adele stopped gushing. "It was strange. She didn't say anything bad. She kept trying to calm Johnny down, dampen his enthusiasm. It was sad watching him rein himself in. He was so exuberant." Adele turned a soulful and questioning gaze to Ambler. "Why wouldn't she let him have fun, be a kid?"

Ambler shrugged. "Did you find out if it was her you saw the day of Nelson Yates's memorial service?"

"She said it wasn't her. She'd never been to Columbia and never heard of Nelson Yates. Yet I would have sworn—" A strange, almost secretive, look came across her face. She leaned closer. "I've been thinking about something. It's impossible; I know. The thing is I can't stop thinking it."

"What?"

"You'll think I'm crazy."

"No."

She hesitated, tossed her head, smiled. "Nah. . . . Forget it."

"Adele, for crying out loud."

"Okay. Johnny's mother's name is Emily."

Her eyes sparkled as she watched for his reaction. He didn't get it, which must have showed because the sparkle left her eyes. "She's the right age. Emily's not such a common name. She went to the memorial service and denied she was there."

"You think she's Emily Yates?"

"She might be. I'm not saying she is. I've gotten a sense of Emily Yates from the research I've been doing. I thought about what she might be like grown up. I saw her having hard times but being resilient, the spunk she had when she was young. A sense I get of Emily Smith is that there's something more to her. She doesn't talk about her past. But you can tell she came from an educated home. It's like she had had a life different than the one she has now. I know it's a stab in the dark—except for the memorial service. I'd swear it was her I saw."

Ambler turned to face Adele. "If her name were Sarah or Eleanor or Barbara, would you have come up with this? Does anything you've discovered in the files about Emily Yates lead you to this other Emily . . . whatever her name is?

"Smith," Adele said quietly.

"If I remember correctly, you saw someone walking across the campus, not someone attending the service—" He stopped because he saw the hurt in her face. "It might be something," he said quickly. "Cosgrove would say, 'You need to rule it out.'"

Anger flashed in Adele's eyes. "Don't patronize me." She started to walk away.

"Wait," Ambler said. "Please." She stopped. "If you think you have something here, go back to the files—to the data—see if anything concrete, anything objective, connects the two Emilys. A photo. Physical description. Hair color, even eye color, you can change. Some characteristics you can't change: Nearsighted? Walk with a limp? Left-handed? Allergies? Propensities. Make a list of anything they might have in common: What type of music did the young Emily listen to? What bands did she like? There are things a person can't change about herself, some things you do unconsciously so you don't think to change. Is pink your favorite color? Do you put salt on your grapefruit? Hate cucumbers? You could consider fingerprints, though Emily Yates might never have been fingerprinted." He paused. "She might have kept things also. But to find out you'd need to look through her things. And you can't do that based on speculation."

"Raymond, I've done a lot of that. You may be the star detective. I've done more library research than you have. I've looked and looked for a photo. You'd think there'd be something in Nelson's files or something on the Internet—but nothing." She turned to walk away again. "You might find this shocking. There's nothing in the files about her feelings toward cucumbers."

Chapter 14

Ambler had run across the high society set at library functions often enough to recognize a member of the species when he saw one. Mrs. Lisa Young, tall, slender, and elegant in a high-strung, over-bred way, swished into the room with a confident stride. A woman about Ambler's age, she was attractive, along the lines of what magazines once called a handsome woman rather than glamorous.

The room she swept into was the King Cole Bar at the St. Regis Hotel on East 55th Street, off Fifth Avenue. Ambler knew she'd arrive there at about that time because McNulty told him she would. McNulty—whose connections to all strata of society in the city through his bartender cronies were akin to those of the Page Six gossip columnists—tracked her down when Ambler told him about Cosgrove's plan.

McNulty's friend, Marcelo, a bartender at the Oyster Bar, told him she was a connoisseur of fine cocktails and New York bars that reminded her of a Marjorie Morningstar past. She made regular stops, besides the Oyster Bar, at Sardi's, the 21 Club, the

King Cole Bar, Bemelmans at The Carlyle, The Blue Bar at the Algonquin, and the Bull and Bear at the Waldorf Astoria. Friday nights during the spring season, it was The King Cole.

Ambler waited until the two patrons at the bar left and she'd finished her first drink before speaking to her. They sat a few seats from one another, she drinking a sidecar, Ambler red wine, studying the eponymous mural behind the bar.

"A merry old soul," he said.

She looked at Maxfield Parrish's mural of the king and his merry men, and then at him. Her expression surprised him, the directness of it and how she lowered her eyelashes so she seemed both shy and provocative at the same time. He liked her smile and how easygoing and friendly she seemed. They talked for a few minutes about paintings, Maxfield Parrish, and New York hotel bars.

When the time seemed right, he told her he worked at the 42nd Street Library and waited to see if she'd mention her connection to the library. She didn't.

"I'm the curator of the crime fiction collection."

She laughed, an easy, pleasant sound. "What an absolutely perfect job. I envy you." She looked at him curiously and then signaled the bartender and ordered them both a refill. "It's ironic, isn't it, that you've had a real-life murder to complement your collection?"

"Two murders," Ambler said. "I prefer fictitious ones."

She lowered her gaze; and her expression, which had been mildly amused, softened into something like sadness. "I'm sorry I sounded flip. I don't mean that at all."

He told her a little bit about what happened and who was killed. She asked questions, seeming interested, but acknowledged nothing about her connection to the library or to Nelson Yates. Still, despite her lack of candor, he felt duplicitous. The more he talked, the guiltier he felt. More than that, something in her expression, a kind of wistfulness or sadness, struck a chord with him, so he began to like her. He took a swallow of wine and plunked the glass back onto the bar.

"I know who you are, Mrs. Young. I should have told you. I know you're a member of the library's Board of Trustees."

Her lips curled in a wry smile. "Is this a fortuitous accident, meeting me here, or have you been following me?"

"I recognized you when you came through the door. I knew you'd be here."

"How did you know that?"

He shook his head. "I can't tell you that."

"I'll get to the bottom of it." She looked him full in the face for a moment while she sipped from her drink. "So you tracked me down. You're a man on a mission. What's the mission?"

He told her about the plan to close the reading room and integrate the crime fiction into the overall library collection.

She knew about the plan to make overall changes to the library but hadn't known about the changes to the crime fiction collection, or even that there was a crime fiction collection. He debated telling her he knew she'd funded the Yates acquisition. Telling her would betray both Harry and Adele, so he hesitated. Finally, he said, "I'm going to level with you."

She smiled mischievously. "Think twice. That might be dangerous."

He did think twice. It was dangerous. He went ahead anyway. "What coincided with the murders we were talking about was the library's acquisition of the Nelson Yates papers—"

Her change in expression gave her away. She knew what was coming. "Go on. Are you reluctant to tell me what you know?"

"Yes."

Something ominous flickered through her eyes. "You're not waiting for me to help you, are you?"

"I think I am."

"Don't falter now, Mr. Ambler. You've been brave, if foolhardy; see it through."

So he did. "What prompted you to make the donation? Why the Yates collection?"

The guarded expression was firmly in place. "It's none of your business why and unethical for you to even know about it." Her tone was biting, her eyes as cold as marble. No matter what else they did, the rich knew how to pull rank when they needed to.

"I'm not going to tell anyone. I want your help."

"I know who told you."

"It wasn't Harry. I found out by accident. You came to Nelson Yates's memorial service. I was curious."

"You're investigating me?"

"No. No. Your secret is safe."

Her eyes didn't focus so well when she looked at him. "My secrets are safe. Do you think so?" She smiled, a pleasant and dreamy smile. "Now, sir. I must go. Please ask the bartender to arrange for a cab."

When he thought about it later, he realized he'd made a mess of his dealings with Lisa Young. He didn't find out anything that would help Cosgrove, and he didn't win her support for the reading room. He told her more than he should have and probably cost the library a patron it couldn't afford to lose—so much for putting your cards on the table. Undercover work wasn't for him; he needed to become a better liar. McNulty told him telling the truth was overrated. The difficult part would be telling Adele what he'd done.

"It's water over the dam, now," Adele said the next morning. She thought about saying more; he could see it in her eyes, the anger—worse, the disappointment. "I'm going to light into Mike Cosgrove for putting you up to this, and I'm going to kill McNulty the next time I see him. He and his bartender cronies are a bunch of busybodies. And I *really* don't want to be around when Harry finds out you told her you know about the donation."

When Ambler got back to his desk, he found a message taped to his computer asking him to come to Harry's office. He stared at it for a long moment. Well, it had to come sometime, but he didn't think it would be this quickly. He braced for battle and wasn't all that surprised to find Lisa Young sitting in the chair in front of Harry's desk, where not long ago Nelson Yates sat after a similar summons from Harry—the conversation that began this trip down the rabbit hole.

"I believe you know Mrs. Young." Harry smiled. "Pull up that chair and join us. We were talking about you."

Ambler looked at the two faces smiling back at him. He didn't know what was coming but chose to take it standing up.

"Mrs. Young is concerned about the closing of the crime fiction reading room. I thought it best if she spoke to you."

Her eyes fastened onto Ambler's, her expression mischievous; the shy, bold look from the night before was back. "I'm meeting with the library president in a few minutes and would like to take you to lunch after that, around two."

He waited for the rest but nothing came. Puzzled, he kept his eyes glued to hers, until she winked. After she stood and shook hands with each of them, she left. Ambler made for the door right behind her.

Harry called him back. "Can we talk for a minute, Ray?" His tone was pleasant, with an ominous undertone.

Ambler halted.

"Sit down. This might take a few minutes."

This time, Ambler sat. Since he had no idea what went on between Harry and Lisa Young, he hoped Harry would tell him.

"I'd like to know what you discussed with Mrs. Young."

"I met her by accident." He'd expected to go in and blurt out the whole truth because Harry would have already heard Lisa Young's side. Now, her smiles and winks threw him off. "What did she tell you?"

"Never mind what she told me. What did you tell her?"

Clearly, Harry's cheerfulness and goodwill had been for Lisa Young's benefit.

"I wanted her to help keep the reading room open."

"Did she say anything about the Yates collection?"

This was the question he dreaded, the moment of truth . . . or the moment of falsity. "About the Yates collection?"

"The papers."

"The papers?"

"The Yates papers." Harry was about to explode.

"Why are you yelling?"

He was being evasive. Harry had to know that, but he didn't come in for the kill. He wasn't built to browbeat, threaten, keep others in the dark, hide his motives, distrust everyone; the pain of doing so was in his eyes. "You don't want that woman as an adversary, Ray. Be careful."

Chapter 15

"You need to ditch that library woman."

"I like her. She's a friend. I can't remember the last time I had a girlfriend. That's what normal women do. They have friends and hang out and talk about clothes, and have lunch and talk about what assholes men are." She lowered her voice conspiratorially. "She has a crush on that library guy you had a run in with. He's too dumb to notice."

"I told you before. You get close to people; you let your guard down. Next thing, you tell 'em somethin'." Dominic shook his head.

"It's not like that. It's a coincidence she works at the library. She moved into the neighborhood. She doesn't know anybody. She don't have any kids. She wants to have a kid, so she sort of took up with Johnny. She's a do-gooder. So what?"

"I saw her on the street. She was watchin' your apartment."

"So what? She lives in the neighborhood. She was probably seeing if Johnny was out."

"If she doesn't know who you are already, she's going to figure it out."

Dominic picked up the leather shoulder bag next to the chair he was sitting in. He pulled a packet of the letters from the bag. "You got these now. Isn't that enough? The library's not going to have them. Max won't get his hands on them."

He reached for her hand. She let him hold it but left it limp and didn't move closer to him. Instead she cocked a hip, a stance like a teenager who's heard it all before.

"Why don't we go away for a while? Let this blow over. You could find someplace for the runt. We could have some fun. I got money comin'."

Her expression softened. "We tried that before, Dom. We can't take more than a couple of days together. We never could. And I won't leave Johnny with anyone, for a short time or a long time."

When Dominic left, Emily finished one beer and got another from the refrigerator. Johnny would be home from school soon, so she started to straighten things up a bit, wash the breakfast dishes, throw away the beer bottles from last night. She got a few things done, stopping when she found a vodka bottle that had a couple of drinks left in it. She got the orange juice from the fridge and sat down with the pile of letters Dominic had left on the table. She was half-drunk and reading the letters when she heard Johnny on the stairs. She stuffed the letters back into the bag and wiped her tears.

The Donnelly woman was so nervous she made Cosgrove jittery, like the Jesuit, a nervous wreck. In this line of work, you got used to giving people the jitters. Lots of people have something to hide and are afraid it will come out when the police get into their business. Even so, usually the folks who got nervous and jittery were not the ones to worry about.

The sure-of-themselves, never-get-rattled folks who swindled widows and orphans, robbed poor boxes, or murdered their families could lie without a drop of sweat.

Ed Ford turned up something on James Donnelly. It looked like he had a thing for young girls. A couple of times at the college, there'd been complaints about inappropriate behavior with a student. No one pressed charges. The college had no record of any discipline or even a warning. They expunged the names of the students.

Cop logic said if Donnelly got caught twice he'd done it more times when he didn't get caught. If someone took him out because of one of those liaisons, it would be hell to try to find out who. Go back through eighteen or twenty years of students to find someone who remembers one of the incidents? Ford talked with current students who thought him creepy, but nothing inappropriate, nothing concrete. Something wasn't right with the guy. Still, it would be a lot less work if the ex-wife turned out to be the killer.

He could make a case for it under the hate-my-ex exclusion, if nothing else. The problem was how to connect her to Yates—he could as easily have pulled in a bum off the street as his suspect—nothing at all, until the skirmish at the funeral. A conversation with the widow the next day confirmed what he'd guessed. You never can tell about these bookworm types once they take off their glasses and let their hair down.

Kay Donnelly sat stiffly in a forbidding-looking wing chair in the sparsely furnished sitting room of the austere and lifeless woman's residence where she was staying. She acted like she expected him to attach electrodes and administer electric shocks if she didn't answer his questions the way he wanted. With those big brown eyes staring up at him, and this demure woman shrinking back from him, he felt like a thug.

"I don't have to talk to you," she said. "My lawyer said I could ask for him to be present."

Cosgrove looked her directly in the eye. "You could. It's up to you. We could go downtown, give him a call, and talk there. I want to ask about Nelson Yates. Do you need your lawyer to tell me about that?"

Her eyes blazed. "There's nothing to talk about. Whatever you think happened is a figment of that deranged woman's imagination."

"You spent time with him not so long ago, she said, visited him at their apartment in New York."

"A few years ago, Max wanted to do an article on Nelson. Nelson wouldn't talk to him—some falling out in the past—so he sent me. I talked with him, interviewed him. It was an assignment. I can show you the notes from the interviews."

"Why would Mrs. Yates think you were sleeping with her husband?"

"Because she's paranoid and delusional—jealous. She married a philanderer. He was married when he took up with her. What did she think was going to happen?

"He made passes at me during the interview. I had to finesse my way out of a number of awkward situations, without making him angry enough to end the interview. On one of those passes, he trapped me on the couch. He had my dress up and had gotten his hand between my legs when his wife opened the door. I should have bashed him between the eyes. I didn't. I giggled like a schoolgirl. She blew up, so I left them to fight it out."

She looked up at Cosgrove. "I suppose I shouldn't have told you this. My lawyer warned me you'd twist whatever I told you to make me seem guilty."

"Did I?"

"No. Not yet. I assume you will . . . or I think you might." Her expression was an entreaty, her voice small. "I hope you won't." She shook her head. "I'm so easy to take advantage of."

Cosgrove hesitated. Was that an invitation? He told himself

it wasn't. She looked down at her hands in her lap as she spoke and seemed to be talking to herself. So what did it mean? He was falling for this innocence act like a novice. What the hell was happening to him? Twenty years on the job, and he's turning into Tinker Bell. He took a moment to look at his notebook. "You didn't like Nelson Yates."

She looked up, speaking softly, no inflection. "He was a good writer. Personally, he was a fraud. I found him disgusting. But I didn't hate him. A giant ego, an insatiable appetite for sex, even as an old man, no wonder Mary hated him. He abused her."

"Abused her?"

"Not physically, psychologically. He acted like she was stupid, like she'd been inflicted on him and he had to put up with her. He demeaned and embarrassed her."

"As he did you?"

"He didn't embarrass me. I embarrassed myself." She raised her gaze to look into his eyes. He didn't like what he saw in hers, defeat; she'd rolled over, belly up, was at his mercy.

He had other questions but decided to wait. He could bear down on her. She was exposed, vulnerable, shame weakening her defenses. He didn't have enough on her to do that. She might give something up. On the other hand, she might not have anything left to give, and he'd leave her there a wreck for no good reason. She'd brought Mary Yates into sharper focus. Maybe it was guile, raising suspicion about the woman's jealousy. Maybe. You couldn't tell. He'd have to look into it.

"So . . ." Lisa Young took Ambler to the Algonquin for lunch. She seemed at home in the elegant dining room, the maître d' welcoming her without being familiar, calling her by her married name, leading them to a table. Ambler suspected the elegant dining room, the trappings of luxury were meant to intimidate him.

"If you think I'm wondering what you're up to, you're right," he said when they were seated.

"I'm a woman of contradictions. As you find out more about me—as I'm sure you intend to—you'll see what I mean."

"I will?"

The waiter appeared. She ordered a romaine salad with poached shrimp, Ambler a twenty-two-dollar cheeseburger. When the waiter left with their order, she sat back and smiled. "So you're not only a curator of things detective, but an actual detective, a counterpart of your fictional heroes."

Ambler sipped from his water glass; it was stemware with a slice of lemon floating in it. "I want to know who killed Nelson Yates, if that's what you mean."

Her face brightened. "You think I know who killed him?"

"Did you know him?"

She folded her hands beneath her chin and leaned on them. "Do you think I know who killed Nelson Yates because I made a donation to the library?"

"Why did you?"

"That's none of your business."

"Do you have something to hide?"

"I don't need anything to hide to tell you something is none of your business." She wasn't angry. She was cheerful, beaming. When she lowered her hands to the table in front of her, the fingers she folded around one another were long and elegant. "Suppose we talk about you? What do you get out of snooping?"

It was a good question. What did he get out of it? He didn't believe justice necessarily prevailed in a criminal case or anywhere else in life. He didn't care for investigative work; much of it was routine, the outcome depending on luck more often than not. What interested him was why: the level of desperation that makes someone murder and the missteps and misfortunes that make someone else a killer's victim, the twists and turns of life's paths that bring them together, this was what interested him. In unraveling all that, outing the murderer, so to speak, was almost a byproduct.

"When I first solved a crime, it was because I saw through something. I saw a murder where most others thought they'd seen an accident. Proving the truth of that was a kind of arrogance," he told her. "Later, I thought if I could solve a crime, understand why a murder happened, I might stop another murder." What he couldn't do was find the words to tell her he did what he did in some part to atone for what his son had done, and what he had done to his son.

She folded her manicured fingers under her chin and leaned on her hands, watching him as if he were about to do something entertaining. "And what do you find? Why do people kill?"

Despite her expression, which might be skeptical, he wanted her to understand. "Sometimes, it's being in the wrong place at the wrong time; other times, a split-second choice, an impulsive act followed by a lifetime of regret. There are calculated, cold murders—for benefit, financial or otherwise; murders from hatred or rage, for slights real or imagined; some people murder because it's their job. Others, I guess, are the sad ones, from pain . . . of betrayal, unrequited love, or love that's too intense to bear."

Her expression became wistful as she listened. She seemed to acknowledge his seriousness and lowered her gaze. "I wonder if someone might commit a crime as bad or worse than murder and the punishment would be simply having to live with it."

He watched the waiter deliver his hamburger—large enough to feed a family of four—and found himself growing angry at this regal dining room with its white tablecloths, wood paneling, wall paintings, and oriental rugs, men in tailored pinstriped suits clinking silverware against china plates and sipping from crystal goblets, people with a sense of entitlement.

"I'm a person of wealth and privilege," she said, as if she read his thoughts. "I'm not especially proud of it. I didn't do anything to deserve it." Ambler searched her face. Impassive, inscrutable, this wasn't a confession. She was a self-assured woman. He didn't understand what she was getting at.

"We're given roles to play," she said. "We don't choose them. When I was young, I thought I could change who I was. Trying to do so drove me insane—I mean that literally—and ruined the lives of everyone around me, everyone I loved." Her voice caught. She blinked a few times before looking down at her plate, poking at the elegantly presented shrimp with her fork. "I want you to hear this now from me, because later, when you know everything, you won't want to understand, or you won't care, or it won't make any difference."

"What do you want me to understand?" Ambler concentrated on his hamburger. For one thing, he was hungry and it tasted good; for another, he'd been brought up not to waste food; and finally, the woman across from him was going through such emotional pain that looking at her felt like a terrible invasion of her privacy.

When he faced her again, her expression was bleak. "I can't keep you from digging into my past. It will be painful for me, and it won't help you find the murderer of Nelson Yates."

"How do you know?"

His question surprised her. It showed in her face. What had been entreaty became confusion. She wasn't trying to put anything over on him. He'd presented a contingency she hadn't considered. She stammered her answer. "I . . . I . . . How could it? Nothing in my past that I know—that I can think of—could have anything to do with Nelson Yates's murder."

Ambler felt sorry for her. "Did you know Nelson Yates?"

From the desperate look flashing across her eyes, he knew before she spoke that her answer would not suffice. She seemed to know that, too. "I think I already answered you," she said brightly enough. "It's no matter." She took a dainty bite from the luncheon plate she'd previously been trying to maul and touched her napkin lightly to her lips. "I have a plan to preserve your reading room." Mischief danced in her eyes again. "Do you own a tux?"

"A what?"

"A tuxedo." She smiled. "I suppose not. A good black suit will do."

Her change in attitude and manner, from the depths of despair to a bubbling enthusiasm, was bewildering. "Why?"

"I'm taking you to the library's spring gala."

"Did you catch up with the society lady yet?" McNulty asked as he delivered a stein of beer to Ambler and one to Adele.

"I did," said Ambler. "I met her in the King Cole Bar. The next day, she took me to lunch."

"She's taking him to the library's spring gala," Adele said.

"She hasn't told me why she donated the money for the Yates collection or if she knew Nelson Yates."

"Why should she?" McNulty said. "People should be able to keep things to themselves."

Adele cast a baleful glance at Ambler. "You'd think that, wouldn't you?"

McNulty was on his high horse. "There's a lot happened in my life I'm not going to tell you or anyone else about."

"Okay, McNulty. I got it." Ambler said.

"She gave money to the library anonymously, right? There you go. If she wanted people to know, she'd have said so."

"I think you've made your point," Adele said.

McNulty walked away in a huff, interrupting two patrons who were arguing about the upcoming election to tell them all the candidates were thieves and ax murderers.

"Mike Cosgrove asked you to talk to her. That's how this began, right?" Adele was angry but not unforgiving, as if whatever there was between them, friendship he guessed, would have to withstand some wrongs he might do. "I hope she never finds out that, on top of everything else, you were investigating her as a murder suspect."

Ambler hung his head. "Not exactly. I'm not going to tell Cosgrove about this yet. He interviewed Mary Yates after the fracas at the memorial service and wouldn't tell me what she said, so we're even."

Adele wrinkled her nose. "If you ask me, Mary Yates makes a better murder suspect than Mrs. Young."

Ambler had been thinking that himself. "The way these things go, when you're looking for a motive, if a murder isn't for love or hate, it's probably for money." He told her what Kay Donnelly said about Mary Yates. "We know she had a motive. That's about it. We won't cross her off the list."

"I haven't come across anything about Mary Yates in the collection, which is surprising. There should be letters, probably other things, unless she took them out."

"See what you can find on Mrs. Young, while you're at it."

"I doubt she'd turn up in the Yates collection, but I'll look. I can check the Social Register, too. She's probably been on the philanthropy circuit since she was a debutante. I wonder if Mary Yates was a debutante."

Chapter 16

On Thursday evening after work, Adele drank a beer by herself at the Library Tavern waiting for Raymond, who didn't show up. She didn't stay for a second one and told McNulty to tell Raymond she went home. McNulty noticed the man who left behind her because McNulty considered it part of his trade to notice everyone who went in or out of his bar.

He didn't like the guy. He'd never been in before, ordered a rum and Coke, which he didn't seem to want, as he left much of it behind, and left a ten for a nine-dollar-and-change tab. He went the same direction as Adele and walked at the same pace. That didn't mean he was following her. There was still daylight and they were in Midtown Manhattan. It was something he noted without analyzing; something he'd remember if he saw the guy again.

Adele walked up Madison and across 42nd Street through Times Square. It was rush hour, the sidewalks crowded, everyone hurrying. As she crossed Broadway, on the island between

Broadway and Seventh Avenue, she felt a man beside her. He didn't touch her and he looked straight ahead.

"I'm going to walk beside you and tell you something. Don't look at me and don't say anything. If you make a scene, I'll disappear and not be so nice the next time."

Instinctively, Adele turned toward him. As if he expected her reaction, he turned away. "I said not to look."

"What do you want?"

The light changed and they joined the crush crossing Seventh Avenue. Just past the corner there was an entrance to the Times Square subway station. She thought about ducking into it but decided not to. The man beside her seemed calm and sure of himself—and vaguely familiar.

"You're bothering a friend of mine and her kid. She wants you to stop."

Now she knew why he sounded familiar. He was the guy Raymond fought with the night they were with Johnny. She began to turn toward him again but caught herself. For some reason, knowing who he was made her braver, maybe because Raymond had bested him. "Why does she want that? Why wouldn't she tell me herself?"

He kept a steady pace next to her. "She told me to tell you to keep away from her and her kid. She's afraid to tell you. I'm not. I'm telling you to keep away from them."

"Or what?" This time Adele did turn. But he was gone, losing himself in the crowd in seconds.

She walked the rest of the block before she began to shiver. As her mind stripped away the traffic noise, she heard his words again, and the tone of his voice. It was Dominic's tone, so empty of feeling, so cold, that caused her to shiver. It was as if a robot had warned her—a message with such inevitability to it.

• • •

"He scared me. That's what he wanted to do—scare me—and he did. Can you go threaten him for threatening me?"

Ambler smiled. "Tai chi doesn't provide for much in the way of threatening."

"What's it good for?"

"A long story. You can leave her alone if that's her wish, and why wouldn't you?" He held up his hand to stop Adele's response. "Or you can check with her to make sure it's what she wants."

"Exactly. Will you come with me?"

The following evening, Ambler and Adele climbed two flights of stairs and stood in front of Emily's apartment. She opened the door and stared at them, the smoke from a cigarette curling up from her hand. Finally, she said, "Yes. Can I help you?" Her eyes lingered a moment on Ambler.

"Emily, this is my friend Raymond Ambler. We'd like to talk to you."

Emily kept her eyes on Ambler, not friendly, not exactly bold but not modest either. She swung the door back and forth in a small arc.

"It will only take a minute."

She turned to Adele. "Is it about Johnny?"

"No," Adele said. "Is something the matter with Johnny?"

"Nothin's wrong with him. What do you want?"

Ambler watched the two women. They were about the same height and build, about the same age. Yet Emily seemed older. Adele radiated a kind of pleasant energy, a spark of life that made you glad to be with her, to watch her go about her work. Emily was harder. She dragged on her cigarette, jittery, tense, but sure of herself in a way Adele wasn't, as if Adele might be an underling, a younger sister.

"Johnny's a great kid, Ms. Smith," Ambler said.

Emily peered at his face as if she recognized something in it. "You have a kid?"

"A boy," Ambler said. "He's a man now."

"What's his name?"

"John."

"You might as well come in." She backed and turned, holding the door for them. "I didn't mean to leave you standing in the hallway."

The living room they entered had an ancient stuffed couch, and mismatched armchairs on either side of a dented wooden coffee table, but the room was clean. When she offered them a beer, Adele looked confused. Ambler said sure. Johnny chose that moment to appear, coming up beside his mom, beaming. Her expression softened when she looked at him. She tousled his hair. When she looked back at Ambler and Adele, the softness in her expression came also.

On a side table against a wall across from the couch was a small—though large for that apartment—cage, housing what looked like two guinea pigs. Adele noticed them first. "Are they yours?" she asked Johnny, who beamed in response.

He crossed the room and extricated one of the furry creatures and handed it to a startled Adele. Ambler laughed. Johnny grabbed the other animal and handed it to Ambler, who held it while it wiggled from its nose to its tail.

Emily came from the kitchen carrying two cans of Miller Lite, handed one to Ambler, who was sitting on the couch next to Adele, and took a sip from the other one. She took little notice of the guinea pigs, until the one Adele was holding worked his way loose and scampered up her chest toward her face. At which point Adele screamed.

"Johnny," his mother shouted, in a kind of weary, motherly tone. "Get that pig off of her."

The boy complied, picking up the animal and sitting down

between Adele and Ambler with his pet on his lap. He offered to take Ambler's also. But Ambler said he'd keep his.

"You didn't come here to pet guinea pigs, did you?" Emily took another slug of beer. "What?" She pulled a cigarette out a pack and lit it.

Adele leaned toward her. "It's about your friend Dominic." She waited for a reaction.

"What'd he do?" She sounded exasperated, a here-we-go-again response, not surprised Dominic did something that would require explanation or apology. Adele told her what happened.

Emily rolled her eyes. "That's Dominic. He thinks he can muscle his way out of anything." Her expression softened. "Did he scare you?" She bent forward and reached to pat the top of Adele's hand. "Don't worry about him. His bark is worse than his bite. I'll straighten him out. He doesn't need to protect me—the jerk."

They talked for a bit about Johnny. Adele was right about Emily's background. You could tell from her vocabulary, her pride in Johnny doing well in school, the way she talked about herself as a young reader, that she'd had a cultured upbringing, maybe not privileged but he'd bet her parents were educated. He wondered where she'd gone off the tracks. Adele pressed her about where she grew up, about her parents, probably because of her suspicion she might be Nelson Yates's daughter, but didn't get anywhere. The only thing she wanted to talk about was her singing.

"I came to the city to be a singer when I was too young," she said. "The East Village beat all that naïveté out of me pretty quick. But I took lessons. I've done okay, not great or anything close but okay. I still get gigs."

"My son used to play music in the East Village," Ambler said. "He was a guitar player."

"Is he cute? Does he have eyes like yours?"

Ambler had to think. "Yes and he has dark, curly hair. I guess he's handsome."

Emily rolled her eyes. "A cute guitar player in the East Village in the eighties. I probably slept with him." She said this in a matter-of-fact way, like she might say they played in the same band or took the same bus. Ambler wasn't sure how to respond, so he didn't.

There was a bookshelf with a CD player and a stack of CDs, and some books—a few hardcover, a lot of paperbacks, bestsellers, romance, mostly women writers; no mysteries; nothing by Nelson Yates, if Adele was curious about that. He noticed a briefcase next to one of the bookshelves; it was open and contained what looked like notebooks, envelopes, and other papers. The briefcase was soft leather and worn, with the initials JXD embossed on it. It was a man's briefcase and didn't seem like something that would belong to Dominic. He wondered if another man had left it. He wondered how many men there had been in her life.

Adele and Emily chatted away. Their effort was forced but they tried hard, especially Adele. Yet it was clear to him, if it wasn't to them, they had little in common. A few times, Emily looked over at him. Her eyes met his and lingered. She was pretty with a kind of vulnerability in her expression that appealed to him, as she must know it would to most men.

"Dominic's been more or less the only constant man in Johnny's life," Emily said. She talked easily about things another person might keep to herself; at the same time, not revealing anything about herself she didn't want to. "He's like a friend of the family."

"He's not Johnny's father?"

Emily shook her head. "His father's in jail." Seeing Adele's look of concern, she said, "He wasn't a bad guy, really, just a bad-luck sort of guy. He was good to me about the kid, if we needed something, before he went away."

A noise at the door startled everyone. The two women froze. Ambler handed the guinea pig to Johnny and stood.

Emily's eyes flashed at Ambler. "It's Dominic. I'll take care of it."

Ambler and Adele watched her walk to the door.

"Don't worry," Johnny said cheerfully. "Mom can handle Dominic." He put the guinea pigs back in their cage.

The door was behind a half wall, so Ambler couldn't see what was happening or decipher what was being said, except for the last thing Dominic said before the door slammed. "It's your funeral."

Emily came back from the hallway and went to the kitchen, coming back this time with three cans of beer, the extra one for Adele. She lit another cigarette.

"Why's he so protective of you?" Ambler asked.

"That's how he is." Emily took a long drink from her beer.

"Why is he worried about Adele?"

Emily was uneasy, not looking at Ambler or Adele. "Who knows? He's not used to me having friends. He'll leave her alone. I told him." She turned to the boy, who was sitting on the couch, leaning against Ambler's arm. "Johnny," she nodded her head toward the back of the apartment. "Go watch TV in my bedroom."

His mouth scrunched up and he let out a small moan. He was gearing up to complain, when Ambler put his arm around him and gently helped him stand. He looked at Adele and his mother before shuffling off. Watching him, they shared a moment that seemed in some way to connect them. The common bond was unspoken, yet it was there.

"It's my fault," Emily said. "In the beginning, Dominic got

the wrong idea. We didn't know what you were up to with the kid, you know? With Johnny's father in jail and all, and things not going so well for me all the time, I thought . . . you know . . . I thought something, someone, might think he wasn't cared for right."

Her voice dropped. "When I met you, I saw you were okay. You aren't a busybody. You're not looking down on anyone." She drank from her beer again. "Dominic hasn't caught on yet." Her gaze went from Adele to Ambler and back to lock onto Adele. "Johnny doesn't really have anybody besides me."

Ambler began to say something but stopped when he felt the intensity from Adele next to him. She was focused on Emily. "Are his grandparents alive?"

Emily, sensing Adele's intensity, too, shifted uncomfortably in her chair. "They're not involved. It's complicated. His father, we weren't married or anything. It was a casual thing with him. I wasn't even gonna tell him I was pregnant. He found out it was him and wanted to help, that's all. He helped now and again with money for the first couple of years. Then he got in trouble and went to jail. We weren't ever together after Johnny was born. So it wasn't a grandparent thing for him. I don't even know who they are."

"What about your parents?"

She looked at Ambler. "I haven't had anything to so with my parents for a long time. They're crazy, and they're not together anyway. I never wanted them to know about Johnny." Her eyes began to tear. "It's sad for the poor kid. It's not his fault. The poor little bastard doesn't have anybody." She sobbed softly.

"I'm so sorry," Adele said. She watched for a moment and then went to her, sitting on the arm of the easy chair, putting her arm around Emily's shoulder. After a moment, Emily leaned toward her and cried against Adele's chest.

• • •

"You never know how things will work out," Raymond said as they walked along 52nd Street.

"She said you could take Johnny to a baseball game. I'm so happy." Adele hopped and skipped beside Ambler.

He started to say something, but touched her arm in warning and seemed to heighten his senses, listening, peering into the darkness, slowing his pace.

She listened with him but heard nothing. They walked toward Ninth Avenue, Raymond, knees bent, walking deliberately step after paused step like a cat.

Soon, Adele had enough. "What is it?"

He didn't answer, so she asked again. And then she heard something, a metallic sound, like a piece of metal sliding into place against another piece. After that, there was silence, a deeper silence than she expected. Parked cars lined the side of the street they walked on. Raymond took her arm and pulled her gently into the middle of the street. It took a moment for her to understand why. It would be harder for anyone to sneak up on them in the street because of the space and light around them.

When they reached Ninth Avenue, Raymond hailed a cab, even though they were only a couple of blocks from her apartment. He opened the car door and climbed in behind her, looking back over his shoulder as he did.

"What was that all about?" she asked as they settled in.

"I heard something. I felt something was wrong."

"Do you have extrasensory perception?"

"I'm a good listener."

"Do you think Dominic was lurking in the alley?"

Raymond shrugged.

"It's over now, right?"

He didn't answer. She liked that he looked worried. He really did watch over her. The cab ride to her apartment around a couple of short blocks and up one long one took longer than it might have because of the traffic and one-way streets.

"I found some things in the Yates collection I want to show you," she said, "photos of Nelson and his daughter when she was very young. I'm hoping I'll find more."

"Do you still think Emily Smith is Emily Yates?"

"I haven't ruled it out," she said with a sly smile.

After she opened the cab door, on impulse, before she got out, she leaned over and kissed him quickly on the lips. The kiss startled him. She couldn't tell what his reaction meant, whether it was surprise, delight, or irritation. It was the first time she'd kissed him since the night her mother died, the night he stayed with her and comforted her, the night they'd never spoken of.

Mike Cosgrove thumbed through the James Donnelly murder book, reading the interviews the homicide team had conducted since the Donnelly investigation began. Somewhere, he'd find a piece of information—a missed observation, a glossed-over fact, an odd remembrance—about this cipher James Donnelly that would tell him why he got himself murdered. That was one of Ray's ideas, and he liked it, not that he'd tell him. At some point in his life, Donnelly did someone an unforgiveable harm—cheated a cousin out of an inheritance, welshed on a bet, inadvertently or purposefully ruined a man's life—hurt someone bad enough to earn the ultimate revenge. It might have happened recently. It might have happened a long time ago. Somewhere along the line he'd wronged someone. The same had to be true of Nelson Yates. Somehow—unless you accepted the improbable but not impossible idea that the murders were unrelated—they must have wronged the same person.

Donnelly wasn't a gambler or an investor, so not likely money was his problem. His bad habit was young women—too young. That could attract a spurned lover, a jealous husband, an enraged father. There'd been a couple of college girls he'd led down the garden path. More interesting was a fling with a high school girl when Donnelly was a young professor—married to Kay Donnelly and a junior colleague of Nelson Yates. Kay Donnelly hadn't mentioned it.

Adele had been walking by Johnny's mother's apartment every few days for a while now, and she wasn't going to stop because some thug wanted her to, especially since Emily wanted to be friends. She'd walk over to Tenth Avenue on her way home, even though it was a long block past where she should turn, and back toward her apartment along 49th Street, lingering down the block and across the street from Emily's apartment for a few minutes.

At the library, whenever she had a few moments, she continued her search for information about Emily Yates. She didn't know what she hoped to find, as she didn't know what she expected to find by walking past Emily Smith's apartment. It wasn't really to spy on her, or see who came and went from the apartment. In a way, walking past the apartment or stopping to linger helped her think about Emily. Perhaps she'd run into her as she left the apartment. They'd go for coffee. She'd ask her about herself, where she grew up and things like that, and check on whatever story she told her.

On this evening, as she sat on a wall across the street from Emily Smith's apartment, she watched a cab pull up in front of the apartment building. She hesitated and then froze, as Harry Larkin got out and brushed himself off, looking up at Emily and Johnny's building before heading toward the door. Stunned, she watched him, not sure what to do. For the first few minutes after he went into the building, she thought about leaving, pretending she didn't see him, that this never happened.

There was any number of possibilities. He might coincidently know someone else in the building or he might know Emily Smith or . . . But she knew what it meant. Harry Larkin would have known Emily Yates, as he knew her father, from his time at Hudson Highlands University.

She sat on the wall for a long time. The sun sunk behind the buildings and the evening grew cooler. She shivered and waited. Finally, the door she was watching opened. Harry came out. Across the street from Emily's apartment building was a Catholic school, next to the wall Adele sat on. He stood for a long moment looking at the school, as if it might help him decide something.

For a split second, when Adele approached him, his face tightened with anger, but it quickly softened with sadness. "Have you been following me?" He spoke so quietly she hardly heard him.

"Of course not."

"Were you waiting for me?" Again he spoke softly.

"I saw you go in."

"Do you know who lives here?"

"I think so. Did you go to see Emily?"

"Yes."

"Is she Emily Yates?"

Harry hesitated. "Do you know her?" Before she could answer, he smiled, taking on a priestly manner that radiated kindness, reminding her of the smiling, bumbling, compassionate parish priest of her childhood. She felt a tremendous sadness, missing her mother. "Oh Adele—" He shook his head like he'd caught her at some mischief. "Is Ray with you?"

"No. I met Emily a few weeks ago. Actually, I met her son. . . ." She stammered her way through the story of her involvement with Emily and Johnny.

"How did you know she was Emily Yates?"

"I didn't until you got here. I suspected she might be when

I thought I saw her at Nelson Yates's memorial service. When I saw you go into her building, it was too much of a coincidence for it to be anything else."

"How strange." He really did look like the kindly village priest, an incarnation of Raymond's Father Brown. "On top of all she's been through, I've led you to her hiding place."

"Why is she hiding? Is she in trouble?"

Harry began walking. "Let's find a place we can sit down."

Adele walked rapidly beside him. "Is she afraid what happened to her father will happen to her?"

Harry kept walking.

"You have to tell me—"

"I don't want Emily to look out the window and see us together."

They found a café on Ninth Avenue and took a table near a large window. While Harry waited for their coffee drinks to be brewed, Adele stared out at the street and pondered how she would tell Harry what she knew about his departure from Hudson Highlands University.

When he returned to the table, she looked him in the eye. "I know what happened in the past . . . to you."

He continued to look at her, his expression meek, as he bent to place the coffees on the table, before he sat down heavily across from her. "I suppose what you've discovered, what you're having a difficult time telling me, is that I left the university under a dark cloud."

"A child accused you—" She looked into a deep pool of sadness.

"If I tell you the accusation was a cry of pain from a wounded child because she couldn't find the words to direct it to where the hurt and harm came from—"

"I see," Adele said. "I'm so sorry. . . ."

Harry smiled, so that his face became cherubic, beatific.

Sometimes, watching him at work, she'd thought he might actually be a saint, and now to hear him speak of child molesting.

"If I told you I was innocent, of course, you'd believe me. But I can't prove it, so there will be doubt, doubt from everyone, even a glimmer of doubt in your mind." He held up his hand to stop her protests.

"Was it Emily?"

"Does anyone else know about Emily? Does Ray know?"

"No one knows. I told Raymond I suspected she might be. He didn't really believe me."

Harry's eyes bore into hers, his face reflecting such agony she expected blood to shoot out of his pores. "Could I ask that you not tell anyone what you found out?"

She thought about her answer for a moment, her chest bursting with the thought of not telling Raymond. Realizing this, she wondered if she was being selfish. Did it make any difference that she knew Emily Smith was Emily Yates? Would knowing this be important or was she just excited at the idea of telling Raymond she'd been right?

"Why Harry? You have to tell me why."

He shook his head. "I know something from hearing confession I can't divulge."

Adele felt a shiver run through her. Harry's expression was ghastly. "Does what you know have anything to do with her father's murder? Is Emily in danger?"

"I need you to trust that I'll do everything in my power to protect Emily." He spoke slowly, choosing his words carefully. "I respect that Raymond and you, too, want only what's best and would feel terrible if your efforts brought suffering and disaster to someone who doesn't deserve such a fate."

She told him she needed to think. She'd give him a day or two while she thought about what he told her and what she should do about it. And she wouldn't say anything to Raymond.

Chapter 17

When the doorbell rang from downstairs, Johnny jumped from the couch, grabbed his glove and his Yankee cap, and headed for the door. His mom cut him off before he reached it.

"Remember what I told you."

"I do! I do!" He was jumping in place.

She put her cigarette in her mouth, reached out with both hands to straighten the collar on his shirt. "You need a jacket. It gets cool at night."

It was thrown over the back of the living room chair. He retrieved it. "I gotta go. I gotta go! He's waiting."

"Remember. You don't talk about the family—nothin' about what happens at home . . . nothin' about me. If he asks anything, clamp your mouth shut and keep it that way."

Johnny ran down the stairs. The man standing at the bottom was smiling. Mr. Ambler was taking him to the ball game. He was so happy to see him. What he liked the most was how peaceful he was, how everything was safe and easy around him, so you didn't have to watch out about anything.

"I'll take good care of him," Ambler hollered up the stairs.

"He has a key," Emily hollered back.

They walked to Columbus Circle to get the train. It was cool, so his mom was right about the jacket. He put it on. Mr. Ambler wore a windbreaker and walked pretty fast. He didn't have to run, but he had to pay attention, concentrate, to keep up.

"You look just like a boy should look when he's on his way to a Yankee game," Mr. Ambler said as they headed into the subway. A lot of the people on the train wore Yankee hats. Some wore jerseys with numbers on the back that he recognized, 2 for Derek Jeter, 13 for A-Rod, 20 for Jorge Posada. A couple of other kids in the subway car carried baseball gloves. The train felt good; a hum of excitement, everyone in a good mood, having fun.

When they came out of the subway, they were pushed along by the crowd that kept getting bigger and bigger because people were coming down the stairs from the el stop above the street, as well as up from the subway. He saw a ball field across from the el and for a moment thought it was the stadium. It was small and dingy with weak lights shining on the field. It didn't look like it could even hold all the people from the subway. He didn't say anything and was glad he didn't because a couple of seconds later the real Yankee Stadium loomed in front of him. It was gigantic and round, a kind of beige color, taking up the entire block, with crowds swarming all around it.

They pushed along with the crowd. Mr. Ambler knew where to go, pushing him through a turnstile in front of them and handing the man tickets. They walked up a cement ramp that was kind of dark, next to walls that were kind of dingy. But all of a sudden they came out of the dinginess, and the diamond opened in front of them. His breath caught in his chest. The field was brighter than daylight, the green grass sparkling, the white of the pinstriped uniforms glowing. He'd never seen anywhere so bright. Nothing seemed real. He didn't realize he stopped and was staring, blocking the path of the people behind, until Mr. Ambler nudged him forward.

Mr. Ambler told him it should be a good game. And he was right. First, the Red Sox scored a run in the first inning. Then, the Yankees came up and somebody hit a home run and right after that A-Rod hit a home run, so the Yanks were ahead.

Next time up, the Red Sox scored again, but the Yankees were still ahead. In the fourth inning, the Red Sox tied the game. Mr. Ambler had a scorecard and a pencil and marked things down. After the Red Sox tied the game, the Yankees scored four runs in the bottom of the inning. Everyone cheered, even Mr. Ambler. But, in the top of the next inning, the Red Sox scored so many runs he lost count, and everyone was mad and groaning and booing and the Red Sox were ahead again. Things looked bad. Mr. Ambler said the Yankees were a bunch of bums, particularly the pitcher who gave up all the runs. But the Yanks came back and scored four runs in the bottom of the fifth and they were ahead again. Everybody yelled and cheered, and Mr. Ambler threw his scorebook up in the air and over his shoulder.

On the way home, Mr. Ambler said, "You'll certainly remember that game, won't you?" And of course he'd remember. He was tired and his head spun when he tried to remember all the runs scoring. He'd eaten two hot dogs, peanuts, crackerjacks, and ice cream. Soon after they got on the subway and sat down, he felt like he was sinking. The next thing he knew, he was holding Mr. Ambler's hand walking up the subway stairs into the lights of Columbus Circle, which used to seem really bright, yet after the stadium lights looked like a dark alley. He saw himself like a little kid holding his dad's hand. He felt dumb, glad none of the kids from school could see him. But he didn't let go.

• • •

Ambler decided to walk home after dropping Johnny off. His mother didn't come to the door. Johnny said that was okay; she was probably asleep. What he meant was she was probably passed out. He waited until the boy signaled from the window before beginning the trek back to Murray Hill. He could have taken a cab but thought the walk might help him beat back some ghosts.

Being at the ball game with the kid, taking him home to his passed-out mother stirred up too many regrets, crystal-clear memories of his son, child of the streets, way too old for his years, as sweet as the boy was. It was uncanny that for a few moments at the game, he'd looked down at Johnny; his heart had swelled; tears pushed against the back of his eyes. He was watching Ron Guidry pitch and his son was sitting beside him.

"I need to talk to Harry and I want you to come with me," Adele told Raymond the morning after he took Johnny to the baseball game.

He looked at her questioningly but didn't ask why.

Harry knew what was coming; Adele was sure of that. He ushered them in and returned to sit behind his desk to face them. No smile. No greeting. No protest either.

"I can't do it, Harry. I have to tell Raymond." She looked to him for help.

He clasped his hands in front of him on the desk. She wondered if he realized it was the way Catholics put their hands together in prayer.

"It would be better if you told him yourself."

"Told him what, Adele?" His expression was blank as a wall.

"About Emily . . ."

"Emily?"

Adele stared at him, her mouth open, and then turned to

Ambler. "Emily Smith is Emily Yates, and Harry knows she is. I saw him go into her apartment building." She faced Harry again. "I'm sorry, Harry. I was wrong to agree not to tell Raymond."

Harry remained impassive. Adele walked over to the front of his desk. "I feel like such a fool. I felt awful not telling Raymond. Now, I feel awful not keeping my promise to you. I lied to Emily, too."

"If you're finished," Harry said. "I have work to do—so do both of you."

"That's it? You're not going to say anything?" Adele glared at him.

"Go to work," Harry said.

Ambler took Adele by the elbow and led her from the room.

Ambler watched Adele stomp off along the hallway toward her desk duty in the catalog room. She was furious because she wanted him to take her shift so she could go back and talk to Harry and he wouldn't do it. He had his reasons for not covering for her.

Not long afterward, from a vantage point around a hallway corner from Harry's office, he watched him bolt out the door, look carefully right and left, and start off down the stairs. Ambler followed at a good distance, waiting until he crossed 42nd Street before venturing down the bottom flight of steps. He had a pretty good idea where he was going so wasn't worried about getting too far behind. Shadowing someone wasn't any more part of Ambler's repertoire than undercover work with Lisa Young; neither was Harry accustomed to being followed. He puffed along at for him a fast pace, the sidewalks crowded enough for Ambler to saunter along unnoticed not quite a block behind.

Harry walked west on 46th Street through the diamond district, past a veritable United Nations of street vendors crowding the sidewalks, hawking gold and jewelry in front of dozens of stores whose windows were stuffed with gold watches, diamond rings, necklaces, and bracelets.

The crowd on the sidewalks thinned west of Sixth Avenue, picked up again near Broadway and Seventh Avenue, where Ambler lost Harry among the tourists gawking through the theater district. He found Harry again near Eighth Avenue and was a block behind when he turned to look behind him before starting uptown on Ninth Avenue. When he turned the corner at 49th Street, Ambler picked up his pace, catching up to him as he entered the doorway that led to Emily Yates's apartment.

"We've been keeping secrets long enough, Harry." He put his hand on the other man's shoulder. "Let's talk to Emily."

"What are you hiding there?" Laura Lee asked her husband.

"It's a .357 Magnum revolver." Max gave her a hard stare as he rewrapped the weapon in a soft black cloth and replaced it in a wooden case.

She stood over her husband. "Who do you plan to kill?"

Max glared at her for a long few seconds before he spoke. "It's for protection. I have a right to protect myself."

"Not with a handgun in New York. Where'd you get it?"

"That's not something you need to know."

"One of your gangster friends from your youth?"

"As I said—"

"Dominic?"

"Not Dominic. Why would you think that?"

"He's your brother."

"I haven't seen Dominic in years." His eyes narrowed. "Have you seen him . . . again?"

Laura Lee sidled up to him. She wore a flowing yellow skirt and a brown blouse, open an extra button at the neck. Laughing that free-spirited, tantalizing, lascivious sound that drove him crazy, swaying her hips gently, she moved closer until her body pressed against his. Hiking up her skirt, she sat down on his lap facing him. She licked his ear and whispered, "I'm only interested in your gun."

He pushed the case away from her. "I told you—"

"Not that one."

Afterward, they lay on the floor in front of the table, Laura Lee's skirt twisted around her hips, her blouse open, bra and panties on the floor beside them. Max's pants were around his ankles, so he had to struggle to sit up.

"How you can be so goddamn passionate and have such a cold heart is beyond me."

Her eyes met his, her expression indifferent. "Help me take off my skirt; I don't want to tear it."

He unzipped the zipper and undid a button at the waist. She lifted her hips and he pulled the skirt out from under her. She slipped out of her unbuttoned blouse and handed it to him. "Please hang them up," she said, lying naked on the floor. "And get me a drink."

He did as he was told, hanging the clothes in her closet, bringing her a vodka and orange juice. Still gorgeous, the most desirable woman he'd ever known. She took his breath away the first time he saw her; an American lit survey class, she sat in the front row, a white blouse, a tight red skirt, red lips, that wispy black hair. She'd crossed her legs and met his gaze with a smile that became a laugh when he tried to look away and begin his lecture. It hadn't taken long.

He should have known the trick with the skirt, the wanton, laughing expression in her eyes wasn't only for him. She came on to most men. How many she actually seduced, he didn't want to know. He hoped it was none. He certainly hoped it wasn't

Dominic. Getting him involved in their lives was a risk; he knew that then. He didn't know she'd find his recklessness so exciting. He thought she'd be repulsed by it. But no, she began flirting with his brother right in front of his eyes.

"The gun isn't going to help you, Max." She lit a cigarette. Naked, she walked over to the couch and sat down. "Why don't you get Dominic to protect you?"

"You'd like that, wouldn't you?"

She took a drag on her cigarette and let the smoke out. Bad enough she smoked. He hated that she smoked in the apartment. She said she wouldn't and did anyway when she felt she had the advantage. "Jealous, Max?"

Emily's face went white when she opened the apartment door. Sizing things up, she tried to close it again. Ambler blocked it with his foot.

Harry spoke softly. "This is Ray Ambler, Emily. He knows who you are."

She glared at Ambler. "I know him. Is that why you've been sneaking around here?"

"No," Ambler said. "I found out today."

"God damn it. Everyone I've ever known has lied to me, tricked me, fucked me over. Why would I think you and that damned woman—who pretended to be my friend—were different? I'm soft in the head." She turned on Harry. "So they know everything, now?"

Harry spoke calmly. "Ray and Adele found out who you are. I haven't told them anything."

Some change came over her, like the wind dying down. Without acknowledging what Harry said, she let go of the tension that had her standing rigid in the doorway. "What do you want?" She aimed the question at Ambler, the sharp edge missing from her voice.

"To ask about your father. I imagine it's not something you want to talk about."

Her gaze was level. "Why do you care?"

"I care that he was murdered."

"Again, why do you care?" Her dark eyes filled with emotion, some powerful passion smoldering behind them. Her nervousness returned, but not a fearful kind, more a fierce energy she didn't know what to do with.

"Do you care?"

She averted her gaze and then met his again. "No."

"You went to his memorial service."

"He was my father—" She turned away from him. "I need a cigarette." She walked away from the door toward a pack lying on a table in front of the couch. Ambler followed. Harry followed him.

She lit the cigarette, taking quick, long drags, exhaling, pushing the smoke out. "It's complicated. He was dead. It was over. . . ." Her voice trailed off.

"Do you know who might have killed your father?"

She made a face, the face a sullen teen makes when she doesn't like what she's being told to do but knows she'll have to do it anyway, not the sort of reaction you'd expect from a woman who'd been on her own as long as Emily. It was as if in talking about her father, in her mind she'd gone back to refight the battles of her teen years.

"Do you remember Max Wagner?"

Something moved in her eyes—doubt, curiosity, fear; he couldn't tell. "He was a friend of my father's."

"James Donnelly?"

She hesitated. "The same. Why are you asking me these questions? What do you want?" Again something changed in her expression—clouds forming, darkness.

What did he want? He'd told Nelson he'd look for his

daughter. He found her. What now? He'd gotten off on the wrong foot, scaring her. Starting with Lisa Young, he'd been doing a good job of blowing people's cover to no particular purpose.

"I'm sorry to spring this on you. You might know something that would help us find out who killed your father. I'd like to talk, to ask you some questions. It doesn't have to be now."

She looked tired, weary. "If I had something to tell you, I would've told you. I don't want anything to do with my father, dead or alive."

"He'd asked me to find you. He mentioned some letters—"

Her expression was sullen, provocative, and unpleasant, again the face of an angry, hurt, rebellious teenager, not what you'd expect on a grown woman, but it fit Emily. "You found me. I doubt he cares anymore."

"The letters?"

She shrugged her shoulders. "I don't know what he was talking about."

"If you—"

"I'm really tired of this. Stop!" Emily screeched, putting her hands over her ears like a little girl might do.

"Please, Ray," Harry said.

Chapter 18

"Sorry to bother you again, Mrs. Donnelly—"

"Somehow, I find that hard to believe. Officer? . . . I don't know what to call you."

"Detective Cosgrove is my official title." He considered her for a moment—her flashes of pretty when she smiled, her scholarly demeanor when she became austere and forbidding, a mask. She'd smiled for a moment when she made the "hard to believe" crack. Funny how you looked at women. She had a pretty mouth, nice lips. He thought she'd be nice to kiss. "People call me Mike."

She turned from him, demurely, as if embarrassed by the familiarity. "My lawyer—"

He held up his hands. "I know. He said not to talk to me . . . and didn't like that you talked to me the last time. This—"

"I didn't tell him about the last time."

Cosgrove hesitated. Something about her expression, the look in her eye, coquettish, a tiny smile, surprised him. The tables turned. She watched with amusement while he regained his footing.

"This is about your ex-husband, not about you."

The mask was back.

He told her about the complaints by young women against Donnelly at the college where he taught.

"James had a fondness for younger women. Is that what you're asking?"

"How young?"

She hesitated. "What do you mean? These were college girls, right?"

"Did you know this about him when you were married to him?"

She snorted. "I was a young girl when I married him."

"I'm talking about very young." His eyes met hers.

"How young?"

"You tell me."

She averted her eyes for a beat or two before meeting his gaze again. Her expression was all business, no attempt to charm him. "If you want me to answer your questions, tell me what you're getting at."

"Does what I'm getting at change what you know to be true?"

She closed her eyes and held them closed. When she opened them, she said, "It would establish that we're speaking to one another as equals. I don't like being tested, as if you're trying to catch me lying."

She had him again. It was either guilelessness or she was a good actor. "I'm a cop investigating a murder. I'm allowed to withhold information and trick people to get to the truth. I can tell you what page it says this on in the homicide investigator's manual." She seemed astonished by what he said. "That was a joke. Like the guy said, 'You can't cheat an honest man.'"

"I'm not a man."

"I know." His eyes moved from her face along her body to her legs and back to her face. He didn't mean to do it and was sorry he gave himself away like that. She looked down at the texture of the couch she sat on. One hand smoothed her skirt, tugging at the hem. The other hand went to her hair, kind of fluffing it up in the back. A clock ticked somewhere in the silence.

"Here's what I know." He told her James Donnelly had been asked to resign as coach of a girl's high school soccer team during the time he was teaching at Hudson Highlands University. He waited for her response. When none came, he asked, "You know what the usual reason is for that, right?"

She nodded. "That whole time we were at Hudson U was unreal. It was a commune of the brainwashed, headed by a flakey guru."

"Nelson Yates was the guru?"

She glanced at him quickly and quickly away. "You're good at dredging up the pieces of my past I'm ashamed of . . . mortified, actually." At first, he thought she was angry, furious. Then, her expression changed, or how he saw it changed, so that he thought she would cry. "I need a minute to get myself together."

Cosgrove thought quickly. If his partner had been with him, he couldn't do it. If anyone else were around, he wouldn't do it. If he weren't already a couple of hours into overtime for the fifth straight day, he wouldn't do it. He'd give her more power over him than he should if he did do it, and she was smart enough to know that. This was not one he'd be telling the boys about over a beer at Hanratty's.

He made his decision in a split second. "How about I buy you a drink?" Raising his eyebrows, he waited for her answer.

She looked astonished. Those inquiring green eyes got bigger and bigger, but she looked pleased.

They found a self-proclaimed Irish pub around the corner on Ninth Avenue. It bright red facade looked like the front of a firehouse, an Irish flag on one side, an American flag on the other side. In back was a section of an alley that passed for an outdoor patio, a beer garden with wrought iron tables, protected from the outside world by a stockade fence. Cosgrove remembered when if you wanted to be out back of a joint on Ninth Avenue you needed a ten-foot fence with razor wire on top.

"You have interesting methods of investigation, Detective Cosgrove." Her tone was teasing, her eyes smiling. "I've never seen a detective take a suspect to dinner on *Law & Order.*"

"I don't watch cop shows. At the moment, you're no more or less a suspect than anyone else." He drank from his pint and set it down. "You were about to answer my question about your ex-husband and a high school girl."

"So I was." She paused. "Everything is so different now. I can't imagine the person I was then." Her expression was sad, pained. "There was a high school—a precocious high school girl. We all knew her. Everyone who knew Nelson knew her. She was his daughter."

Later, Cosgrove would think about the world Kay Donnelly described. It was like the stories he'd read as a kid in his mother's Somerset Maugham book, where the colonists lived in their own world insulated from the life around them that the colonized people lived. Her description of Emily at fourteen, pretty, precocious, encouraged by her parents to socialize with the adults—and sleeping with at least two of them—got him to thinking about teenage girls like his daughter. The world came at them—young pretty girls—too fast. They woke up one morning and discovered they had something men desperately wanted.

Kay came clean about her and Nelson Yates. She'd slept with him, despite what she'd said earlier, during that time at the college when she was young. Most of the girls who were part of their literary circle slept with him.

"Nelson was an evangelist for free love. When he was younger, he'd been a follower of Wilhelm Reich—orgone energy and all that—and he still believed in it. Nothing crass or vulgar, Nelson was charismatic. " She paused, searching for words. "It sounds ridiculous now. The aura he created was amazingly seductive." She looked away modestly. "That's all I'm going to say about that."

When she looked at him again, she seemed sad, contrite. "I don't think he wanted his daughter when she was that young to become part of his free-love movement, but it was inevitable she would. She was gorgeous and impressionable and had no restraints. Men salivated over her, including my husband."

Ambler found Adele at the reference desk when he returned to the library. He told her he and Harry had spoken to Emily Yates.

She gave instructions to a middle-aged man with a gray beard who was interested in Antarctica and turned her smile on Ambler. "See. You didn't believe me."

"I did believe you, or I wouldn't have followed Harry. What's hard to believe is she's been in the city within walking distance of the library where her father was murdered and kept her identity secret."

"She'd kept who she was secret for years," Adele said. "Why would his dying change anything? I hope you didn't bring that up when you talked to her. It was bad enough following Harry and sneaking up on her."

Ambler shifted his gaze, looking anywhere except at Adele. "Well, I did actually." He finally met her gaze. "I probably shouldn't have. It's likely if we knew why she ran away from home—"

Adele rolled her eyes. "You need to take a break from Ross Macdonald. Why Emily? What about his son, the one Nelson thought he saw in the park that day? Why don't you bother him?"

"He was traveling with the ballet in Europe when his father was murdered. He flew back for the memorial service, and returned to Paris right after it."

Adele prepared to tackle another reader who was charging toward her from one of the computers across from the reference desk. "I hope you haven't ruined things with Emily."

When Adele wasn't digging through the Yates collection, she was at the Social Register office on Park Avenue South searching through the archives. Who knew there were so many yacht clubs, polo clubs, fencing associations in Manhattan? Each name in the register had a string of abbreviations following it. When she found herself getting bored, she'd guess what an abbreviation might stand for and then look it up, wasting time, like when she was in library school.

She found out that Raymond's new friend Lisa Young's husband had relatives who fought in the Revolutionary War—on the side of the British. Lisa Young was born into the Hathaway family, which traced its roots in America back to the 1600s and made the family fortune raising tobacco in Virginia with the help of slaves.

Once she got the last name, things began to move. Lisa Hathaway was introduced to society at the International Debutante Ball in 1976. She was prominent in the New York Junior League. Her photo turned up in the *Times* in the society pages and in an article about Virginia horse country in *Town & Country*. Then, nothing! Nothing after 1976 until a marriage notice to Mr. David Young appeared in the *Times* in 1992.

So what next? She didn't have any luck finding the names of the attendees at the 1976 debutante ball. There were archives somewhere; no one she talked to knew where or how one got access to them or if they'd include a list of debutante ball attendees. She thought she might do better with the Junior League. Fortunately, the League didn't take the term "Junior" literally. After a few phone calls, she tracked down a woman who'd known Lisa Hathaway. The woman turned out to be chatty, was fond of her memories, and liked gossip. They chatted about this and that, the woman assuming Adele a kindred spirit, until the chatty woman dropped the bombshell.

"She ran off with a writer, dear, a man old enough to be her father. The scandal of the year—I can tell you."

Adele thanked the woman. "I knew it," she said. She ran to find Raymond.

Mike Cosgrove knew Ray Ambler was holding back something. It riled him but he understood that he would. All of these librarians and researchers had skeletons rattling around in their closets. He'd gotten better cooperation from car thieves and whiskey hijackers than this crew of seekers of truth. Once again, he was stalled in traffic, getting onto the Queensboro Bridge. He should have known better. Left the car at the precinct and taken the express bus. Then again, right there, idling a couple of cars in front of him was an express bus. He'd be sitting in traffic anyway. Besides, he thought better by himself in the car. Traffic began to move, at a crawl, but steadily.

Tomorrow was pretty well set. He'd talk to the woman whose husband the Yates girl was with when he was killed. Ford had gone upstate to look through whatever the police from that time had come up with. Kay Donnelly hinted that the professor who was writing the book about Yates, the guy Ray didn't like—Wagner, Max Wagner—had fooled around with the Yates girl, as James Donnelly had. Grown men, intelligent men, college teachers. You'd think there'd be some virtue in that, that these guys would take the high road, and here they were fucking a fourteen-year-old, something they could go to jail for.

The first time for him it was with a fourteen-year-old girl actually. Of course, he wasn't a grown man; he was seventeen and she was in love with him, and he with her. Probably, at seventeen, he shouldn't have been with a girl that young—a friend's sister. In just about all ways though, except years, Anne was older and wiser than he was. More to feel guilty about was that he was still in love with her and she with him—both of them married to someone else.

"Adele, you're sure?"

"Well, not a hundred percent. I'd say only ninety-nine point ninety-nine percent. Who else could it be, Raymond?" She'd pulled him away from an interview with a new reader.

"Any number of people. John Updike. Bernard Malamud. Ross Macdonald. Nelson Yates isn't the only writer someone could have run away with."

"Ross Macdonald?"

He shrugged.

Adele grabbed Ambler's arm, turning him toward her. "You can't be serious. This is too much coincidence even for you." The expression on her face was magical, color in her cheeks, her eyes glittering with excitement. "I'll tell you something else. I found a letter from Mary Yates to Lisa Dolloway, a thank-you note after a visit. So she knew her." Adele became pensive, thinking something through before she spoke. "Or Harry. He would have known all along."

"That's just it. Why would he say anything now?" Ambler looked back into the reading room. "I've got to finish here."

"Should I wait for you?"

"You can, or you can go ahead yourself. You've gotten this far without me."

Adele looked confused for a second. "You mean . . . Oh my God! I'll come back at five-thirty."

Laura Lee hung up the phone and sat thinking. The goddamn detective wanted to talk to her again, and Max afterward. Talk to each of them alone. That's what the police did to get one suspect to turn on the other one by telling lies to the first one. Anyone who watched television knew that.

It was probably nothing. Max's freaking out was the problem. In his panicked state, he'd surely give the cops reason to think he was guilty of something. Ever since he decided Emily killed Jim Donnelly and was out to get him, he was going nuts. Still, he wasn't nuts enough to tell the detective what he was thinking. He knew what would happen if they arrested her and she told them what she knew.

If the police talking to Max wasn't problem enough, the pain-in-the-ass librarian who thought he was Sherlock Holmes was nosing around like he actually knew something. Harry was afraid of what the librarian might find out and scared Max into being afraid of him, too.

Max was supposed to be so smart—Columbia and all. And here he was scared of this Casper Milquetoast librarian. Though, when she thought about it, something about the librarian—the way he was quietly sure of himself; easygoing; no need to impress anyone—was appealing . . . quite appealing. She wondered if she could handle him. She'd come across few men she couldn't handle. He might be different. The odds were he wasn't.

As she expected, Max fell apart when she told him he had an appointment with the police. He reached for the Beefeater bottle. "It's no big deal, Max."

"No big deal? He wants to meet us separately?"

She laughed. "It's okay, honey. A wife can't be forced to testify against her husband."

He looked at her hollow-eyed and slopped some gin into the glass. "Against me? Against me for what?"

"Jesus, calm down. It was a joke." After all this time, he didn't trust her. He was at least smart enough for that.

"This is on top of everything else. The world's going crazy. . . . I swear to God that was Lisa Dolloway I saw with Ray Ambler."

"It couldn't have been."

Mary Yates greeted Ambler and Adele in the doorway of the brownstone where they'd dropped off Nelson Yates what seemed such a long time ago. She held the door partially closed. She didn't recognize them.

"We knew Nelson from the 42nd Street Library—" Adele began.

Ambler watched the fury rise in the woman's face, color in her cheeks, eyes rounding into a glare. Adele wasn't watching her closely enough and didn't see it coming.

"My God, you're the ones!" she screamed. "You'd come here now after what you've done?! After you all but murdered him?!" Her voice increased in pitch and volume with every word.

Adele froze.

For Ambler, this was the third time he'd been in the woman's presence, and the third time she'd been raging against the world, always aggrieved.

"We're sorry Mrs. Yates—"

"He was an alcoholic and you let him drink."

Ambler watched the fury rise in Adele's face—the same fire in the cheeks, blazing eyes. "He wasn't a child. We didn't lead him to anything." She bit off the words.

Mary Yates turned from Adele's fury to glare at Ambler. After a moment, she said. "You couldn't understand what it was like to live with that man." The rage was gone. "You're wrong," she said, turning back to Adele. "He was a child—a vengeful, violent child, who couldn't be trusted by himself." Her voice trailed off into almost a whisper. "I guess you couldn't have known that." She didn't invite them in, but seemed less likely to slam the door in their faces. Ambler was content to stay where they were. "What do you want?"

"Frankly, we want to be clear about your wishes for your husband's collection," Adele said. Ambler listened as curiously as Mary Yates did. "Maximilian Wagner is using the collection by virtue of a letter signed by your husband before he died." Adele asked if her wishes for the collection and for Max to write the biography had changed as a result of Nelson's death. "We thought you might want to suspend work on the papers until the circumstances around Nelson's death were cleared up."

She seemed to buy what Adele was saying. It even sounded good to Ambler, who knew better. He wondered how she was going to get around to asking about Lisa Dolloway.

"Did you know Nelson's daughter Emily?" Adele asked.

"No. I asked once and he told me never to mention her name again, so I didn't. He didn't have any contact with her."

"His ex-wife, Lisa Dolloway?"

Mary Yates shook her head. "Slightly. I met her twice. Nelson had a great deal of past life. After the first few discoveries, I decided I was better off not knowing about it."

"Do you know anything of what happened to her?"

She shook her head.

"Is it possible she died?" Ambler asked.

She turned to him with a strange expression. "She's very much alive, or was a few days ago. She attended Nelson's memorial service."

"I knew it!" Adele said, louder than she intended. She turned red. "Could you describe her?"

"She's tall, thin, gray hair. I don't remember what she was wearing—something expensive. I caught a quick glimpse."

"Ray?!" Harry squawked into the intercom when Ambler announced himself after leaning on the buzzer to his apartment. "What in God's name are you doing here?"

"We need to talk to you."

"You have no right to . . . to come here." His voice trembled. "It's . . . it's . . . a violation—"

Ambler's own voice was shaking. "I'm sorry, Harry. This is about Lisa Dolloway."

A long silence was followed by the buzzing of the entrance door lock. Ambler and Adele trudged up the stairs.

Harry sat stiffly on a straight-backed chair at his glass dining room table; Adele and Ambler sat together on the couch. Harry's expression didn't change as Adele spoke.

"It's true, isn't it? Lisa Young is Lisa Dolloway. Nelson Yates's ex-wife provided the funding for the Yates collection."

Harry tented his fingers, an unconscious priestly pose; he appeared resigned. Adele tilted her head, bending forward to try to meet Harry's downcast gaze. "Why the secrecy?"

"Lisa didn't want to create a new scandal. She didn't want anything to do with Nelson. I don't think her husband knows about that part of her life."

"You were the intermediary?"

"I knew them both, Ray. They trusted me." Harry shrugged. "I expected difficulties. Who would have thought it would come to this?"

Adele leaned forward. "When you said her husband didn't know about that part of her life, did you mean he didn't know she had a child?"

Harry nodded. "I suspect he doesn't know any of it."

Adele was about to ask something else, but Ambler spoke over her. "What do you mean difficulties?"

"Mary, Nelson's wife, wanted the collection to go to Max Wagner. James Donnelly said Nelson authorized him to write the biography. Em—"

Ambler and Adele both noticed he'd caught himself.

"Did Emily contact you about her father's collection?" Adele asked.

Harry looked helplessly from one to the other.

"Are we back to that confession thing again?"

Adele put her hand on Ambler's arm. "Don't, Raymond."

Ambler paced the few feet in either direction in the tiny apartment. "This is a murder, Harry. For God's sake. Religious beliefs are fine. But—"

"Raymond!" It was a command from Adele.

Ambler stared at her.

"You're wrong, Raymond." Her tone was softer.

He didn't ask again. Nonetheless, there was a connection he hadn't thought of. The wheels were turning.

Chapter 19

"I'm surprised my first husband's death keeps coming up in—"

"Someone asked about your first husband's death?" Cosgrove sat across from Laura Lee, notebook in hand, in an office he'd borrowed from Harry Larkin.

She brushed off the question. "Oh, it's nothing. One of the librarians fancies himself an amateur detective."

"You mean Ray Ambler?"

"As a matter of fact, I do." She crossed her shapely legs.

"Yeh, Ray's a curious guy."

She raised her eyebrows, catching the double entendre.

"Suppose you tell me what you told him, unless you've thought of something new in the meanwhile."

Her expression changed, the lines in her face deepened; the smile left her lips. "Mr. Ambler had the fanciful notion that Emily Yates might have killed Arthur, my husband. I told him that wasn't possible." She met Cosgrove's gaze. "What I didn't tell him—what I haven't told anyone—is that Arthur didn't fall. He leapt. Arthur committed suicide."

Cosgrove moved cautiously. He'd opened up wounds questioning witnesses in the past and had things go bad. He didn't want her to drift off into a funk of painful memories or break down in tears. He wanted her to keep talking. "That's a tough load to carry. I'm sorry. The police investigating didn't consider suicide?"

Irritation flashed in her eyes. "Of course, they considered it. Of course, they asked. I don't know what Emily told them. She would have known. I don't know why Arthur wanted to be with her when he killed himself."

"How do you know it was suicide?"

She took a deep breath. "He told me he would. I didn't believe him. I thought it was a bluff to save our marriage. Arthur was despondent. He took up with the little tramp because his life was in ruins. His academic career was going downhill. We had financial difficulties. Our real life was behind blank walls. I told Arthur I was leaving him. Not something I'm proud of, after the fact. Nothing I wanted to think about or talk about, that my leaving might have deepened his despair, might have been a cause of his death. I preferred being the wronged woman, as embarrassing as that was, to being seen as the cold-hearted woman who drove her husband to his death."

"I'm going to ask you some questions," Cosgrove said. "You're not charged with a crime. If you think you might say something incriminating, you have a right to have a lawyer present."

The man in front of him was a mess, the panicky, hangdog look of the guilty. "How would I incriminate myself? I haven't done anything wrong."

"Good. Tell me about James Donnelly."

"I told you the last time you asked."

"I've found out some things since then, a different side of him, say."

"A different side?"

"What do you remember about Emily Yates?"

"Emily Yates?"

This guy was a trip. Talk about evasive. Don't volunteer anything; you might not get into trouble. Right. Nice for him if it worked like that. "Emily Yates. What do you know about her?"

Wagner leaned forward, his manner grave. "What do I know about her?"

Cosgrove almost laughed. Wagner didn't realize what he was doing and how obvious it was. "You know, Professor, in these things, the truth comes out. If you don't tell me, someone else will. Then, what do you look like? You look like a man with something to hide."

Wagner tried to resemble the most surprised person on earth. "No. I don't."

"You knew James Donnelly. You knew Nelson Yates. You knew Emily Yates. Did you know your wife's first husband, Arthur Woods?" He'd seen that trapped expression a zillion times before. Usually, he knew why the person he was questioning felt trapped. He knew what he or she was hiding. This time, he had no idea. He didn't make Max Wagner for either of the killings. No evidence pointed to him, except the academic rivalry Ray talked about. He didn't buy it. Maybe he'd need to rethink that. More likely, this guy was afraid of something in the past.

"What are you hoping I won't find out?"

Wagner averted his eyes.

"Did you have sex with Emily Yates when she was a teenager?"

Wagner went rigid. "Of course not. I don't have to answer a question like that."

"You just did. You don't want me to find out you're lying, do you?"

The first time he'd interviewed Wagner, the guy was arrogant and aloof, as if a dumb cop couldn't catch the nuances of the answers provided by a learned professor. Now, the professor squirmed like a grade school kid in the principal's office.

"Did James Donnelly?"

"I'm sure I wouldn't know."

"I'm pretty sure you would know." Some liars he could take. This guy wasn't one of them. "How well did you know Arthur Woods?"

"Arthur Woods?"

This time Cosgrove did laugh. "Were you and his wife having an affair at the time of his death?"

"Of course not. Our relationship developed much later . . . after a time. She was devastated by her loss."

"She told me she was going to leave him."

"She did not."

Cosgrove laughed again. Wagner was driving him nuts. "Mr. Wagner or Professor Wagner or whatever you prefer to be called, I don't care about family secrets or indiscretions. I'm trying to catch a murderer. Why don't you tell me what went on with Emily Yates? She was a teenager involved with older men. You take it from there." He watched Wagner wither in front of him.

Ambler waited for Lisa Young in front of the library. Floodlights and arc lights for the film crews gave the white marble of the facade a sense of unreality. Women in deep-colored evening gowns, dripping with jewelry, and men in tuxedos exited taxis and limousines and climbed the steps to the library entrance in the ghostly light via a red carpet that had been unfurled for the occasion. He half expected the lions to climb down from their pedestals. They'd fit right in, strolling among the literati and their patrons.

She came by herself, stepping out of a limousine, the car door held open by the driver, whose black suit wasn't so different from Ambler's. Other men wore suits and ties, so he didn't feel as conspicuous as he might have among the gowns and tuxedos; some of the younger men didn't even wear ties. She wore a floor-length evening gown, deep green, maybe satin, a solid color but it seemed to shimmer and change hues as she walked. A black lace shawl over her bare shoulders, her hair framing her face, that shy and flirtatious smile in her eyes and on her lips, taking long graceful strides, she came toward him. Holding out her hand, she leaned forward, brushing his lips with her cheek, as he reached for her hand.

"Relax, Mr. Ambler—can I call you Raymond?"

"Ray."

"Ray. This will be fun. You'll charm the pants off the board members."

"I hope not."

She laughed gaily, her eyes locked on his. "They rarely get a chance to hobnob with a real librarian. They'll love it." She put her arm through his and gave him a tug. "Give us a break. We don't have to do this. We care about the library. Everyone will want to speak with you."

She was right. He strolled beside her among the benefactors, the affair not so different from the few other receptions he'd attended—tuxedoed waiters and waitresses slithering through the crowd with trays of wines and canapés, elegant and relaxed men and women chatting in groups that formed and broke up as new groups formed. The air crackled with self-assurance. Her hand on his elbow, she steered him from group to group, introducing him to people whose names he forgot seconds after hearing them. At each introduction, she talked about the ill-advised plan to close the crime fiction reading room. Most everyone she spoke with seemed interested, asking questions, nodding, wrinkling their foreheads as if this certainly was something to be concerned about.

"See," she said as they sat down to dinner. The long library tables in the Rose Main reading room, decorated with white tablecloths and vases of flowers, held china plates and crystal stemwear. "Your crime fiction has more support than you thought. By the end of the evening, you'll have a fan club."

Ambler wasn't sure he believed her. Nodding sympathetically, patting a worried librarian on the back, didn't cost anything. These folks didn't get rich by letting sentiment overrule business decisions. Perhaps he'd won some support by showing up. Most likely, it would dissipate once he brought up Lisa Young's past life as Lisa Dolloway and asked about her dead ex-husband and estranged daughter.

All evening, she'd carried herself with an air of cheerfulness and good nature, smiles and tinkling laughter, moving through this sea of evening gowns and tuxedos, money and sophistication, air-kissing cheeks, whispering greetings, embracing everyone she came across. If she wasn't the belle of the ball, she was close to it. As they took their seats, her expression changed to something warm, and familiar, as if they were old friends and could relax and enjoy their time together now that the formalities were over.

"You seem to enjoy this hoopla," he said.

"To an extent. I enjoy it in ways I doubt you'd understand." Her expression shifted; the smile was there but something like sorrow lurked in its shadows. "To whom much is given, of him shall much be required."

"Was God talking about financiers?"

The smile flickered. "I told you when I was younger I didn't think I deserved wealth—"

He took a deep breath. "When you were Lisa Dolloway?"

The sorrow lurking in the shadows of her smile took over. Even so, her expression was noble as she gathered her thoughts. "It was a matter of time; I knew that from the evening we met."

A man in a tuxedo approached her from the side opposite him, kissed her on the cheek, whispered something. A bright flash of smile, a small laugh from her as he straightened up. This time, she didn't introduce Ambler. "We'll be interrupted often this evening. Can we wait until after dinner to discuss this?"

Every now and again, someone stopped by the table to greet Lisa Young. Between visits, she chatted easily with the person on her right. Ambler spoke uncomfortably to the person on his left, who'd never heard of the library's crime fiction collection and complained about so many of the tourists visiting the library on any given day being Asian.

"They must have a lot of money in China these days for so many to be traveling."

"I'm glad they like the library," Ambler said. "I wish more American tourists did."

"Of course, they do." Her tone was a rebuke. "The Chinese don't have libraries. That's why they're fascinated by ours."

Lisa Young took a moment to bend closer to him. "Don't fret. Enjoy your dinner."

After the dinner and the speeches and presentations, Ambler took Lisa Young or Lisa Dolloway to the Library Tavern, where they could talk. Instead of the booth he suggested, she chose a corner barstool. It was late, the dinner rush over, and McNulty's late-night regulars were yet to arrive. His greeting, while not formal, was less informal than usual. He made their drinks and moved a discreet distance away, not letting on by as much as a raised eyebrow that anything was different.

"It was simple, really. Nelson wanted to keep his collection away from Max Wagner. He contacted Harry. Harry, at

Nelson's suggestion, asked me for a donation to pay for the acquisition."

"Why would Nelson think you'd do that? Why would you? How did he know where to find you?"

"I always thought Nelson was a brilliant writer. I never hid from him. I changed my name. Not really a change, I dropped Dolloway—it was a nom de plume—and restored my family name. It's not difficult to disappear from public view. After a short time, everyone forgets you. If Nelson hadn't been murdered, no one would have cared where the money came from." She drank from her snifter of cognac.

"I asked you not to dig up my past. What good has it done you? I don't want to be a Page Six exposé." She was quiet for a moment. "I was a selfish young woman. The consequences, I brought on myself."

"I'm not interested in telling the world about your past—"

Her face softened into an ironic smile. "The police?"

He hesitated. "That's more difficult." He told her about Cosgrove, how telling him wasn't the same as officially going to the police. "He asked me about you. He'll ask again. I don't want to lie to him."

"I see."

She did see, at least as well as he did. If he told Cosgrove about her, the information could get out. The murder was high-profile enough, the story salacious enough; reporters would jump at it.

"If we got to the bottom of this—the murder, I mean—he wouldn't care about you."

She threw up her hands. "Don't you think I'd tell you if I knew anything about Nelson's death?"

"If you tell me about Nelson, his friends, and more particularly his enemies, you might be telling me something about his death. I'd also like you to tell me about your daughter."

"Emily?" Her voice was a shriek. On her face was the horror-twisted grimace of a mother watching her child run into the street in front of a car.

As he walked home after putting Lisa Dolloway into a cab, Ambler felt the loneliness of the darkness and the empty city sidewalks. That riches don't protect you from suffering was never more apparent. Lisa Dolloway suffered more than her share; she paid heavily for her mistakes.

He told her he'd found her daughter. She wasn't sure after all this time she wanted to see her. Too much had happened for things to be put back together.

"I should never have been a mother," she said. "I was young, terribly self-centered; I'd never had to be responsible for anything. I didn't want a child. The baby scared me to death. It got worse as she got older. She was a smart and defiant little girl. She knew I was afraid of her. She'd stand there saying no, her eyes burning into mine, and I'd swear she was possessed.

"Nelson loved it, that I couldn't handle her, couldn't control her, because then she was all his. I told him, 'Fine. She's yours.' She had him wrapped around her finger. He loved her to a fault. It's just—" She finished what was in the snifter in one swallow and signaled for another. "With Nelson, his caring, his tenderness—" She looked at Ambler, waiting for him to understand, to say he understood. But he didn't want to say that. He didn't want to understand.

"You had to have known Nelson then. He was charismatic, a glow of peace around him, and—difficult to say now—love. People flocked to him. Everyone loved him. I loved him. And, of course, Emily loved him." She drank from her snifter again, staring in front of her, watching McNulty, who was making a couple of fairly complex concoctions for three women who'd finished dinner and come to the bar for dessert drinks.

"She traveled with him. On one trip, she didn't want to go—" Lisa Young threw back her head and closed her eyes. "She said it felt funny in bed. Daddy took up too much room—I didn't want to hear." She finished her second snifter of brandy. "She never brought it up again. I never asked. When she got older, there were older boys, and then men. I thought of sending her away to a boarding school. And then the tragedy with that professor."

"Let's compare notes," Cosgrove said. "I'm on my way to the library. Can we talk in your office?"

"It's not an office but we can talk. I'm on the second floor," Ambler said.

Fifteen minutes later, he watched Cosgrove open the door of the crime fiction reading room. He walked softly, tiptoeing, like a penitent entering a church, surveying the bookshelves with a kind of reverence.

Ambler cleared some books off of a chair. Cosgrove sat and without prompting told Ambler about his conversation with Kay Donnelly.

"There's your connection. All of these folks were part of a cult involving some sexual abuse of a minor. The minor was Nelson Yates's daughter. She keeps coming up. Why did you ask me to look for her?"

"Her father asked me to help him find her."

"Did he find her?"

"No. He was killed shortly after I asked you about her." His answer was the truth but disingenuous. Amazing that Cosgrove would ask about Emily now; it sometimes felt as if this cop could read his mind and ferret out his secrets. This was partly because they often thought along the same lines. Still, it was unnerving. At the moment, he was shaken by what Lisa Young told him about Emily and her father. He wasn't sure if he wanted to ask Emily about that. And he'd told Lisa Young he'd try to keep her name out of the investigation if he could. So he wanted to sort some things out before he told Mike what he'd learned. He was sorry he'd agreed to meet with him and now had to be evasive.

"The first victim, Donnelly, had a thing for young girls, including probably Nelson Yates's daughter. You might think he'd be the one to do Donnelly in for what he did to his daughter. But Yates, I'm told, headed up the sex cult. I'm thinking there might have been other girls. They might have done something to some girl together. Years later, someone discovers what they did—the girl's father finds the truth; she confesses to her husband why's she sexually screwed up; her brother discovers what happened. Boom! Someone sets out to right the wrong."

Cosgrove waited for his reaction, nothing triumphant in his expression, a kind of weary craftsman's confidence instead.

"What do you expect Emily Yates to tell you?" Ambler asked in place of telling Cosgrove what he knew.

"She was abused. Someone close to her might be the avenger. If not that, she might know other girls involved. Another reason is there's something fishy about the death she was witness to when she was teenager. Your friend Wagner's wife, Lou Lou or something—" He reached for his notebook.

"Laura Lee."

Right. She changed her story, says now the guy, her husband at the time, jumped. The Yates girl was never properly interviewed." Cosgrove shook his head. "She was hysterical when the investigator talked to her. He wanted to talk to her again but never got the chance. So we don't know for sure what she saw."

"So?"

"Fell, jumped; maybe the new husband gave the old one a shove." Shrewdness flickered in Cosgrove's eyes, like a not-so-good poker player pulling his full house closer to his chest. "You should like my thinking on this. In some ways, I'm spouting one of your theories, connecting the monkey business that went on back then with the current murders."

Ambler smiled, feeling uneasy. "If we're comparing notes, I don't have much to give you at the moment. I might have something helpful soon, maybe not. I don't know who your source is—"

"You don't need to know."

"I wasn't asking. If James Donnelly was a serial abuser of young girls, it's reasonable to think someone would make him pay for that. The Nelson Yates connection is possible. You don't know. You don't have an explanation for why the murders took place at the library. Professional jealousy or greed—in the case of Max Wagner or Mary Yates involving a significant amount of money—can't be discounted."

He told this to Mike in good faith—somewhat stretching the definition perhaps—because it was a possibility. No real evidence connected anyone to anything yet. The field was open, yet he now had some disturbing questions to try to answer.

Later that day, on his way back from the deli on 40th Street with a container of coffee, Ambler came across Benny sitting at a table on the terrace behind the library that overlooked Bryant Park. He hadn't spoken to him since his abrupt departure from the Library Tavern a few nights earlier. He walked over. "Why aren't you inside?"

Benny bowed his head. "I don't like going in there. It feels funny if I'm not going to work, like I don't belong." He shifted his position to look out over the park. Ambler followed his gaze.

"Sorry about the other night—"

"It's okay. Kay's been on edge. She's afraid to cross Wagner." He was quiet for a moment. "I was thinking about that guy getting murdered." He pointed out into the park. "He got killed right over there."

"Right over there," Ambler thought back to the moment

when he knew instinctively that Nelson Yates had been murdered.

"It's funny," Benny said. "I talked to him on the phone the day before. He sounded like a nice—"

Ambler's heart started to race. "You what?"

Benny turned a worried expression toward him. "Back before everything got crazy, Ray, you asked me to do a favor, try to find something about his daughter." He eyed Ambler carefully. "Don't you remember? I found her, or I found Emily Smith, who I was pretty sure was her."

"You found Emily Yates and you told him? You told Nelson? How did you know it was her? What did you tell him?"

"It was actually pretty complicated. I did about six different database searches and didn't find anything. Then I got lucky. It was—"

"What do you mean you talked to him on the phone?"

"You gave me his number. I called and gave him an address. I didn't know if it was good or not. I told him that. He was really appreciative. I really liked his—"

"What was the address you gave him?"

Benny wrinkled his brow. "I don't remember exactly. Somewhere in the West Forties?"

Too much was coming at him too quickly—snatches of conversation, pieces of information, snapshots of places. He saw then what he remembered. "Benny, this sounds foolish and someday I'll explain. Would you call Kay Donnelly and ask her what her husband's middle name was?"

Benny looked at Ambler curiously while he made the call, which took longer than it might have because of the questions she had that he didn't have answers to.

"Ray wants to know."

"I don't know why."

"Why don't you just tell me? What difference does it make?"

Finally, he hung up. "Xavier," he said.

Chapter 20

Leaving the library after talking to Ray, Cosgrove had a sense the case would break soon. He couldn't say he knew this because he didn't. It was a feeling, like you might sense that a rainstorm was waning. Though it still rained as hard or almost as hard, a change in the color of the clouds to a paler shade of gray and a barely perceptible slackening of the wind hinted at the end of the storm.

Often, in a case like this, you'd be heading down one blind alley after another. Then one day, you realized you'd been heading down this alley for quite a while now and hadn't hit a wall; the alley was leading you someplace. It would be helpful to find the Yates girl, though that might not be so easy. Max Wagner could tell him something and soon probably would. It might be worth putting a tail on him; not so much that he'd lead them to anything, more to let him know it was there so he'd become more nervous than he already was. The ex-priest was a bundle of nerves also. He'd get to him sooner or later, too. Now, Ray had something up his sleeve. He didn't often withhold anything, and it made him uncomfortable when he did, so you could most of the time tell. When push came to shove, he'd come clean.

He was about to call in the request for a tail on Max Wagner when his wife called. She'd been drinking, so it took a few tries for her to tell him his daughter had run away. She was angry to the point of vengeful, stemming from her guilt, of course, guilt she wouldn't admit.

"Stop screaming, Sarah, and tell me what happened. Did she say where she was going?"

"Of course not, you asshole. She ran away."

"Did she run out the door or did she take some of her things?"

"How the fuck should I know? Let her go. She'll come back soon enough when she figures out how good she has it here. It's your fault. You never stand up to her." She let loose with a string of grievances against him and Denise. While she berated him, Cosgrove turned his car toward Queens. He hated dropping the case—but that had always been his problem; he'd hated dropping the case, and too many times left Denise to deal with her mother's tirades alone.

Sarah finally admitted they'd had a fight and she'd slapped her daughter. He needed to find Denise; he was afraid of what she might get herself into. The problem with being a cop and a father was you expected the worst because that's what you saw all the time. No one called the cops when they were having a good time at a kid's birthday party. It was the birthdays where the estranged father showed up to put a bullet through the mother's head that cops got to go to.

"You want me to steal from her?" It had begun raining, so Ambler and Adele took the subway to her apartment. At the moment, she stood on the platform with her hands on her hips, glaring at him. "How do you know she even has a briefcase?"

"I saw it the night we went to her apartment." A train headed for Queens rumbled into the Bryant Park station on the opposite track, so he waited for it to stop and the noise to subside before he answered. "I want to know what's in it."

"She's going to hate me. She might not let me in. I made friends with her and then tricked her. Why would she trust me? And why do you want to know about the briefcase?"

"It's an incongruity. A worn leather briefcase, why's it in her apartment?"

The train arrived and they pushed their way into the crowded car for the one-stop trip to Times Square.

"You don't think it's hers? Who do you think it belongs to?"

Ambler used the lurching of the train and the jostling of the crowd to avoid answering, and then there was the rush up the stairs. As they walked through the long underground tunnel from Times Square to the Eighth Avenue train, she asked again. "Whose briefcase?"

He took her arm and moved her along. "If you look in the briefcase, you'll know more than I do."

After leaving the subway, walking together under one umbrella in a rain that poured straight down from a leaden sky battering the gray sidewalk, they found themselves with their arms around each other's waists. One second, they walked side by side, the next second they were entwined. Later, he remembered, they both realized what they were doing, some acknowledgment came, an awkward second of realization, after which they continued to hug one another until they reached Adele's doorway, where they separated. Ambler shook out the umbrella. For a moment, in the vestibule, something passed between them. Adele gently brushed his wet hair back from his eyes. He looked into hers. The moment passed.

"I could ask her about it," Adele said when they were seated at her tiny table in the space between the kitchen and the living room drinking tea.

"You could."

"But she might not want to tell me."

Ambler sipped his tea.

An hour and a half later, Adele returned from Emily's apartment. Ambler stopped reading and looked up. Her expression was ashen. "The papers in the briefcase—" Her eyes met his. "You knew, didn't you? You knew and didn't tell me." Her voice, shrill and shaking, rose. "What if I hadn't looked? I almost didn't. I almost didn't look. If she hadn't been crying, hadn't gone to the bathroom, I wouldn't have."

Ambler stood and reached toward Adele, a message of peace, an apology. "I didn't know what was in the briefcase. I had a suspicion. I hoped I was wrong. I didn't want to alarm you if I was wrong."

"But now you know you're right, and what does it mean?"

"I have to tell Mike."

Cosgrove double-parked his car and burst into his house, going immediately to his daughter's room. As he passed, Sarah pressed herself against the wall across from the stairs as far from him as she could get, her face tear-streaked and blotchy. She put up a front of false bravado anyway. "Well, well, the hero's home. Big Officer Mike. He'll take care of everything! That's why she has no respect for me. You—" Her voice wavered. Something cold and scared lurked beneath the angry words.

A quick search of Denise's room turned up enough to get started. In her rush to leave, she hadn't turned off her computer or logged out of Facebook. She had dozens of friends, photos of her and her friends, school pictures, group shots, gag photos, and hundreds of photos of celebrities and rock bands. Almost all of her friends were girls her own age, a couple of boys, a couple of bands, nothing alarming. He went through the photos quickly to find girls he recognized and matched those to names in her friends list. He came up with four who he'd guess were her closest friends.

"Where are you going?" Sarah's voice was quieter now, the challenge gone.

"To look for Denise."

"Can I come?"

Her plaintive, contrite tone stopped him; he felt sorry for her, a deeper sympathy than he thought he could muster. "I'll do the first run myself. If you get some sleep and get yourself ready, I'll come back for you in a couple of hours."

She nodded and reached a hand out to touch his arm. There was a time it might have meant something, but that time had passed. He left her standing in the doorway.

Denise's friends would lie to cover for her. But they wouldn't be very good at it. He'd met most of them—giggles and too much dark eyeliner, tight jeans or short skirts and skinny legs, brash and secretive. Everything they talked about was at the Oh My God level. They were polite enough, called him Mr. Cosgrove, but leery of him; a dad was bad enough; a cop way too much. With luck, he'd scare the truth out of one of them. His first stop was Jenny. She lived closest, and Denise talked about her more than the others.

If Jenny didn't work out, he had an ace in the hole. Anne's daughter was on the list. The kids weren't close but they had the same circle of friends. Cosgrove didn't encourage closeness between the families because of how things were between him and Anne. They tried not to see one another more often than every couple of months when they could spend a night together, Anne pretending she visited her sister in Connecticut, Cosgrove taking sick leave when he was on the overnight shift.

Jenny was scared to death, as was her mother, who begged her to tell him what she knew about Denise, probably thinking he'd throw the whole family in jail if she didn't. Jenny didn't make eye contact, mumbled monosyllabic answers, and insisted she knew nothing. With her mother standing beside her, he couldn't grill her. If she'd lifted her gaze from the doorstep for more than a fraction of a second, she'd have seen how poorly her act was going over. When he ran out of polite questions, he told her to look at him. He spoke so sharply she jumped—as did her mother—and did look at him.

"If you think of anything, Jenny, you call me any time of the day or night—and I mean any time." He handed her his card and turned to her mother. "Maybe you could help her remember. Same goes for you; call me any time with any tiny piece of information you come up with."

He sat in his car for a few minutes watching clouds closing in, followed by rain pelting against his windshield. Talking to the other girls on the list was probably a waste of time. Going to Anne on this was risky; talking to her daughter without asking the girl's father wasn't how one cop approached another cop's family. But he didn't have time for explanations. He wouldn't have to explain to Anne. She'd know the risks, too. And she'd help him anyway.

When he took out his cell phone to call her, he saw Ray Ambler had called twice. Something was breaking with him, too. Wouldn't you know it would all come down at once?

Ambler closed his cell phone after getting Mike Cosgrove's voice mail a second time.

"Are you sure we can't ask Emily about the briefcase?"

He looked at Adele's wrinkled face, like a child's who was about to cry. "I'm sorry. It's almost certain she knows who killed James Donnelly."

"Her friend Dominic?"

"We have to tell Mike what we found."

Adele's voice rose dangerously. "What about Johnny? What's going to happen to him when you take his mother away?" Tears trickled down her cheeks; sobs mangled her words. "How can you do that? How can you take his mother away? You have to talk to Emily."

He wasn't taking Johnny's mother away. Emily did it to herself. No sense trying to tell Adele that, no sense reminding her of what she knew. The outcome of this would be misery for a lot of people. Didn't a murder always do that? Cast a pall far and wide over everyone connected to it.

Chapter 21

She should've listened to Dominic. You couldn't trust anyone; you took care of yourself; no one else would. She trusted Adele; look what that got her. Something was going on the way she acted, sneaky, like she was up to something—like she'd been caught snooping when Emily came back from the bathroom. That's what it was; she was snooping. What could she find that would tell her anything?

The briefcase! She rushed to open it. What an idiot she was! Jim Donnelly's manuscript! Did Adele look in the bag and find his name? She dug through the briefcase. Everything had his name on it. Adele could've taken anything. Her father's letters! They seemed to all be there. Maybe Adele didn't know what was in the bag. Maybe she didn't take anything. But she knew too much. Dominic would go nuts when she told him what happened. He was already freaked out. They'd argued about Max again. Dominic thought Max was so smart because he had a Ph.D., even though Max treated him like dirt. Laura Lee made excuses. That was bullshit, too. Max didn't want anything to do with Dominic.

Max was the first one, a filthy liar like the rest of them. She was a little girl. What did she know? A couple of years ago when one of his books came out, she heard him on the radio and almost threw up. His voice made her sick, his pompous tone, like he was born an aristocrat, instead of the son of a two-bit hoodlum from the Bronx. At least Dominic owned up to where he came from. If people knew what Max was really like—how he'd been with her when she was thirteen—he'd stop being a big shot pretty quick.

What she needed to do was show Dominic what a bastard his brother was, so Dominic would hate him too. He was already sleeping with his wife. Laura Lee had been with him, for sure. Women were a sucker for Dominic. She was herself when she was young. At least Dominic didn't tell her he loved her. Dominic didn't love anyone but Dominic. That's what Laura Lee was like, too. Poor Arthur said that a long time ago. Little did he know how right he was. Boy, that was a trip. Sitting on his lap one minute, the next minute out of the woods comes Dominic and over the wall goes Arthur. She'd have been right behind him, too, if she hadn't already opened her blouse and taken off her bra, so Dominic got distracted by her tits. Turned out he wasn't any worse than the rest of them. Better. He took care of her. She was an idiot. She loved them, all of them; she really did. None of them loved her back. So look what happened. Because of them!

The librarians knew who she was now. There it was. Adele wasn't her friend, after all. At first, she was mad but now she was sad. She didn't remember ever having a friend like that. And Johnny loved Adele; you could see that. She wasn't jealous; she knew Johnny loved his mother more than anyone, despite how horrible she'd been sometimes. She'd thought about telling him to go to Adele if anything happened to her. She might still do that. If she got killed or was in jail, the state might try to find her mother—the mother who wouldn't take care of her own daughter. Despite everything, Adele might be best.

Maybe nothing would happen to her. If they could get by this thing about Max, when it was over Dominic still might want to take her away. The thing was, he didn't like kids. He'd never laid a hand on Johnny. He knew what would happen if he did. But he might. As Johnny got older, a teenager, he'd be harder to handle; who knew what Dominic might do? She wondered if she should talk to Adele again now that the truth was out . . . not all of the truth. No way she'd handle all the truth.

Cosgrove put off the call to Ray and reached Anne Gannon on the first try.

"I was so happy to hear from you, and now I'm so sorry," she said.

"I shouldn't have called you. I'm desperate—"

"Of course, you should call." Listening to her calmed him, always had since they were kids. Even when she told him she couldn't be with him anymore, he knew it was right because she said it. "I'll talk to Kate. You know the coffeehouse on Greenpoint Avenue? Meet me there in an hour."

"Are you sure? It's too close to your neighborhood."

"We can't worry about that, Mike. It's raining. I can't think of anywhere else. Gary will know I've seen you anyway. Kate will tell him. He'll have to live with it."

"I don't know, Anne—"

"In a half hour."

He'd ordered his second cup of espresso when he saw Anne on the street walking toward him, wearing a tan trench coat and dark slacks, wrestling with her umbrella. Her dark hair was shorter than the last time. Over the years, she'd filled out—not the wisp of a girl with long black hair she'd been as a kid—still gorgeous to him. He felt a kind of joy watching her come toward him. He signaled the waitress and ordered a tea for her.

When she came through the door, he stood but didn't know what to do. What he wanted was to take her in his arms, kiss her, and hold her. She came close to him and seemed uncertain, too. For a second, they looked into each other's eyes. She kissed him quickly on the lips and put her arms around him. He hugged her tightly, and gently pulled her head back to kiss her again, knowing anyone watching would guess they were lovers not merely friends. He couldn't help it.

"Sit down, Mike." Her tone was gentle. "Denise went to the city. She went by herself, but Kate thinks she knows people there—guys in a band from Sunnyside. They're older and have an apartment on the Lower East Side."

A sharp, shooting, painful sadness gripped Cosgrove's solar plexus.

Anne bit her lip. "Guys in their twenties, Kate said. They played at a couple of the kids' parties last summer. All the girls are crazy about them—Facebook fans and all that. Denise and some of the girls began following the band, going to the clubs where they played."

"Does Kate know where they live?"

"Not the address. Danny O'Neil is one of them. He's a nice boy, Mike. His father was a fireman, died in 9/11. Gary and Danny's father were friends. He tried to look out for the boy after his dad passed but not much came of it. . . . Gary isn't much of a touchy-feely guy."

"And Denise? Did something go on between her and this Danny?"

Anne measured her words. "Denise is wilder than some of the other girls, more adventurous." Her eyes filled with sympathy. "She looks older than the others, acts older."

Cosgrove stared at her. "She's thirteen."

She reached out across the table for his hand. "She won't say it, Mike. She may not even know it. But she wants you to find her. Danny O'Neil, Lower East Side."

Cosgrove stood; he bent to kiss Anne one last time, until he noticed from the corner of his eye Gary Gannon standing outside the window watching them.

Adele told him Emily would be singing that night at a bar on 23rd Street. She'd convinced him he had to talk to her. Ambler knew the place. It wasn't far from his apartment, across from Madison Square Park, in a block of storefronts that had been there forever. He'd walked by it plenty of times, the music loud and raucous pouring out into the street. One night a week, a string of motorcycles—Harleys—lined up out front. With smoke-clouded storefront windows, a neon sign above the door, it was the sort of place where the only thing you'd want to order would be a beer, and from a bottle at that.

There was a chance Emily wouldn't talk to him. Yet the couple of times he'd seen her, he'd had a feeling she wanted to. Everyone, at some point, wants someone to know her side of the story. He peeked through the door, past the rowdy crowd, to the small stage at the back. The music and the mob of young people shouting over it was deafening, the cacophony attacking him as soon as he opened the door, bringing painful memories of suffering through CBGB back when he was trying to hang on to wild and wanton Liz.

He took a step inside, shook off the rain, looked up, and there she was. Tiny and pretty in a short jeans skirt and low-cut blouse, she looked like a child in the glaring, colored spotlight, against the bandstand's garish background—the massive set of drums, the guitars and amplifiers, and the bare-chested, longhaired men gyrating across the stage. The music was grating and angry, her voice low and thick, an old-time whiskey voice, but melodious and sweet. Sipping a beer, he worked his way slowly to the front. If she saw him, she gave no indication.

After the set, the last for her band, which had opened for a better-known group waiting in the wings, he blended back into the crowd and watched the band gather up its instruments and pack up its equipment. Emily sat by herself in a booth near the stage, taking sips from a longneck beer bottle. When she walked to the bar to get another beer, he approached.

"You're out of your element, Mr. Librarian," she said over her shoulder. "Out without your girlfriend?"

He hadn't thought she'd seen him.

"You stick out like a sore thumb." He expected anger, but she smiled at him with her eyes. "Did you come to see me?"

"Can we go somewhere and talk? It's loud in here."

"What would Adele say?" She raised her eyebrows, a teasing rebuke.

From that look, he didn't know where this was going. At least, she'd talk to him. The rain had mostly stopped, the sidewalk along 23rd Street still wet, reflecting the ragged bright colors of the bar's neon lights. She led him a couple of blocks down a more dimly lit Park Avenue South to a late-night French-style eatery where they shared a cheese plate. Ambler had a glass of white wine, Emily another beer.

"So what do we talk about?" She popped a piece of cheese into her mouth and leaned on her elbows. Something shrewd in her expression suggested she might know that Adele found James Donnelly's papers in her apartment.

"Your father came to your apartment." He didn't know this for a fact, so he watched for her reaction. He didn't get one.

"What are you getting at?"

He treaded carefully. "You didn't tell anyone your father found you before he was killed."

"Why should I?"

"Did your father know he had a grandson?"

She shuddered. "No. Not—"

"Not?"

Alarm flashed in her eyes.

"Not until he came to see you shortly before his death?"

She paused. Something changed in her expression, her eyelashes covering her eyes for a second. When she looked at him next, her eyes had taken on a new and kind of beguiling depth. She leaned across the table toward him. "Do you find me attractive?"

He should have known this was coming. The truth was he did find her attractive. Emily was practiced in the art of attracting men. It was her defense.

"We could get a bottle of vodka and go to your place."

"We could." Ambler leaned forward so that his face was close to hers. "That's not what I'm here for. You're in trouble. I was about to go to the police. Adele asked me to talk to you first."

Emily signaled the waiter for another bottle of beer and finished drinking the one she had. She sat back stiffly, looking away from him.

Adele thumbed through the swath of papers she'd taken from Emily's apartment. They looked like manuscript pages, not enough of them to tell what they were from. A story, from the point of view of a young girl, but the pages weren't consecutive and nothing of much interest until she came to a passage and was frozen to her chair.

> He would come and sit on the side of her bed. He would stroke her hair and her back, her chest, her legs, between her legs; he would bury his face against her stomach and kiss her along her stomach, below her stomach, and into

> the place between her legs, where he'd push his mouth tight against her, pressing her center against his mouth. She felt a reverberating current of pleasure, shudders of pleasure, before the shame. He rubbed something against her, rubbing, rubbing, and then she was gagging on it, the hard and soft-textured, thick, bulging thing like an inflamed and swollen finger he pushed into her mouth.

She'd read enough. She could put two and two together. But she didn't want to believe what she was thinking until she knew who the man was who sat on the little girl's bed.

Ambler tried meet Emily's gaze but she wouldn't look at him. "James Donnelly was carrying a briefcase when he was killed. The briefcase disappeared. A briefcase belonging to James Donnelly is in your apartment."

She leaned back against her chair, raised her face toward the ceiling, and blew air out between her lips, like a whistle, before she faced him, glaring. "So that's why Adele was snooping around, pretending to be my friend, both of you, lying, conniving—"

"You knew James Donnelly."

The glare faded; her icy stare melted; the fire went out of her eyes. What he thought he saw was disappointment. "I thought she was my friend. I'm still a sucker—"

"She is your friend—"

Emily sneered. "Did I know James? You bet your ass I did. When I was a teenager, he—what do you call it—he statutory raped me."

He wanted to say he was sorry for what happened to her. Yet he couldn't, the sadness and embarrassment that colored her face stopped him.

"So now you know." She stared at him with lifeless eyes. "What else do you want?"

"Why do you have his briefcase?" His voice caught in his throat.

"He gave it to me."

He couldn't tell anything from her face, which had relaxed into a mocking expression, nothing from her tone of voice, which was quiet and steady. What she said could be true; he didn't know for sure the briefcase in her apartment was the one Donnelly carried at the time of his death. Stranger things had happened.

"It's complicated." She sighed. Her eyes met his, the mocking expression replaced by something innocent and vulnerable. "James found me a couple of years ago. My life was a mess. He told me he was still in love with me. . . . He was lying, of course. And I, of course, was stupid enough to fall for it all over again. He wanted to write a book."

"Was the book about your father?"

She nodded. "About my father and me. My father didn't know that part. James said we'd collaborate. I gave him some things, personal things. I trusted him. After a while, I didn't like how it was going. I didn't want to do it anymore. Whatever I thought was going on between us wasn't. I told him it wasn't working. He was okay about it. I guess he'd grown tired of me—and the book—so he gave me the stuff I'd given him and the manuscript. That's why I have the briefcase. That's what's in it. He gave me the manuscript and the briefcase to carry it in."

"When was that?"

"I don't know, six months . . . a year ago—" Color rose in her face; the expression in her eyes hardened. "What? You don't believe me? Ask the people at the college, his secretary or something. They'll remember I was there with him. It doesn't have anything to do with him getting killed."

"Slow down, Emily. If it turns out Dominic didn't—"

She swallowed what she'd intended to say. "The police think Dominic—"

"The police don't think anything. I haven't told them—" He knew he'd made a mistake as soon as he said it. He didn't need to see her expression turn wily. "Emily, you need to trust me. You could lose your son."

Ambler's cell phone rang. It was Adele.

She didn't bother with "Hello." "If you're with Emily, don't say anything. Go somewhere you can talk."

He looked at Emily over the top of the phone. "I have to take this. I'll be right back."

Adele began talking before he'd gotten outside. "Does Emily know I took those papers from her apartment?"

"Yes."

"Did you talk about what's in them?"

"No."

"Don't. I read some things I really need to ask her about. I'm on my way to her apartment to wait for her. But don't tell her."

"Hold on—"

"I'm sure Johnny will let me in, so I can wait. I don't think she'd let me in after what I did. And I really need to talk to her."

"Wait, Adele. It's not a good idea to go to her apartment—"

"You didn't have any trouble sending me before when you wanted to trick her."

"You don't understand. Dominic—"

"Dominic doesn't live there."

"Wait."

She hung up.

When he got back inside, Emily's chair was empty. He thought about the ladies' room. On his way to check, he asked the waiter, "Is there a back door?"

"A side door onto 20th Street."

Chapter 22

"What's this?" Gannon's hard stare went from Cosgrove to Anne and back to Cosgrove. Gannon was a big guy, broad shoulders; Cosgrove had known him since they were kids. A couple of years younger, a cowboy, a loudmouth; not someone he'd ever liked.

"His daughter ran away, Gary." Anne looked frightened.

"And you came to console him? You said nothin' was goin' on . . . my imagination. This ain't my imagination."

"I asked her for help, Gary. Your daughter, she knows Denise."

"Why not ask me, Mike? Who the fuck you think you're kidding?"

"I'm looking for my daughter. I don't have time for this." He made to walk by the bigger man. Gannon's arm shot out and grabbed the front of his jacket, bunching it into his fist. Cosgrove stumbled as Gannon yanked him. Anne jumped up and tried to come between them, clawing at her husband. He swatted her away with his other arm. "Come sniffing around my wife again, you son of a bitch. Let's go outside."

"I'm going to find my daughter."

Gannon laughed. "A chickenshit for a father; no wonder she'd run off." He let go.

As Cosgrove walked toward the door, he saw Gannon grab Anne's arm and pull her toward him. He kept walking.

Ambler tried to call Adele. She didn't answer. He crossed the street, the phone pressed against his ear, and tried to flag down an uptown cab. Dozens streamed past, none of them with a vacant light on. He finally got a cab that was headed downtown, almost breaking his leg stumbling across the foot-high cement barrier median on Park Avenue South.

There was no reason to call Cosgrove again; he'd left messages. He could call the precinct. But it would take half the night to explain what was going on. Closing his eyes, he tried to bring himself back to the evening Nelson was killed and remember Cosgrove's truculent protégé whom he'd had a run-in with at the time. Mike had confidence in the guy, if Ambler didn't. Not like Cosgrove, thickheaded, but he was working on the case and knew the players. Now what the hell was his name? It was short. Detective Blank. Detective Stout. . . . Font. . . . Bart.

The cab swerved and screeched almost to a stop, the cab-driver fuming. "Did you see that asshole in the Ford—"

Ford! That was it. He called Cosgrove's number at the precinct and pushed 0 for an operator. "Detective Ford, please."

She put him through. The cab crawled in traffic uptown on Eighth Avenue approaching the Port Authority, cabs piled up double and triple into the street in front of the terminal. He stomped his foot impatiently on the floor of the cab.

"Ford."

"You may not remember me. Ray Ambler from the library, a friend of Mike Cosgrove's."

Silence. Ambler could picture the cop bristling. "Yeh. So?"

"I can't reach Mike."

"He took some time off."

Cosgrove take time off in the middle of a homicide investigation? Ford wasn't about to volunteer anything, so Ambler bit the bullet. "Something's come up. Some information's come my way."

"I get it. You've outsmarted the dumb cops again."

Ambler stomped again, staring at the ceiling of the cab. Why the hell did Mike have to take time off now? In a second, he knew why. The only thing that would take Cosgrove away from a case at a critical time: something happened to his daughter.

"A woman might be in danger. And it's my fault. I need help."

"Cut the bullshit. Who's in trouble? Where is she?"

Ambler told Ford about the briefcase in Emily Smith's apartment and that she was Nelson Yates's daughter living under an assumed name. When he told him about Dominic, he realized he didn't have anything concrete to tie Dominic to anything.

"Does this Dominic guy have a last name?"

"I don't know it."

"Don't know where he is right now?"

"No."

"Where he lives?"

"No."

A moment of silence, before, "What you're doing is stupid."

"I—"

"What your lady friend is doing is even stupider. If you weren't Mike's friend, I'd hang up. . . . I'll ask the precinct to send a squad car to bring this Emily person in for questioning. You thinking you found someone's briefcase isn't enough to go barging in. If the uniforms happen to come by for something else, they'll smell trouble if it's there. She'll have to agree to come in. If she's been around the block more than once, she'll know she doesn't have to."

• • •

"My mom said not to let anyone in when she's not here. . . . I don't know if it's okay even if it's you."

"Johnny, I'm trying to help your mom." Adele stood in the doorway, fighting off the temptation to push past him. "I know this is hard to understand."

Johnny hesitated, his eyes searching hers for some kind of answer to a question that was too hard for him.

"You can let me in now. I'll wait with you until your mom gets home and explain what I'm doing. I'll tell her it was my fault that you let me in. She won't be mad at you."

Johnny lowered his voice. "It's not just mom—"

"Dominic?" Adele heard the alarm bells, saw the flashing red lights. "Is he here?"

"He's coming."

Adele turned to go but it was too late.

"What the hell are you doing here?" Dominic climbed the stairs purposefully, his rock-hard gaze locked on her.

"I was just leaving." She hated the tremble in her voice; she knew he'd hear it—and Johnny would hear it, as he'd hear her lies and excuses.

"That ain't what I asked you."

"I came to see Emily. She isn't home, so I'm leaving."

Johnny's face was expressionless.

"She'll be here. You can wait."

Her heart beat faster and louder, loud enough that she thought he could hear it. She had to get out of there. But how? If she tried to walk by him, he'd grab her. One look at his stance and his expression and she knew he not only expected her to try to get by him; he wanted her to.

"I'm sorry. I can't wait." She took a step toward the stairs.

He shifted his legs, a wider stance, taking up more space on the landing. On his face a smile, or sneer, or leer, or whatever it was, a challenge and a threat. "You wait. Your boyfriend goes downtown to see Emily and you come here. You think we're idiots?" He turned toward Johnny. "What did she ask you?" His tone was threatening enough to scare anyone, certainly a child.

Johnny flinched but stood his ground. "She asked for mom." He wanted to help her, he tried, but his wavering voice gave him away.

"You lying to me?" He took a step toward the boy.

Adele stepped in front of Johnny. "You're not going to hurt him."

"What are you going to do?" His face tightened with sudden rage. "What the fuck are you going to do? I'll hurt you and him both if I want." He rolled his shoulders. "You're—" The sound of the downstairs door opening, followed by the sound of voices, interrupted him.

One of the voices belonged to Emily; it was high-pitched and agitated. Adele couldn't make out what she was saying. The other voice, a man's, was muffled, maybe more than one voice. Dominic cocked his head toward the sound.

Footsteps slapped against the steps, along with creaking, rattling, and jangling. Adele couldn't take her eyes off Dominic, who looked trapped. He paid no attention to her, focused entirely on the sound coming up the stairs.

She took a deep breath as she saw something dark blue float in the space at the top of the stairs, first morphing into a face, and then into the form of a uniformed New York City police officer. Behind him, leaning back over her shoulder to complain at a second officer, Emily was in high dudgeon, demanding a search warrant and telling them they couldn't come into her apartment.

"We're not searching, ma'am. We don't need a warrant.

We're not going into the apartment unless we see something's wrong."

Hearing this, Dominic started for the apartment door.

"Hold it, fella," the officer said. "If you go in, I'm coming in after you."

Emily, Dominic, and Adele stood together on the landing in front of Emily's apartment door, with the two police officers seeming to surround them.

"What's the problem here?" The older cop looked at Adele. She started to answer. So did Dominic and Emily.

"One at a time," the cop said.

"Nothin's wrong. Nobody has a problem," said Dominic.

"Is that right?" The cop looked at Adele.

"Not exactly. If I could leave, that would be fine."

Both cops stiffened.

"Leave." Dominic seemed to growl rather than talk. "Who's stoppin' you?"

"You were—" The buzzer from the downstairs door interrupted her.

Johnny, still in the doorway, looked at his mom.

"Open the door," one of the cops said.

Johnny pushed the buzzer. Everyone turned to see who would come up the stairs.

Adele saw him first. "Raymond?"

"Are you all right?"

"Who the hell is he?" the older cop asked Adele.

"My friend Raymond Ambler."

After a few minutes, the police sorted things out and told Emily they wanted her to come with them to the precinct to answer some questions from the homicide detectives.

Ambler nodded toward Dominic. "I think Detective Ford might want to talk to him."

The cop appraised Ambler. "How would you know?"

"I spoke to him—"

"I think we'll do what we were asked to do." He turned to Dominic. "Can I see some identification?"

Dominic showed him something, glaring at Ambler as he did.

"I don't want to go to the precinct." Emily folded her arms across her chest. "They want to ask me something, let them come here." She spoke louder than necessary and her voice shook.

"Ma'am, you're not under arrest. We'll give you a ride if you want to talk to Detective Ford. If you don't want to come with us, we won't force you."

Ambler tried again. "Would you please check with Ford? I'm sure he'd like to talk to Dominic and Emily."

"Who the fuck asked you?" Dominic rolled his shoulders.

"The talkative cop turned to Adele and Ambler. "You two can leave."

"I don't think—" Ambler began.

The cop folded his arms, a copy of Emily's stance.

As soon as he and Adele reached the bottom of the stairs, Ambler called Detective Ford on his cell phone. "Dominic is here. They're letting him go. They won't listen to me."

"Good for them," Ford said. "I'm in the neighborhood, maybe I'll stop by and say hello if he's still there.

"What are you doing?" Adele asked as Ambler ducked into a doorway across the street from Emily's building.

"Making sure Dominic waits for Detective Ford."

"That's a stupid idea. He's dangerous."

"We don't know where he lives. He might have given the cop a false address."

"What are you going to do?"

"Talk to him."

Adele squinted, lowering her eyebrows, as if she wasn't seeing him quite right. "Somehow, I don't see that working out."

Ambler's cell phone rang. It was Benny. Benny never called him. "Of all the times—" He flipped the cell phone open. "Benny? Sorry. This is a bad time. I'll have to call you back."

"No." Benny's voice was hushed. "You can't. I'm at the runaway center. I'm not supposed to do this."

The door to Emily's building opened. Dominic! Ambler cupped his hand over the phone and whispered. "I can't talk now. Call back and leave a message on my voice mail."

"Wait here," Ambler told Adele and headed after Dominic, who walked quickly toward the blur of lights and traffic sounds of Ninth Avenue.

"Say, Dominic," he called. No cars moved on the street. The sidewalk was empty. The streetlights reflected off the windshields of the cars parked along the curbs on both sides of the street.

Dominic stopped and turned. He looked past Ambler at the police cruiser parked in front of Emily's apartment. "You're pretty brave when you got backup, librarian. One of these times, I'll get you alone." His eyes met Ambler's, his expression eerily lifeless. "How about we take a walk together over toward the river? Nobody bothers us over there."

"I want to talk to you about Emily."

Behind Dominic, the Ninth Avenue traffic hummed, punctuated by blasting horns, lights flickering as headlights passed the intersection. The air around them was still. Dominic shifted his stance. "You're gonna be sorry you ever laid eyes on her."

"If you're trying to protect her, you're doing a lousy job."

Something changed in Dominic's stance, a flinch, a flicker in his stone-like glare. "You don't know nothin' about Emily."

He moved closer to Ambler, inches from him. He was taller, with the sloping shoulders of a weight lifter, his neck thick.

Ambler stood his ground, though he shifted his stance—legs shoulder width, most of his weight into his front leg, knees bent. "You do take care of Emily, don't you?"

Dominic moved back a step. A deadly seriousness replaced the bluster. "What's that mean?"

"How much do you know about her past?"

"More than you—" Another deadly pause. "Maybe not. I asked you what you think you know."

"Did you know James Donnelly?"

The coldness of Dominic's stare was unsettling, different from the earlier standoff when it was a man-to-man thing. Ambler felt he was looking into the eyes of an executioner. "Sometimes you know too much."

"Whatever it is," Ambler said. "You could leave Emily out of it." As he spoke, he sensed, heard, rather than saw a car behind him. A nondescript gray Dodge pulled up alongside the parked cars in front of them.

Dominic turned when he heard the car. "Fuck," he said, and turned to walk away.

Ford was out and had Dominic jacked up against a parked car in a flash. He patted him down and stood him up. Turning to Ambler, he said, "Take a hike."

Ambler joined Adele next to the cruiser parked in front of Emily's apartment. He watched another nondescript car pull up behind Ford's and two men get out, young, husky guys, one white, one black, dressed like they might be longshoremen or truck drivers. Shortly after they arrived, the uniformed officers came out of the apartment and joined Ford and the other two men. They talked together in something resembling a football huddle for a minute until the uniformed cops walked back to their car. The talkative uniformed cop beckoned to Ambler.

He looked up to see the door to Emily's building closing behind Adele and started to follow her, but the cop flagged down a cab that had emptied down the block. He held the back door open for Ambler in a way that brooked no resistance. Once in the cab, Ambler checked his voice mail, hoping to find something from Cosgrove. Instead, he found Benny's message. After listening, he called Benny.

"She's leaving."

"Keep her there."

"I can't, Ray."

"Can you find out where she's going?"

"We try to find a friend or relative they're comfortable with. She didn't come up with anything."

"You're going to let her go out into the night, just like that?"

"I'm trying to talk her into letting us contact her parents."

"Can I talk to her?"

"I'll ask her."

"Hello?"

"Denise. It's Ray Ambler. Will you wait there for me?"

"Not if you'll tell my father."

Ambler hesitated. "I won't."

Chapter 23

Emily opened the door, a cigarette in her hand. Dragging on the cigarette, she met Adele's gaze and quickly looked away. Scared and nervous, she seemed fragile.

"You poor kid," Adele said.

"What do you want?" Her tone was gruff, but the expression in her eyes told a different story. She was close to tears.

"I want to make sure you and Johnny are okay."

Emily stared into the empty space of the hallway, sneaking a peek at Adele. It was impossible to tell what she was thinking. After what seemed a long time, she swung the door open and walked into the apartment. Adele followed and waited next to the couch while Emily went into the kitchen. She came back with a bottle of vodka, two glasses, and a carton of orange juice. She poured two drinks, mostly vodka.

Adele took a sip. The drink tasted awful but she took another swallow anyway.

"Johnny's asleep finally. Why'd you come here when I wasn't here? What were you looking for this time?"

Adele told her the truth. She'd read something in the papers she'd taken from the briefcase that Ambler thought might belong to James Donnelly.

"He thinks Dominic killed James. Does he think he killed my father, too? It's a different briefcase. I told him."

Adele hesitated. "I read something disturbing—"

Emily sat still, staring beyond Adele. "I don't know what you read. I told your boyfriend. I was helping James. We were writing something together. I changed my mind. I didn't want to do it anymore. He gave me back the book. James and I were okay. Dominic didn't kill him."

"It's true? What I read?"

Emily looked at the wall beyond Adele. "Our super-close, father-daughter relationship?"

"No wonder you ran away."

Emily continued to stare at nothing. "I'm sorry you read it. What happened is no one's business. That's why I didn't want to do the book. It's why— You're not helping me. I don't need pity."

"I didn't read it on purpose." Adele took another swallow of her drink, this time for fortification. "Emily, all of this is awful and terribly unfair. But you need to think of Johnny. You need to take him and get away from Dominic—no matter what he's done for you, no matter what you think you owe him."

Emily finished her drink and poured another one. "Everything I did, I couldn't help doing. It was decided long ago, everything I'd do. You don't understand. I was evil. I was born evil—possessed. I didn't hate my father. I wanted to be with him—me and him."

Adele reached for Emily. "You're not evil. You loved your father. You felt what little girls feel—"

Adele heard the door to the apartment open. So intent was she on getting through to Emily she didn't think about what it meant until she saw Dominic. The police hadn't taken him in.

• • •

Mike Cosgrove watched his hands shake as he sat in his car. It was guilt. Shame. Rage. He was a fucking fool, like one of those slimy, behind-the-back street punks, stealing from people worse off than they were, ratting on a partner the first time push came to shove. He was wrong, and being wrong had no courage. He loved Anne. She loved him. Why couldn't they stand up and say so? Take their lumps. He'd made a mess of his life. Now, Denise would follow in his footsteps. He started the car.

On the way back to Manhattan, he called the Missing Persons Squad and asked for George Ehnes. He'd worked a couple of cases with Ehnes, sad ones, when homicide compared notes with the runaway team. "My daughter's missing . . . ran away," he said after the briefest of preliminaries, the most difficult admission he'd ever made.

He gave Ehnes the particulars, said he'd drop off a photo later, and headed down the BQE toward the Williamsburg Bridge and the Lower East Side. The LES had become trendy, beyond trendy now, the shooting galleries and flophouses of years past overrun by gentrifiers, except for the building here and there where rent stabilization protected a few longtime tenants.

Danny O'Neil was probably a good kid, not some degenerate who picked her up at the Port Authority and put her on the street. Now, he was kidding himself, whistling past the graveyard. He drove up one teeming, narrow street and down the next—from Delancey to Houston, from Bowery to the projects. At one point, he parked on Ludlow Street and walked the narrow sidewalk of Rivington Street, sticking his head in the doors of bars, walking the aisles of small, stuffed-to-the-gills grocery stores.

He knew what he looked like to the few people he happened to ask. He'd seen people like himself too many times, the haggard expression, the begging eyes, the fading hope that a missing husband or son or wife or daughter wasn't dead, that there was some mistake. Now, it was his turn, he who all his child's life knew the dangers beyond the walls of home, saw each day how evil lurked everywhere. He who knew better than anyone, in the end, couldn't protect her. When his phone rang this time, he saw that it was Anne, and answered.

"I found Danny O'Neil's address." She gave it to him, speaking in a hurried whisper.

"Are you okay?"

"I'll be all right."

That wasn't the same. "Do you need to get out? I can find somewhere for you to go."

"One crisis at a time, Mike. I can't leave Kate and her brother, and he wouldn't let them go. He'd come after us. It'd be war."

"We can't keep on doing—"

"Find your daughter, Mike. Gotta go."

The address was on Rivington Street, a few blocks back the way he'd come. He walked quickly, working out what he'd do if Denise was there. And if she wasn't, he'd have to judge real quick whether the guy was lying about knowing where she was.

He rang the bell for the apartment, on the third floor of what was once a tenement, above an art gallery. Right away, someone buzzed the door open. No intercom. When he reached the apartment, he took a deep breath and knocked.

A male voice asked who was there, naturally enough. The tone was calm, easygoing, a kid's voice, not someone who had an argument with the world.

"Mike Cosgrove—" He was about to explain who he was to the closed door, when the lock clicked and it opened.

"You're looking for Denise?" He was a normal enough looking kid, no shaved head, no tattoos, no rings in his nose. His eyes met Cosgrove's; his expression was earnest.

"Is she here?"

The boy shook his head. "She called. When I first met her, I didn't know how old she was." The boy had trouble holding Cosgrove's gaze. "I never went out with her . . . just hung out. Someone told me she was thirteen, so I stayed away after that." His gaze steadied. "She was nice to talk to, smart. When she called, I told her she couldn't come here. I'd get in a lot of trouble. I told her to go home. She wouldn't, so I told her about a runaway center near Port Authority." He looked at Cosgrove. "I went there once, years ago when everything was crazy in my life."

Cosgrove took out his business cards and handed one to Danny O'Neil. "I'm sorry about your dad. If I can ever do anything, you call." He turned and left.

"I promise, Denise," Ambler said to the slim, pretty girl in front of him. She seemed older than thirteen when he first saw her. But when she began to talk, her eyes shifting away from his, her voice quiet and uncertain, she seemed a shy young girl. "Let me buy you dinner. I won't call your dad until you tell me it's okay."

She'd remembered him, of course. They'd been pals when she was younger, when her dad took her to a Knick game or Yankee game with Ambler. He hadn't seen her much in the last couple of years. She'd outgrown ball games with her dad.

As they walked up Eighth Avenue, Ambler suggested a couple of places they passed, Chinese, Indian, a French-style bistro; she held out until after a few blocks they found an all-night Greek diner. With a laugh and a little dance, she asked, "Can we go here?" holding her hands together, a playful supplicant. "Dad goes to these hoity-toity gourmet places. When I was little, he took me to the diner in the neighborhood and I loved it. I know exactly what I want."

When she relaxed and smiled and chatted, he remembered her cheerfulness and chatter when she was a youngster at the ballpark or the Garden. The sullen, taciturn girl he'd come upon at the runaway center was hard to like. The high-spirited girl with her head buried in the giant plastic menu, cheerful in spite of herself, was cute and likeable. He for damn sure wasn't going to turn her loose on the street again, not until she said "uncle" and he could return her to Mike.

"What are you doing?" Emily screamed at Dominic.

He'd grabbed Adele as she ran for the door. She'd done it instinctively. Now, his hand over her mouth was rough and smelled of stale cigarettes and something else repulsive. It constricted her breathing as well as muffling her screams; his arms were strong and hard, sinewy, so it hurt when she struggled, like banging against a fence post. She tried to kick at him but couldn't stand well enough to get any power into the kick, and he'd push his hand harder into her face and mouth and squeeze her arms tighter with his other arm when she tried.

"Get me something to put in her mouth."

"Let her go," Emily screamed. "Leave her alone."

"Get me something to put in her mouth, God damn it, or I'll put her lights out—" He tightened his grip on Adele. "Stop screaming or I'll smack you—"

"She'll stop. Leave her alone." Emily went up close to Adele. Her breath smelled sour, too, of vodka and cigarettes. "Shut up," she said. "Shut up for a minute."

Adele did. She stopped screaming and stopped struggling. Dominic didn't let go, but he relaxed his grip. All three of them were breathing hard.

Emily moved up face-to-face with Dominic. "What'd you do that for? Why'd you grab her like that? We were talking."

"You're an idiot. She's onto you. We got to do something with her."

Emily closed her eyes and shook her head. "You aren't going to hurt her, you fucking asshole! No sir. You can't hurt her."

Dominic balled up his fists at his side, twitching from head to foot, looking first at Emily and then at her like he'd batter each of them in turn. He snorted through his nostrils like a horse.

Hearing something, Adele turned and saw Johnny, small and white in his pajamas, his eyes ovals of wonder, watching from the doorway of his room. Her movement must have alerted Emily. She turned also.

"Look what you've done." She half pushed, half punched Dominic in the chest and moved toward Johnny. "Go back to bed!" He looked helplessly at Adele and turned back into the darkness behind him.

"Okay. Okay." Dominic shoved Adele onto the couch. "Stay put. If you get up, I'll drop you before you get to the door, so help me."

Adele measured the distance to the door. He'd caught her once, faster on his feet than she thought he'd be. In a strange way, it felt better doing what he told her, safer, even as she feared what he'd do.

He pushed Emily toward the kitchen, standing in the doorway where he could talk to Emily and watch Adele. Grimacing, gesturing, he spoke heatedly in a sort of growling whisper, so Adele couldn't understand what he said. She didn't hear Emily's voice at all. She looked at the door, her escape, and waited. Strangely, she was calm, believing something would happen that would tell her what to do next. She didn't think making a run for the door was it.

Whatever happened in the kitchen was over quickly and Dominic and Emily were back in the living room. Dominic looked like he wanted to rip her apart but he didn't come any nearer. Without any change in his menacing expression, he nodded toward the door. Her heart jumped. What was he telling her? She didn't dare to hope.

"Get out," he said.

"I don't care what your fucking rules are." Cosgrove spoke through gritted teeth. He knew he was wrong, abusing his authority, but couldn't stop. "This is my daughter."

"I know. All I'm willing to tell you is she was fine and she left," Benny said.

"You're a fucking librarian, not a social worker. What the hell do you know?"

"I'll get the social worker."

Cosgrove shook his head. Benny was easier to deal with than a social worker. With him, he might have some leverage. "Look. I know what you think about why kids run away . . . their families, abuse and neglect and— This isn't like that. Denise is rebellious. Her mother gets on her. They fight."

"Kids run away for a lot of reasons." Benny's tone was sympathetic. "Right now, she's not ready to go home. I can tell you she's safe."

"Do you know where she is?" Before he answered, Cosgrove knew he did. "Let's say you do know and you won't tell me. I can bring you in for harboring a runaway."

"I don't think so." His answer surprised Cosgrove. He didn't know what the law was on runaway centers; he should've asked Ehnes. "And if that's what you need to do, okay. It won't do you any good. She's safe. I hope she'll call and tell you that much. I asked her to. But she's mad at you, so she might not."

Cosgrove considered his options. There weren't many. Standing in front of Benny, his hands balled into fists, he felt a wave of exhaustion and something else, something weird happening with his eyes. Benny began wavering, bigger, smaller, closer, farther away; the room was spinning, shimmering walls . . . a confused sound of voices, nothing he could understand. . . . Darkness.

Chapter 24

"Dad used to say baked chicken in a Greek diner was one of the best meals in the city." Denise was chattering away about anything that entered her head. They'd finished eating and walked along 42nd Street without a destination in mind. He wanted to take her to Adele's, but Adele wasn't answering her phone. The first time he'd called she'd answered—or someone answered—and when he said her name, the phone was disconnected. Now when he called, he got her voice mail.

"I'm hoping you can stay with a friend of mine until you decide what to do next, but I can't get her on the phone." They waited to cross Sixth Avenue, Bryant Park and the library in front of them, traffic charging up Sixth Avenue.

"I'll be okay," Denise said. "You don't need to find a place for me."

"Oh? And where would you go?"

Her smile faded. "I have friends . . . I haven't been able to reach them. That guy at the center said I could crash there, but it's sort of creepy."

He stopped to look at her and realized she was exhausted. The burst of energy from dinner was gone. She yawned. Her eyelids drooped. Her face became a child's again, a child about to drift off to sleep. He hailed a cab.

"Where are we going?" She hesitated next to the cab door he held open for her.

"To my apartment. You can rest until I reach Adele."

Her face lit up, not gleeful, but close, as if she'd gotten something she secretly wished for. "Are you sure I won't be too much trouble?" she asked politely, stepping into the cab.

Searching through her pockets as she ran down 52nd Street toward Ninth Avenue and the bright lights, Adele realized she'd left her phone in Emily's apartment. She wanted desperately to call Raymond. She'd thought he'd follow her up to Emily's apartment and didn't understand why he hadn't. She'd gotten away because Emily insisted. That wouldn't keep Dominic from coming after her again when Emily wasn't there to hold him back.

She looked for a pay phone, something she hadn't done in years. Apparently, no one else had either. They seemed to have disappeared, like typewriters. She headed toward her apartment, not that far away—she could call Raymond from there—until a realization stopped her. She searched her pockets with a growing sense of dread. Her phone and her keys were in the same little bag she'd dropped on Emily's couch when she tried to slip out the phone while Dominic was in the kitchen with Emily. And the photos of her mother were on that phone, the last photos she'd taken, last summer at Gravesend before her mother got sick. She should have downloaded them before and she hadn't. Now they were lost.

She reached into her jeans back pocket. Thank God, her

credit card was there. She flagged down a cab. She could try Raymond's apartment. It was unlikely, but he might have gone home. A better possibility was the Library Tavern. Maybe he went there to wait for her. If he wasn't there, McNulty would help her.

Ambler watched Denise falling asleep on his couch. She'd taken a shower and he'd given her a pair of pajamas to wear. For a few minutes, she pretended she wasn't tired, but her eyes closed as she talked, sometimes in the middle of a sentence. Now, she lay curled up on the couch, swallowed up by the pajamas, a sheet, and a blanket, her features relaxed, eye shadow and liner and lipstick scrubbed off in the shower. Her pink, scrubbed face was peaceful and pretty, in repose.

Sitting in an easy chair across from her thinking about children growing into adults, he remembered his son John, a small boy growing into a bigger boy, and one day a stranger, neither man nor boy but a creature, ungainly and uncertain, in between. The most shocking changes weren't physical. It was that this person you once carried in your arms and bounced on your knee, whose dependence for so long was absolute, had grown into someone independent of you.

The phone rang.

"Where have you been?" he said when he heard Adele's voice. "Are you all right?"

"Where have you been?!" she shot back. "I need you to come with me right now."

He explained why he couldn't.

"You're in your apartment with a runaway thirteen-year-old girl. Are you crazy? Have you called her father?"

"I told her I wouldn't until she said it was okay. I was waiting for you. I tried to call. Why didn't you answer?"

"No reason, really . . . except maybe I was being murdered!!" She told him about Dominic at Emily's apartment. "I think he wanted to do away with me. She wouldn't let him. I swear looking into his eyes was like staring at death."

"You got out of there, right? You're safe."

"Yes. But I have to go back. My mother's photos are on my phone, Raymond. I have to get it."

"You don't have to get it now. You can get the phone later when this is over."

"What if they're not there? What if the phone gets lost or broken? They'll be gone forever."

Ambler tried calming her. She grieved for her mother. She was impulsive to begin with and now she was irrational, at least about her mother. She wasn't to be dissuaded.

"I need to go. If you care so much, you'll come with me."

"I can't. I have Denise here."

"Send her home and come and help me." She sounded panicked.

He felt panic rising in him also. He looked at Denise. "You come over here and stay with her. I'll go get Emily and your phone."

"No. I have to go. Let me talk to the girl."

"She's asleep on my couch."

"It doesn't look good anyway, Raymond. What are you doing alone in your apartment with a young girl?" Her tone was nasty and suggestive.

He ran his hands through his hair. "Let me think for a minute, Adele."

"No. I'm going to go."

"Don't go alone."

"I'll ask McNulty."

"Please wait for me."

"No."

• • •

Sometime later—he wasn't sure how long—his phone rang. It was Benny.

"Your friend, the cop, the girl's father, is here. He knows she was here. He passed out but won't go to the hospital."

"Did you tell him Denise is safe?"

"I did. Not good enough."

"'Tell him Denise is with me."

"No. She told me she doesn't want to go home. Sometimes, home is the worst place for a kid. You don't know why she left. If the kids can't trust us, they can't trust anyone, so then what happens to them?"

"Oh, for God's sake! Let me talk to him."

"If you tell him without asking her, you're violating her trust. You shouldn't have taken the responsibility if you were going to do that."

"Okay. I'll ask her."

Mike Cosgrove worked to get his body under control. He didn't treat it very well, rich food, too much wine, not enough exercise. But it never let him down like this. And he wasn't going to let it give out on him now. He heard Benny talking on the phone, and he was sure he was talking about Denise. The last thing he heard sent a chill through him. It sounded like, "Okay, Ray."

Of course, it made sense. Ray was protecting Benny. He'd protect Ray. He couldn't believe Ray would help Denise hide out. They hadn't seen each other in years. Right? Of course it was right. All this crap with sex and teenage girls was driving him nuts. He sat up.

An EMS technician stood over him, pushed him back down to a prone position. He was hooked to an IV line and had already refused to go to the hospital.

"I'm okay," he said. "Let me get up."

"Sure, you're okay . . . taking a little nap on the floor." The EMS tech was a short, stocky black guy with a West Indian lilt to his voice but a no-nonsense tone.

"I'm okay now."

"You lie there until I tell you. I need this IV to finish. Your blood pressure too low."

"Then I can get up?" He felt foolish asking permission.

"We'll see, man."

When the IV was disconnected, Cosgrove waited a few minutes for his head to clear. He dialed Ray's number.

"What's up?" he said when Ray answered. "You've been calling."

"I've got a lot to tell you."

Cosgrove took a deep breath.

"We've found Emily Yates." Ambler told the detective about Adele discovering Emily Smith's true identity, about Dominic, and about James Donnelly's briefcase in Emily Yates's apartment. "She had an explanation for why it's there. I'm not sure I believe her—"

Cosgrove cut him off. "You've been holding back a lot. You better hope it doesn't come back to bite you."

Something was off with Cosgrove's voice. It was strained, tight, under pressure, holding in a barely controlled rage. Ambler was beside himself with discomfort. He knew the strain Mike felt. He was a father, too, and remembered the agonized, helpless sorrow and rage he felt when his son began running away. He could save Mike a lot of heartache. But he needed to wake Denise and tell her before he told Mike.

"Look. Give me a minute. I'll call you right back. I have to do something."

Cosgrove tried to control his tone of voice, but Ambler could hear the rage seeping through. "Your guy is Dominic Salerno."

"And?"

"You're right he's mobbed up. You're wrong in making him for the murders—Donnelly and Nelson Yates. He was somewhere else. He's accounted for."

"That changes things," Ray said. "Emily might be telling the truth about the briefcase. Or, if she isn't—"

"Do you have anything else to tell me?" Cosgrove interrupted.

"No. I need to call you back." He hung up.

Chapter 25

"I close when I want," McNulty said. "It's busy, I stay open. It's slow, I close."

"You'll come with me?" Adele had that look of pleading innocence. You could put up with it from a pretty woman if there was a chance you'd sleep with her. The thing was he wasn't going to sleep with Adele. So why he thought he needed to put on a Sir Galahad or Sir Lancelot or Sir whoever-the-fuck-it-was act, was something he'd go over with his shrink—or more likely with Marcelo over a martini at the Oyster Bar.

No one buzzed them in at the apartment Adele took him to. They stood in the vestibule inside the street-level door while she rang the bell a second and then a third time. "I'm scared," she said. She didn't have to tell him. The fear was etched into her face.

He went back to the street. It was too late to start pushing doorbells and too late to hang around expecting to follow someone who opens the door. There should be a super because there was a pipe for steam heat at the end of the hallway; steam required a boiler, which required a stationary engineer. No super was listed on the register they were looking at. These walk-ups a lot of time ran in packs—one super for three or four of them. He went toward Tenth Avenue checking a few doorways; then came back toward Ninth Avenue checking a couple more. In the third doorway, he found a bell for a super. Pushing it would produce one pissed-off guy, who probably wouldn't speak English, but— He pushed the bell and held it, waited a few seconds, pushed it again and held it longer.

The panel of bells and mailboxes, like the others on the block, didn't have an intercom system. Most of the time, supers lived on the first floor, if not in the basement with their boilers. He was about to push the bell for a third time when a strip of light appeared under a door at the back of the first-floor hallway. A minute later, a grizzled old gent, short and stocky, wearing a Knick shirt and boxer shorts came shuffling along the hallway toward him.

After a lot of muttering and what was undoubtedly cursing in Spanish, the super went for his keys and a pair of pants. They found Adele standing in front of the door to Emily's building.

"I told him she was sick, might be passed out. You're her sister. She called you. I'm your husband." He watched the super go through his stack of keys at an agonizingly slow pace, trying one after the other in the lock of the downstairs door. "I don't know why I bothered making up a story. He didn't understand half of it. But there you go." McNulty gritted his teeth watching the guy's stumbling efforts with the keys. "You'd think he'd know how to get into his own fucking building."

With the door finally open, they followed him up the stairs. On the way up, he said a couple of things back over his shoulder that McNulty didn't catch. Years of working with Salvadoran and Dominican kitchen workers and bar-backs taught him the secret was to nod and either smile or grimace depending on the other guy's expression. This one called for grimacing. At Emily's door, the super knocked a couple of times and began the ritual of the keys again. This time, the results came more quickly.

The lights were on in most of the rooms of the apartment, except toward the back where it was dark. Adele called Emily's name and then again louder. Silence was the answer. She took a few steps in. The entryway to the apartment had a half wall that blocked the view of the interior of the apartment. She peered around the wall and screamed, frozen where she stood. When the screams became a whimper, she put her fist to her mouth and ran into the apartment. McNulty followed a couple of steps behind, turning the corner in time to see Adele fall to her knees in front of the couch where a woman lay.

Her position was unnatural; her neck extended in a way that seemed impossible, her head lolling off the cushion inches above the floor, her face toward them; her expression was peaceful; her eyes open and red where they should be white. No marks on her head or neck. A pillow lay beside her.

Adele lifted the woman's head so that it rested on the arm of the couch and stroked her hair, softly speaking her name, Emily. McNulty stood over her. The super came far enough into the room to see the body on the couch and no farther.

Adele sat up and screeched, "Johnny." Jumping to her feet, she ran to the back of the apartment. In a few seconds, she came out of the darkness ran into the kitchen, and then back to where McNulty stood watching her. She grabbed the front of his jacket with both hands.

"He's not here." She wailed into his face.

He looked into unseeing eyes. "You gotta stop. Calm down, Adele! Where's your phone?"

She stood face-to-face with him for a moment as her eyes began to focus. "It's here," she said. "It's here somewhere. . . . I left it here." She began tearing around the apartment. McNulty ran behind her trying to grab her. Finally, he half-tackled her and held her pressed against the kitchen wall.

"You can't touch anything. You gotta stay still."

"My phone's gone. Johnny's gone. My wallet. My keys."

McNulty held her against the wall with one arm, and hollered and gestured to the super, asking for a phone. Luckily, he had one. McNulty dialed 911.

When he finished with the 911 dispatcher, he asked Adele if she knew Ambler's phone number. She gave it to him and he called.

"McNulty?" Ambler said when he finally caught on to who was calling.

"Bad news, Ray. This girl is dead."

"What girl?"

"I think her name is Emily." He told Ambler where they were and what they'd found. "The cops are on their way."

"The boy? What about the boy, Johnny?"

"He seems to be missing."

"Missing? Is Adele there?"

"She's not in very good shape." He still held her against the wall; she breathed in short gasps like a trapped animal but grabbed for the phone, so he handed it to her.

She talked for a minute or two, telling Ray the same things he'd already told him.

"Raymond said we should search the stairwells," Adele said. "Johnny might be hiding somewhere."

"Would he go to someone's apartment? I'll check the stairwells. You wait for the cops. Tell them. It's better if they go knocking on doors than if we do."

Ambler had been about to wake Denise when McNutty called. Hanging up the phone, he sat for a long time despairing. He pictured Emily, how fearful and vulnerable she was, the desperation that seemed a permanent part of her, as if she'd seen death and had her own appointment in Samarra. He was a fool—a damn fool. He knew she'd be killed, as he knew her father would be.

He paced the small living room, unable to shake loose the picture of doomed Emily, cold and dead, as she seemed to know she would be. He should have stopped it. He shouldn't have left her alone. He didn't care what she did. He shouldn't have let her die. He'd set out to stop a murder before it happened, and he couldn't do it. Instead of following his instinct, he analyzed this and theorized that. Adele told him Emily Smith was Emily Yates. He knew in his gut she was right. If he'd only—. He let out a sarcastic laugh, mocking himself. Stopping in front of his bookcase, he took down his worn copy of Martin Innes's *Investigating Murder.* He looked at it for a moment, and then flung it, slamming it hard against the far wall.

The bang of the book against the wall, like a loud backfire, woke Denise. She sat up, startled, her eyes wide with fear. Wrapped in blankets and pajamas three sizes too large for her, a patch of her dark hair sticking straight up on top of her head, she looked childish and fragile and vulnerable.

He went and sat on the couch beside her. "Sorry," he said. "I was mad. I threw a book."

"Mad at me?" Her voice was small.

"Not at you," he said gently. "At me."

She yawned, reaching up to loop her arm around his neck, pulling his face down against hers. "Thank you so much," she whispered and lay back down, asleep before he pulled the blanket back over her. He'd wake her soon enough.

The detective who'd been talking to Raymond and Dominic on the street a couple of hours earlier barged in a few minutes later, as did what seemed like a hundred other people who did whatever official people do when someone is dead murdered. Tons of equipment that seemed unnecessary and intrusive—lights, cameras, people with leather bags like doctors once carried, people with big metal cases—too much of everything and too many people bumping into one another, pushing someone else out of the way; the scene was eerie, grotesque, sad, and depressing, as if the person who died was a specimen, part of an experiment.

The detective—Ford—said how hard this must be for her, and he was sorry but he needed to ask her some questions. Once the grilling began, she didn't believe he was sorry at all. He didn't care about who was dead. He didn't miss Emily. He wasn't shocked and sad he wouldn't see her anymore. He wanted to catch whoever killed her. That's what he wanted. It was a challenge. Something he needed to do, like climb a mountain. He was calm and calculating and unfeeling, like a machine, and eager to get going on his quest. She didn't like him.

"I told you everything that happened," she said, when he began asking questions about what she'd already told him. "I want to go look for Johnny."

"The patrols will be looking for him. Can you tell me about the boy's relationship with his mother?"

She didn't understand his question.

"Was he angry at her? Was he unruly? Hard to handle?"

Adele felt a rush of blood, a blinding anger. "Are you crazy? . . . Is that what you think? He's eight years old." She glared at him.

The detective's expression didn't change. No anger. No apology. "We're gathering information."

Rigid with anger, she stood up. "You're not gathering any more from me."

"Please sit down, ma'am."

"No. . . . Go find Dominic, instead of asking stupid questions."

"We're looking for him. Talking to me might help us find him."

She looked at his broad face. He had a large, almost square head, a thick neck, sandy hair. Probably, he was handsome. Probably, a popular football player when he was in high school—popular with the boys because he was bigger and stronger than they were; with the girls because popular high school girls like big, beefy, heedless, handsome boys like him. Narcissism and insensitivity was so appealing; they wanted romance to be superficial like they were. She shook herself. Why was she thinking like this? Why did she dislike this man so much? He was doing his job.

She was filled with rage that Emily was dead because Emily had become her friend. She was going to help Emily get away from Dominic and help her raise Johnny. Now she was dead, and it was her fault. Dominic wanted to kill her and Emily wouldn't let him, so he killed her instead.

Detective Ford got a phone call on his cell and told her he had to leave but would be in touch with her again in the morning. He offered to arrange a ride home but she said she'd walk.

A loud knock on the door surprised Ambler. The street door buzzer hadn't rung, so he thought first of Dominic. He told Denise to go to his bedroom and approached the door cautiously.

"Open the door, police!!"

Cosgrove filled the doorway, his eyes ablaze, boring past Ambler into the apartment. "Where is she?"

"Easy, Mike. She's fine. I couldn't tell you—" Ambler turned to see Denise standing in the doorway to his bedroom. He turned back to Cosgrove and caught his large meaty fist full in the face. Staggering backward, he heard Denise's scream, "Dad!" His head cleared in time to avoid the next couple of punches, by sinking and turning, finally pushing the winded Cosgrove off balance onto the couch.

"I know," Ambler said, breathing hard. "Cops see the worst, think the worst."

By now, Denise stood beside Ambler. "I hate you," she screamed at her father. "You're an asshole. He took care of me to make sure nothing happened to me."

"Denise—" Cosgrove said. "Denise."

She put her hands over her ears. "I'm not going with you. I'll run away again. Have me arrested. I'd rather be in jail than go home."

Denise pouted and yelled and cried. But in a while, she went back into Ambler's room to get dressed. Cosgrove, sitting among the bedclothes on the couch, looked up at Ambler. "What was I supposed to think? You didn't tell me." His eyelids drooped over his bloodshot eyes.

"Worse things happened," Ambler said. He told him about Emily Yates's murder.

Denise hugged Ambler when they were leaving. She held him for a long time. He kissed the top of her head.

Cosgrove seemed to want to say something but was unable to get it out. Finally, he said. "After I drop her off, I'll talk to Ed Ford. Find out what there is about the murder."

"I'm going to find Adele," Ambler said.

Chapter 26

Max was getting stranger and stranger, turning into Macbeth, paranoid and delusional. Laura Lee didn't trust him around anyone other than herself. It was as if he'd run into Banquo's ghost.

"You're acting like a little girl."

He hugged the Beefeater bottle like it was his favorite doll. "We need to leave here . . . travel until my sabbatical runs its course."

"What about the book?"

Dominic called him a couple of days ago, out of the blue, first time in years. Since then he'd been ducking around corners, about to dive under the bed when the doorbell rang with the Chinese food delivery. In the library, he hid in one of the reading rooms or the stacks, changing locations every hour or so like he was in the witness protection program. He'd started carrying that stupid gun, which she told him was a felony in New York.

The strangest thing was Dominic calling him, rather than calling her, and neither of them telling her what it was about.

Sleep with your brother's wife maybe. But the family secrets—especially that family—stay secret. Max seemed to have forgotten she was there. You'd think that would be a blessing, rather than his usual panting after her. Yet, strangely, she worried about him. Then, the other night, out of the blue, he told her he was going to Atlantic City for a couple of days, so he could relax. Whatever was going on, someone better tell her soon. Left to their own devices, those two were disaster bound.

Dominic ignored her calls. Not something she couldn't get around. Her last message on his phone was simple: "Let's get together at the Liberty Inn. Max won't be back from Atlantic City until tomorrow afternoon." Whatever else was happening, Dominic wouldn't miss a chance to bang his sister-in-law.

"You look good," he said when he opened the hotel room door. Wearing light-colored slacks and a tight-fitting black T-shirt that accentuated his muscular arms, powerful shoulders, he looked good, too. He groped for her but she slipped past him and ducked into the room.

"Anything for a girl to drink?" She never fooled herself that Dominic's interest in her was anything other than lust. He sometimes pretended to an interest on a level above the animal. When he did, she played with him, as in this instance, if she wanted something. It was akin to getting a dog to do tricks and withholding the treat until he did.

Dominic took the champagne bottle from the ice bucket, twisted off the top and filled a flute glass for her.

She took the glass and said, "Come sit down here beside me and tell me about this hush-hush stuff with brother Max."

"You don't want to get into that—"

"Yes I do." She smiled.

Dominic took a deep breath. "You know what's up, Laura Lee. Or you should."

"Let's say I'm naïve."

"I'm not going to say anything out loud. Maybe you're wired."

Laura Lee laughed. She stood and began to unbutton her black blouse. "Well, I can put your mind to rest on that." Dropping the blouse on the bed, she reached for his hand. "Come. Feel." She pressed his hand against her flat stomach, sliding it along her midriff and over her black bra.

He leaned his face against the bra and reached behind her back to undo the hooks.

"Find anything?" She pushed his head away from her breasts, holding him at bay. "It might be in my pants—"

He reached for the waistband of her skinny-leg jeans, sliding along the bed as he reached, so that he was almost on the floor as he worked to undo a button. She lifted her knee and turned slightly so that he slid to the floor at her feet.

"You're panting, Dominic." She walked to the far side of the room, undoing her jeans as she walked. "Now, tell me what this is about, so we can have some fun." She took off her shoes, and pulled her jeans down. In her tiny black underpants she did a pirouette, dropping the panties to her feet. "See, no wire." She kicked the underpants toward him. "You can spill the beans while I blow you." She walked toward him.

He pulled himself onto the bed. The expression on his face as he undid his pants made her laugh. Pushing his hands aside, she undid the buckle herself. "Well. Well. Look at that! Now talk . . . and you better tell the truth. If I think you're leaving something out, I'll bite." She bent down to him.

"It was about Emily—"

"It's nice of you to walk with me," Adele said. "You don't have to."

"What I have to do is get my head examined," McNulty said.

"You shoulda let that cop take you home, with your key missing and a murderer on the loose."

"I didn't like him."

"Good reasoning." McNulty rolled his eyes but she didn't catch it. Adele was grieving. He didn't know what to say to comfort her, didn't have the words to get across what he felt, much less the words that might make someone who was grieving feel better. He thought about putting his arm around her but didn't know what good that would do either. He did anyway, so she leaned against him, her eyes glistening with tears when she looked at him. They walked the final two blocks like that.

Her apartment was on the fourth floor, the elevator tiny, slow, and groaning. She'd gotten the key from the super—the second super they'd woken up that night. McNulty listened to the tumblers click as she turned the key in the two locks, one after the other. Thinking he'd watched too many private-eye shows on TV growing up, he touched her shoulder and moved her aside, so he could enter the apartment first.

He looked left and then right. The hallway ran straight through the small apartment and lined up with a window on the far wall of the kitchen. Some faint light beyond the window formed a lighter gray backdrop to the darkness of the kitchen. Against that lighter backdrop, a silhouette darted across the darkness.

Instinct took over. The light in the doorway behind them would make him and Adele targets, so he pushed her out into the hallway. Adele being Adele, she bounced right back. Without thinking, he headed into the darkness; first, he moved gingerly, flattened against the wall in the short hallway; then, he made a dash for the kitchen. Catching a glimpse of the silhouette, he threw himself at it, squeezing his eyes closed, waiting for the explosion he expected would be the last thing he ever heard.

Instead, he barreled into a human form that crumbled as if from a blind-side tackle. The small body beneath him made an oomph sound but nothing else. He drew back his fist to smash whoever it was, but held back because the form beneath him was small and not struggling. Adele switched on the light and he saw he'd tackled a boy.

"Johnny!" Adele cried.

He'd made a fool of himself in front of Ray, and embarrassed his daughter. Denise didn't speak to him on the drive back to Queens. He knew better than to speak first, except to say he was sorry, but saying it, he knew being sorry didn't change anything.

When he stopped the car in front of his sister's house, he said, "I know I was wrong. You think there's no way I can make it up to you. I'm still going to try. Promise me you'll stay with Aunt Mary. Promise you won't leave."

She turned to him as she opened the door to get out. He waited for the promise. "I know about Anne," she said, climbing out and slamming the door.

So that cat was out of the bag. Anne's husband knew. Now Denise. If Sarah didn't know, she would soon. Or maybe she already knew and pretended not to. Why not? Why wouldn't she let them go on being trapped in their misery?

Jammed up in traffic, merging onto the 59th Street Bridge ramp, he thought it might be good to forget about his family for a while. Hard to believe tracking down a killer could come as a relief. Light rain fell, hard enough for windshield wipers; the road glistened. He called Ed Ford, who filled him in on Emily Yates's murder. When he disconnected, he headed for 49th Street. Even if the apartment had been cleaned up, everyone gone, the show over, he needed to see where the murder happened. Like a bloodhound, he'd go to the beginning to get the scent.

A patrol car sat outside the building, so the apartment was sealed. He slipped under the yellow crime-scene tape. In the half light from a window that opened onto an airshaft, he took in the apartment—gloomy, a threadbare rug in front of a worn couch. Not a tidy place, nothing on the walls, no photos or knick-knacks, nothing welcoming or comfortable about it. It reeked of sorrow, as the rooms where murder happens often do.

As usual, he didn't know what he looked for. The lab team gathered in anything that might be evidence: hair samples, stains, glasses, cigarette butts. Ford had gone through the place, drawers and cabinets, clothes and bookcases. Remnants of the dust from the fingerprint kits remained on a windowsill and the coffee table. What he looked for was something different—something that would tell him why this person died at this place at this time. What he saw was a lair of unhappiness.

He found a briefcase someone must have not thought important. Letters and papers. Ford should have taken that along. But he was called away to a different homicide. Someone slipped up. He took a handful of papers from the briefcase and sat down with them, instantly gripped by what he read—the sexual history of a teenage girl. Reading, he couldn't help but think about Denise.

McNulty was on the floor eyeball-to-eyeball with the kid, who didn't blink. Neither did either of them speak. McNulty figured he was owed an explanation and didn't think he needed to ask. He didn't know what the kid thought. For all the expression on his face, he might be waiting for a bus. But something in that expression was familiar. He'd seen those eyes before. Who was this kid?

Adele moved things along by rushing over and trying to pull him off the kid, something he was willing to do, get off the kid, as soon as he got his legs under him. Diving across rooms and tackling someone, even if it was a kid, was not something he trained for, so he wished to make sure all his moving parts were working before he put himself in gear. He attempted to explain this to Adele.

"Get off him, you lug. You'll squash him."

McNulty rolled to the side. "The youngster, I think, is better equipped to roll around on the floor than I am. I need a moment to take inventory. The missing boy?" He cocked his head toward Johnny. "You okay?"

The boy nodded.

"Wanna go another fall?"

The kid's eyes widened and then he smiled.

Adele knelt beside Johnny and helped him to his feet. When he was up, she hugged him. The kid looked dazed but held onto her for dear life. He probably didn't know about his mother. Adele would have to tell him—and how do you do that, tell a kid his mother is dead? Tears trickled from her eyes. Not from the kid's, though. She wasn't telling him anything yet but in a quiet voice asking him what happened. He sat down across from them and waited.

As the boy talked, McNulty tried to fight back waves of sadness but didn't do so well. He thought about his son, Kevin, being told he was dead. Tears welled up behind his eyes. He stifled them. Bartenders don't cry. When they'd been in the apartment only a short time, the downstairs bell rang. It was Ray. McNulty opened the apartment door for him, and Ray stood in the doorway watching Adele and the boy for a minute. No one spoke and then the kid got up and ran to bury his face in Ray's midsection. Ray looked at Adele. There was a good deal going on in both their faces.

For a while, the three of them sat on the couch, the kid in the middle. The kid had told Adele what happened but he told it again to Ray.

A man was coming to the apartment, the kid said. Mom said he was going to give her money. Whoever he was, Mom was scared. She told Johnny to go before the man got there. He didn't know where to go, so he grabbed Miss Adele's keys and her phone and took off. He passed the man on the street and watched him go into the building. He didn't think the man saw him come out of the building. He couldn't call Miss Adele because he had her phone and he didn't know how to call Mr. Ambler. He remembered where she lived from the day they went to the zoo, so he went there. When she didn't answer the bell, he went up to her apartment and opened the door with the key.

That was it. Sitting across from them, McNulty felt pretty much forgotten. Which was okay, he didn't have anything to say to anyone. Still, it didn't seem right to leave. Adele and Ray had to tell the kid he didn't have a mother anymore. What do you say about that? People came to bars sometimes when they were grieving. More than a few times, a guy's halfway through his third drink and pipes up that his father had passed, or a good buddy threw a seven the night before.

It happened with Ray the night after the writer Yates was killed. Ray stayed longer and drank more than was his wont talking about the guy. He never knew what you said when someone started talking like that. He guessed the job was to listen, let the guy kill his snakes. Nothing could comfort him when he was a kid and his mother died. She wasn't murdered. Her dying was slow. He got to watch her waste away until the time came when she didn't get out of bed, when she was skin and bones and hardly awake at all. Everyone knew, even him, she'd be dead soon. He knew it and couldn't imagine it. Until it happened. She was dead. Gone to return no more. He went numb. His dad woke him up in the morning, put food in front of him, sent him to shower, took him to school. He didn't think. He was empty. Thinking back now, what he remembered was darkness.

So he guessed he knew something about how the kid would feel. Him being there wouldn't help. The kid wouldn't know it, would never remember. But he felt like he should anyway. It would mean something. It might help somewhere. So he stayed, not saying a word, sitting in the silence, while Adele and Ray told the boy his mother was dead.

If Cosgrove had seen this diary before the girl was murdered, he'd have figured her for the murders at the library. First, she had the briefcase that was missing from the murder scene. And she certainly had a motive. Still, there was something not right about the diary. Why was she writing this? For herself? For someone else to read? It was as if he'd found the diary on a bookshelf in a bookstore, like one of those unexpurgated books when he was a kid, *Tropic of Cancer* or *Lady Chatterley's Lover,* shocking, explicit sex. He'd need to talk to Ray about it. Thinking about Ray, he flushed with embarrassment. It would be hard to face him again.

He called Ed Ford to ask about Dominic Salerno. Ford hesitated because he didn't want to piss off the RICO task force again.

"Pick him up," Cosgrove said. "The kid might be with him."

"You know where to find him?"

"Ask the organized crime guys."

He didn't like most of the possibilities for the kid. You could hope he'd missed the whole thing. Or he might have left when the bad things began to happen. In either case, why didn't he come back? He didn't get himself a hotel room. The best outcome would be that he went to someone.

Ray had visited Emily Yates before she was killed, so had Dominic Salerno, and so had Ray's friend Adele. Adele and the bartender McNulty found the body. He could start with any one of them, and Adele's apartment was only a couple of blocks away. He headed over. On the way, he got a call from Ford.

"They dropped the surveillance after I questioned him the other night. They're still pissed off, and they don't know where he is—or if they do, they won't tell me."

"This is a hell of a gathering." Cosgrove stood in the doorway of Adele's apartment. The four culprits stared at him from the interior of the apartment, as if he'd come to haul them away. He hadn't slept, except for the few minutes on the floor of the runaway center, and couldn't remember the last time he'd eaten. He didn't feel much like chitchat.

Adele told him about finding Johnny in her apartment and recounted what Johnny told them about the man who came to his mother's apartment. Cosgrove asked the boy to describe him. The description was vague, as might be expected from a scared kid.

"Would you recognize him?"

Johnny shrugged his shoulders.

"I'm going to bring you down to the police station with me to look at some photographs, okay?"

Johnny looked from Adele to Ambler.

"Who do you want him to look at?" Ambler asked.

Cosgrove met Ambler's gaze. "Let's not prejudice this. I want him to look at some photos."

"Can it wait?" Adele put her arm around Johnny. "Why don't you go and arrest Dominic?"

"Sooner's better than later. It's not for sure Dominic's the killer." He looked from her to Ambler and back at her. "I have to take the kid with me anyway."

Adele reacted like he'd pulled a gun on her. "What? Why? You can't take him. Where would you take him?"

"Child protective services."

The boy's eyes went wild. If Adele hadn't tightened her grip on him, he would have bolted. Talk about fear and loathing.

"That's the procedure when we don't have a relative."

"He can stay with me. His mother sent him to me."

Cosgrove rubbed a spot on his forehead between his eyes, feeling a headache coming on. He was a cop. He didn't make the laws. He was supposed to follow them. That's how it was. So, there you go, another problem with having friends. Cops shouldn't have friends. They'd be better off without hearts.

"C'mon. I didn't make the rules." He was angry at the protocols, at himself, and at them. "I gotta contact child services. Maybe someone there, they'll say it's fine for the kid to stay with Adele."

They stood, and the bartender, who'd been sitting off to the side watching the encounter like it was a boxing match, walked over to join them and whispered something to Ambler. Ray then whispered something to Adele. Cosgrove's hackles went up. Whispering meant trouble.

"Okay," Ambler said. "We'll go downtown—all of us. You can show Johnny your photos. The child welfare people can meet us there."

"I don't know. They should come here and pick up the boy."

"C'mon, Mike."

He gave Ambler an exasperated look and headed for the door.

At the bottom of the stairs, in the vestibule between the inner and outer doors, Ambler called Cosgrove back, and they let McNulty, Adele, and Johnny precede them out the door to the street.

"What?" Cosgrove said.

"Really, Mike. Do you have to do this now?"

"The boy's an eyewitness." He opened the door.

Ambler put his hand on his arm and pulled him back. "Did anyone find a briefcase at the murder scene?"

Cosgrove turned to Ambler. "You know what's in the briefcase?"

Ambler nodded. As he did, Cosgrove caught the glint in his eye and knew he'd been had. Yanking open the door, he rushed out to the sidewalk, looked up the street and then down the street. McNulty, Adele, and the kid were gone.

Chapter 27

The next morning, after only a couple of hours of sleep, Ambler went to the library to tell Harry the terrible news. He found a small fleet of police cars parked in a kind of mishmash constellation on Fifth Avenue. At the top of the marble steps, in front of the giant bronze doors, was the sort of chaotic scene you find during police action. A crowd gathered; uniformed officers pushed the crowd back while folks in the crowd pushed back against the officers, craning their necks, jostling for position. Ambler was stopped from going up the steps, so like everyone else he craned his neck to see what was happening.

A wave of blue uniforms came through the revolving door and seemed to flow down the steps. Behind them, flanked by plainclothes detectives, his hands cuffed behind, nothing to shield his expression of mortification, came Harry Larkin.

"Harry!" Ambler shouted as the entourage moved close to him at the bottom of the stairs.

Harry turned his pale face toward Ambler, his expression

like the frozen, pasty face you see on a corpse. Ed Ford, Cosgrove's partner, steered him by the elbow. From him, Ambler got a quick glance and a flicker of irritation.

"Where are you taking him?"

Harry's entourage ignored the question.

"Probably Central Booking," a voice behind him said.

"Harry. Don't talk to anyone about anything. I'm getting you a lawyer."

Ed Ford flashed him another sour look. Harry's expression didn't change.

Remembering McNulty's lawyer friend, Ambler headed for the Library Tavern.

"They arrested Harry?" McNulty said. "They might as well lock up the Blessed Mother." He called his lawyer friend and after some difficulty getting through argued with him for a while. Eventually, he hung up.

"He's talking about conflict of interest because he's representing the other guy from the library. I won him over when I said Harry was a boss and might be a paying customer. He'll try to spring him, but it'll take a few hours, maybe longer."

Ambler called Mike Cosgrove.

"Not now," Cosgrove said.

"What's the charge?"

"He hasn't been charged." Cosgrove sighed into the phone. "I know he's your friend—"

"Why would you take him out in handcuffs?"

"Let me do my job, Ray? I can't talk now." Cosgrove paused and Ambler could hear him grumbling to himself. "They cuffed him because he resisted. . . . He ran."

Kay Donnelly and Benny Barone were watching TV at the Liberty Inn on Tenth Avenue, appropriately enough in the Meatpacking District. Kay took the morning off, so they availed themselves of the two-hour rate, and were comfortable enough with one another to enjoy watching TV in bed, like a real couple, once they'd completed the mating ritual.

When Benny went to the bathroom, Kay switched to NY1, idly watching until a bulletin flashed on the screen and she learned that Emily Yates had been murdered.

"My God!" she screamed.

Benny ran from the bathroom and stared at the TV. "Another murder? Who's she?"

Kay wrapped herself in the sheets. "Nelson's daughter."

"Oh, that's right. Why? Why did someone kill her?"

She looked into Benny's eyes but didn't answer.

In the lobby, as she and Benny were leaving, Kay bumped into a handsome but dangerous-looking dark-haired man, who was vaguely familiar. When she turned to apologize, she stopped in her tracks. The man's arm was looped through the arm of Laura Lee.

Kay stared. Laura Lee smiled sweetly. "Hello Kay." She tightened her grip on the man's arm and pulled him closer to her. "Nice to see you let your hair down." She turned her smile on Benny.

Benny gawked at her.

"Emily Yates was murdered," Kay said. She wanted to shock Laura Lee. She didn't expect the reaction of the man with her. His expression hardened into the scariest she'd ever seen—the face she'd been terrified she'd one day see looming above her as she was about to be raped and murdered.

He yanked his arm loose and turned on Laura Lee. "You fucking son of a bitch. You're a shill for my brother?"

"No! Dominic, no!" Laura Lee voice rose to a hysterical whine. She reached for his arm with both hands. He grabbed her wrists, held them in a grip that looked as tight as a vise until her face twisted with pain; then, he shoved her away so that she careened off the wall, leaving her there, cringing, rubbing her wrists, a wreck of her former cocky self. He pushed past Kay, stopped for seconds to glare at Benny, who'd taken a step forward as if he might intercept him, and pushed past him also. In seconds, he was gone.

As she watched Laura Lee run out to the street and flag down a cab, moments, if not seconds, after the man she'd been with had done the same thing, Kay turned to Benny. "I know that man," she said. "I've seen him before . . . with Max."

"You don't have to talk to me until your lawyer gets here." Cosgrove pulled up a straight-backed chair across from Harry Larkin and sat down. The ex-priest, sitting up straight in his own chair, stared at the blank wall behind Cosgrove. "I don't want any crap about you not getting your rights. You can remain silent. What you say can be held against you. Someone told you all that, right?"

Harry pulled his chair closer to the metal table between them, rested his elbows on the table, and buried his face in his hands. Cosgrove wondered if he might be crying. People did that when the life they've built on a lie begins to crumble. From the outside, all you see is a little bit of erosion or some rotting at the base. From the inside, they see the whole thing coming down, not visible yet, but already started.

"We're being recorded. You got that. On the video, everyone will see I'm telling you you don't have to talk to me if you don't want and if you do talk what you say can be used against you. Your name's Harry Larkin, right?"

Harry sat back in his chair and looked at the ceiling. In his expression, no anger, no hate. He was a soft guy, no chip on his shoulder, no grudge against the world. Not so unusual for soft guys to murder someone. When they did, usually they didn't fight you. The murder was the end for them. What happened afterward, they didn't care.

"From the beginning, I didn't believe you on what happened in the office." Cosgrove kept his tone conversational.

Larkin looked at him blankly.

"You had to see the shooter. So why not say so? I didn't get it right away. Now, I do. If you told on her, she'd tell on you. Maybe she'd think you keeping quiet evened the score." Cosgrove stood and pushed his chair back. "We know about the pedophile charge." He paced the room, not looking at Harry.

"That wasn't true. There was no charge."

Out of the corner of his eye, Cosgrove saw Larkin following him with his eyes, so he turned to face him. "I suppose you were never in Emily Yates's apartment either."

"I was."

"Fingerprints," Cosgrove said weakly. Not what he expected. Instead of him catching the look of surprise on Larkin's face, it went the other way. Something about the ex-priest made it easy to believe him—the you-can't-cheat-an-honest-man aura. You couldn't sweat a guy like this. He knew that, but he wouldn't have enough to hold him if Ray lawyered him up like he said he would, so he might as well try.

He told Harry the scenario he'd come up with: a sex scandal, a cover-up, shipped to a new parish, like with the rest of the pedophile priests. Emily Yates turns up after all these years. She could expose him. Maybe the statute of limitations had run out; even so, there was the embarrassment; maybe a civil suit; living the rest of his life marked as a pervert. Kill himself if he's exposed. Kill her, he doesn't get exposed.

That might not be 100 percent right. But the elements were right: sex, revenge, the past refusing to stay in the past. He was close. "Why not confess? Get it off your chest."

Harry remained silent, inscrutable.

"The seal of confession keep you from admitting to a murder, too?"

Harry's elbows rested on the table, his chin in the palms of his hand so his fingers were splayed out against his cheeks, thoughtful, cherublike. "Emily's death confirms that innocence doesn't protect you from the consequences of the evil that others do."

Cosgrove slowed his pacing. Like a hunter come upon his prey, he tried to blend in with the surroundings, barely taking a breath, doing nothing to alter the landscape, to make it as if he weren't there, that the prey was safe in his natural environment. Larkin was talking. He needed to keep talking until it all came out.

"Emily was sexually abused when she was young. Perhaps you didn't know it began with her father."

"Only since her murder," Cosgrove said.

"She knew I knew what he'd been doing to her. She knew it was wrong. She didn't know how to stop it. She turned to me for help, yet I couldn't reveal what I'd learned in the confessional. I told her to tell the authorities, someone at her school." He paused. Even if his voice was steady, he squinted his eyes closed every few seconds, as if something was hurting him. "Her parents were Catholic—not what you'd expect from their behavior—mystical, no rules. Emily thought if she divulged her sins in the confessional . . . What she didn't consider was that others confessed to me."

His silence this time was longer. The temptation to urge him on was hard to resist. Cosgrove clenched his teeth and waited.

"She blamed me and, of course, herself, angry at me because I didn't help. She got the idea that if she accused me of what was being done to her by someone else, I'd reveal what I knew to save myself."

He was through talking. He might be lying. Cosgrove didn't think so. It didn't matter. Emily Yates was dead without recanting. Whatever denials he made would be baying at the moon.

"She never forgave you." Cosgrove said. "She tried to kill you. She was the shooter in your office. Took out her revenge on Donnelly for what he did to her, and later her father for what he did, and tried to get you, too."

Larkin looked at him blankly.

"You knew she'd try again, so you got to her first."

"What happened?" Ambler asked.

Kay and Benny began talking at once, standing in front of the library table in the crime fiction reading room.

"Slow down. You were where when you saw Laura Lee and this man?"

They looked at each other and then at the floor. "A hotel downtown, the Liberty Inn." Benny mumbled, his eyes downcast. "That's not important. It's what he said when Kay told him the woman had been murdered. He acted like she'd murdered her—"

"No." Kay interrupted him. "He said she was a shell—or something like that—for his brother."

"A shill?" Ambler asked. "She called him Dominic? Can you describe him?"

They combined forces to come up with a description that might fit Dominic Salerno but would also cover half the men his age on and around Arthur Avenue, many of them also named Dominic.

"Do you know what he meant by a shill for his brother?"

Kay turned from Ambler to face Benny and looked at him for a long time. "I'm sorry you have to hear all this, Benny." She turned to face Ambler. "I remember where I saw him. Upstate. During the time we were at Hudson Highlands. He came to meet Max twice. It was strange. They met at a rest area, a scenic overlook on Route 9-W. Max had told me his father was a gangster and so was his brother. He'd broken away, changed his name, and had nothing to do with them. I thought it was bragging, part of the bad-boy image he cultivated. When I saw him with this man, Dominic, I didn't think it was bragging anymore. When Arthur Woods died right after that and Max dropped me and picked up with Laura Lee—"

Benny's expression clouded. "You were with Max Wagner?" He cocked his head, like a dog listening to something he couldn't quite make out, maybe his master's voice from far away, waiting for her to clear things up.

Kay kept her eyes trained on Ambler. "They got out of their cars to talk. I thought it peculiar . . . and sinister."

Ambler needed to sort things out. Dominic Salerno knew Max years before. He was in Hudson Highlands when Laura Lee's first husband, fell, jumped, or was pushed off a cliff. Dominic spent the morning at an hourly rate hotel with Laura Lee— and when he found out Emily had been murdered suspected Max of the murder. It was a lot to digest. "Was Max having sex with Emily at Hudson Highlands?"

Kay's expression hardened. "Yes. Everyone was, including my husband and her father."

Benny stared at her. She kept her eyes averted.

Ambler had trouble keeping his voice under control. "You knew this?"

"Not until after Emily ran away." She paused, squeezed her eyes closed, and seemed to steel herself. "Nelson and Max did something with Emily. I finally got out of Max that they'd taken pubescent, erotic photos. After she ran away, Nelson went nuts. He didn't know Max and James and Arthur were having sex with her, and I guess Max told him."

The puzzle was coming together for Ambler. He needed one

more connection for everything to add up. "Did Max ever see Emily again after she ran away?"

Kay took a deep breath. "I'm sure Max didn't because he was looking for her. But James did. He found her a couple of years ago but none of us knew that until the day before he was killed. He tricked her into giving him letters her father wrote to her trying to get her to forgive him for what happended to her when she was young . . . what he'd done to her. After a while, Emily caught on to what James was up to and told him she wanted the letters back."

"Did he give them to her?"

"No."

"Are you sure?"

Kay nodded. "That's what the argument Benny overheard was about. James had the letters. He showed them to Max. He wanted to make a deal, coauthor the biography. Max said no." She smiled weakly. "Max was never very good at sharing. He wanted to interview Emily for the book. He wanted her quotes. The letters weren't enough for him. When James was killed, and then Nelson, Max began falling apart. He thought the murders were retribution. He convinced himself that Emily was the murderer . . . and he was next."

Benny stared straight ahead. He listened to Kay, not interrupting, not commenting. Ambler didn't know how much he'd known about her past. From his dazed expression, you'd have to guess not much. They might still work things out. A lot of people have pasts they'd rather keep in the past. Better for Kay if some things had been left unsaid. But there it was.

A few minutes later, standing in the hallway outside the crime fiction reading room, he watched them walk away, heads down, not speaking to each other. "A shill for my brother?" Max and Dominic Salerno brothers? He found Frank Robinson in the Milstein history and genealogy division room on the first floor.

Frank had a sixth sense that pointed him in directions others couldn't see, so he was often sought out by the amazing number of people searching for their roots.

"It's a follow-up, Frank. Adele did the research a couple of weeks ago. Something came up we didn't think of."

Twenty minutes later, Frank Robinson called Ambler. "A great family tree—three generations of criminality, at least one felony conviction a generation, sometimes two or three. Dominic Salerno has a brother, Anthony, graduated from Fordham Prep, valedictorian, scholarship to Notre Dame. Didn't graduate from Notre Dame. A Maximilian Wagner did."

Ambler stared into the space in front of him. Of course, Emily! He'd half known it all along, sidetracked, blinded, because Dominic was a killer for hire and Emily a mother, because he couldn't believe she'd kill her father. She'd practically told him, if not in words, by her reactions.

He punched Mike Cosgrove's number on his cell phone. He was uncomfortable calling him after all that had happened—with Denise and then Adele taking off with Johnny. Mike had a hard shell to begin with. It took years to develop any trust with him. Now, circumstances might have blown it all away.

"I came up with the girl myself." Mike's tone was cooler, more formal, than it had been, not as stiff as it might be. "She had every reason to want revenge. And she wasn't finished. That's why she was killed. Friar Tuck in the next room could nail it down, but he won't talk. My guess from the beginning was he saw the shooter. He wouldn't come clean because she had too much on him."

"Harry didn't kill Emily. He didn't have any reason to. He was trying to help her. He told Adele—"

"Oh?" Ambler could see Cosgrove's eyebrows go up. "The

fugitive? Is this the Adele we're talking about? Don't think I'm not going to lock her up when I find her."

"She's keeping the boy safe, Mike. Emily killed the men who molested her. Max knew he was next. In all likelihood, years ago he had Dominic kill Laura Lee's first husband. Max Wagner and Dominic Salerno are brothers."

"I didn't see that one coming." You didn't often hear surprise in Mike's voice. "Brothers, eh? I'll look into it when I can get to it."

"It may not wait. Dominic might kill his brother because he killed Emily."

After a long pause, Mike said, "It's not that I don't respect your instincts on this. But what you have here is instinct, not proof. I have something else I'm trying out. Emily Yates killed the men who abused her, including her father. We both got that. And the priest, the ex-priest—"

"Adele can tell you. It's not true."

"Neither you nor Adele is high on my trust list right now. We have physical evidence on Larkin. And he's the only one she actually accused of—"

"What kind of physical evidence?"

"I can't tell you."

"It's too soon for DNA. . . . Prints, right? You found his fingerprints. Harry was in Emily's apartment. He was there a couple of times, once with me. Question Max Wagner."

"His brother Dominic is a gangster and you don't like him, any other reason?"

"Because he has a motive."

Cosgrove was silent for a moment. "Let's say he does. Friar Tuck's still the favorite. She tried to kill him."

"Harry isn't going anywhere while you follow this up. And you might save Max's life."

After another pause, "I'll talk to him. That's all. Any idea where he is?"

"He should be at the library." He gave Mike the address he had for Max and Laura Lee on the Upper West Side. "If he's not here, he might be there."

When Ambler finished on the phone, he went to look for Max. He often worked in the Manuscripts and Archives reading room. The curator at the desk told him the Yates collection reader would come and go a few times a day, never staying long at one time. He tried the Berg reading room, also on the third floor, as well as both halls of the main reading room. Next, he checked the Frederick Lewis Allen Room on the second floor. On the first floor, he checked the periodical reading room. He was on the main staircase between the first and second floor when Laura Lee caught up with him. She grabbed his arm, a wild expression in her eyes, her face bloodless.

"Have you seen Max?" Her question was simple. The way her eyes begged for an answer changed the question utterly.

"No. Is something wrong?"

"His brother—" She froze. She searched his face. It didn't take her long. A flash of rage—or hate—narrowed her eyes. She understood he knew. Wasting no more time on him, she continued her dash up the stairs.

Ambler returned to the crime fiction reading room and called Cosgrove's cell phone to tell him Max and Dominic were in the library.

"We're not there yet," Cosgrove said. "I got to clear up something before I can go after Dominic Salerno."

"What's that mean?"

"Internal stuff. It's complicated. Stay away, like I told you. I'll get after him as soon as I can."

"Could you get a warrant for Max Wagner?"

"And what do I tell the judge to get a warrant—that you have a hunch he killed the girl? I've got to clear something. Damn it, Ray! Let me do my job."

When he disconnected, Ambler saw Benny and Kay in the hallway outside the crime fiction reading room and brought them in.

"Laura Lee's trying to stop Dominic before he kills Max," Kay told him.

"Where's Max?"

"No one knows."

"Call 911," he told Benny. "Tell them a man with a gun is loose in the library." He called Cosgrove and told him the situation had changed.

"I'm on my way."

"We have to warn Max," Kay said. Her face was a mask, the expression she wore when he first met her, the attitude she wore like a severely cut business suit.

"It's too late for that," Ambler said, "and too dangerous. The police need to handle it now."

Benny put his arm around Kay. She slid out from under it. He stood back from her, seeming both surprised and embarrassed. "Why do you care, Kay?" His tone was sharp, irritated. "Let them work it out."

"You don't understand." Her eyes blinking rapidly gave her a look of uncertainty. "I'm not sure I understand myself." Her glance went back and forth from Benny to Ambler. "I owe some loyalty to Max. Don't I?"

Ambler tried to sound sympathetic. He'd known Max a long time also. Like or dislike him, he didn't want him murdered. If you could keep someone from being killed, you'd have to do that. "The police are on their way. Laura Lee is trying to warn him. If you know where he is, that's one thing—but you don't want to get in between him and Dominic."

Kay's eyes locked on his, as she weighed what he said. For a few seconds, she seemed frozen in place and then she was out the door.

"Where are you going?" Benny shouted after her.

When she looked back at Benny, her eyes, wild, unhinged, she was already running, her heels echoing against the marble hallway. Benny ran after her.

For a moment, Ambler watched the empty space in the doorway, not thinking but knowing what would happen, and what he would do now.

Chapter 28

Ambler hadn't been in the stacks for months. Wending his way down the narrow, iron stairs from the third-floor reading room, he came to the top level, the seventh floor. The cast iron and Carnegie steel shelving stretched out before him for two city blocks, nearly a hundred miles of shelves.

If Max holed up down here, he'd be safe. No one came down into the stacks except library staff. Benny would know how to get in. Laura Lee could probably charm her way in. Max couldn't know for sure the police weren't after him, though if he saw them taking Harry out of the library in handcuffs, he might think he had breathing room. Did he think Dominic would come after him?

The Yates papers were part of the Manuscripts and Archives Division so they were stored under Bryant Park. The tunnel to those stacks was on the ground floor. Yates's collection of first editions signed and inscribed by his writer friends, which Max had been going through, was shelved beneath the main reading room. He didn't remember which level.

As he made his way down the narrow stairway to the next lower level, he heard the unmistakable echoing report of a gunshot. Before the thought fully registered, another shot rang out. At the moment of the first shot, he felt a rush of adrenaline, a strange, physical sensation of something rushing through him—instinct, developed over millennia, took over.

He paused in his steps down the stairs, his hand on the thin iron tubular railing. After the pause, he took another step and paused again. After each step, he paused, and after each pause, he stepped again. He could die if he kept going. Never before had he thought dying was imminent. Of course, he'd thought about dying but abstractly. Now he could be dead in a matter of minutes. A man with a gun was down in the stacks and he was walking toward him, thinking he had to do this, that it had become his duty to stop the shooting, so he kept going down the stairs and when he passed the sixth floor and was on his way down to the fifth level, he hollered, "Dominic!"

"Ray!" It was Benny. "He's got a gun. Go back up. He's already shot—"

Ambler dropped down the last few steps to the fifth level. The rows of shelves were close together, the concrete ceiling low, the aisles in all directions narrow, so it wouldn't be so hard to dodge someone. He didn't have a plan but crouched and maneuvered between the rows of shelving. He might distract Dominic and give Benny and Kay a chance to get out. Dodging between the rows of shelves, he might keep Dominic at bay until Cosgrove got there. He had the advantage of knowing help was coming. With that knowledge came hope and confidence. This moment might be why he'd practiced tai chi for twenty years. Yet, when push came to shove, he didn't know if the tai chi moves he'd practiced for years would work if he had to disarm someone with a real gun and an intent to use it.

Another shot rang out, amazingly loud again, the bullet pinging and clanging off the iron and steel of the bookshelves, probably embedding itself in a book. He wondered if one day he might hold up a bullet-pierced book at one of his lectures and recount the true-crime adventure that ended in a shootout in the stacks. More likely, someone other than him would hold up the bullet-pierced book and tell the audience how the 42nd Street Library lost its first crime fiction curator.

It made no sense for him to be in the stacks dodging someone with a gun, but here he was, something inevitable in his moving forward. Shadows flickered among the rows of shelves, so he wasn't the only one crouching and creeping among the stacks. He worked his way toward the farthest wall, where he expected to find someone who'd been shot, most likely Max. When he saw a body on the floor in the distance, he rushed toward it because it was moving. Turning into an aisle, he realized he was watching Laura Lee, scrabbling along the roughened floor like a crab.

He heard a sound behind him and turned to see Dominic behind a pillar. Laura Lee crawled, barely moving, pulling herself with her hands and arms, dragging her legs, leaving a swath of blood on the floor behind her. Her breath made a gurgling sound. Something clicked behind him again, so he crouched and ran past Laura Lee and around the next iron pillar.

The place was vaultlike, rows of iron pillars and tiers of steel shelving stretching out into the distance like an interminable cellblock. He ducked behind a second row of shelving, putting another aisle between Dominic and him. When he peered through a space between a row of books and the shelf above them, expecting to see Dominic creeping along the next aisle searching for him, he saw him kneeling on the floor next to Laura Lee.

Bent over her, he spoke softly, in the sorrowful tone reserved for the time when you're no longer being heard. "Why?" Ambler heard. "Why, Laura Lee?"

When Dominic stood again, a gun in his right hand, down by his waist, his expression was different than Ambler had seen before. The cold, robotlike mask that showed no feeling was replaced by sadness that might even hold a strange brand of wisdom, the face of a man with a distasteful task in front of him; not one he'd chosen but something he'd have to complete.

Dominic spoke softly as if whomever he addressed was not far away. "She's dead, Max. That's what you got out of this." Lifting his head as if to speak to a larger audience farther away, he said, "Whoever else is down here, don't get in my way. Lie down on the floor and stay put. This is me and Max. Nobody else." Even louder, he hollered, "She's dead, Max. You got that? Dead instead of you. You could've stood up like a man."

Intent on listening, Ambler didn't realize Dominic had moved toward him while he spoke. When it was too late, he heard him—and saw the muzzle of his gun, a few feet away pointed at him through a shelf of books.

"Stay right where you are, librarian." Dominic came around the section of shelving holding his gun on Ambler. "Who else is down here?" Before Ambler could answer, he said, "Tell them to get down on the ground."

"Benny," Ambler called. "You and Kay stay where you are. Lie down on the floor."

A moment of silence and then, "What about Max?" Kay Donnelly's voice shook.

Dominic flashed a look of exasperation at Ambler. "The guy's a prick. You know him. Now, everyone wants to take a bullet for him. I don't get it." He took a breath and shouted. "What about Max is I'm going to kill him."

Ambler waited, not knowing what he waited for.

"He's got a gun, too, you know." Dominic's eyes were bright with heightened alertness. He seemed to ask for understanding . . . for forgiveness. No. Not forgiveness. He asked for permission, for Ambler to agree that killing Max was the right thing to do. Max murdered Emily and he had a gun, so you could concede a sort of law-west-of-the-Pecos logic to Dominic's thinking.

Risking his life to save Max from a deserved fate wouldn't benefit humanity in any way he could imagine, yet he'd have to do what he could to save him. What that would be, he had no idea. Somewhere in his memory was a tai chi move designed to disarm an opponent with a weapon. Getting into the bow posture might help him remember how to do it, so he bent his knees and shifted his weight to see if anything came to him.

Dominic would have to be close enough to him for him to reach the gun, which at the moment wasn't the case. Next he'd have to grab the gun and spin to the side so the gun wasn't pointed at him. Then twist his arm until the gun dropped. It was easy enough in the exercises, with a compliant teacher, likely to be different in real life, with a professional killer.

Dominic noticed his change of stance. He took a step back and raised the gun. "It's time for you get on the ground, librarian." He pointed the gun at the floor to emphasize his point.

"Do you want—" Ambler was trying to stall, when, out of the corner of his eye, through a gap in the bookshelves, he saw movement. His reaction, because it was instinctive, was unguarded.

Dominic followed his gaze. "What was it?"

"What?" Trying to distract Dominic wasn't going to work. He tried anyway. "Do you want me to get down on the ground?"

"What'd you see?" Dominic shifted his stance, trying to get a better look through the shelves and keep an eye on Ambler at the same time. He was bending this way and that, stooping one second, standing taller the next, trying to see through the shelves, when a mournful cry, a sobbing wail of hopelessness and despair, shattered the silence of the tomblike stacks. A few seconds behind the wail, a single shot rang out close enough to be deafening.

Dominic moved toward the sound, as if he had started toward the wail and was hurtled forward by the shot, his reaction unthinking, instinctive. Distracted, he allowed his arm, the arm holding the gun, to brush against Ambler. Ambler would think later that he too reacted unthinkingly, that Dominic's arm with the gun brushing against him triggered a reaction that required no thought—that allowed for no thought.

He grabbed Dominic's wrist above the gun and twisted, at the same time turning on his waist and twisting Dominic's arm in a circle and pulling him in the direction he was already going. He had his hand on the gun, on top of Dominic's. It went off. He let go of the gun and spun on his right foot, completing a circle, and used the force of the spin to kick with his left leg, knocking Dominic's legs out from under him. As Ambler spun onto the floor and Dominic fell, the gun went off again.

And then stillness. For a second, he thought he was shot. When he realized he wasn't, he looked at Dominic, lying still. Ambler didn't move, letting the enormity of what had happened sink in. He began shaking. Somewhere, something made a sound. Next he heard a scream. Soon, the sounds of activity increased. He hadn't moved from the spot on the floor in the narrow aisle he'd ended up in. He began to feel pain in his shin where it had met Dominic's shin in his last kick, pain in his shoulder and in his hip. He should move, stand up, but he didn't.

Dominic was dead. He knew without going nearer the body He'd killed a man. That seemed not possible. He went back over what happened, trying to recall every detail in sequence. He couldn't. He'd spun and twisted Dominic's arm. The gun went off. Dominic was dead. It happened fast. He wasn't sure he'd even been there.

Next, Mike Cosgrove was standing over him. "Don't get up."

Ambler shook his head. "Is he dead?"

"What the hell happened?"

Ambler shook his head. "Dominic. Is Dominic dead?"

"If that's Dominic, he is."

"I killed him."

"We'll sort out what happened. First, we need to know if you're hurt." He called to the medics, who came to look at Ambler.

Chapter 29

Cosgrove watched the medics examine Ambler. They looked for bullet holes first. Surprisingly often, folks have a bullet hole in them without realizing it. Ray's face was ashen. Pain. Shock. Whatever happened took a toll on him. If he did kill Dominic, as he said, it would weigh heavily on him. Bad enough for anyone, even a cop. You don't get over killing someone. Most people never know the feeling. Not even cops. One in a thousand, not even that. His bad luck to be one of them; years ago, and the nightmares still woke him. For Ambler, it would be worse—for all his interest in crime, if there ever was a never-hurt-a-fly person, it was Ray; he'd be a mess. Made no difference the guy deserved it.

What they had down here were three deaths, all by gunshot, one self-inflicted. Maximilian Wagner ate the gun. The woman was shot in the chest. With Wagner beside her, it looked like a murder-suicide. But the woman took more than one bullet. Same with Dominic, shot more than once. His gun was a semiautomatic. The gun in Wagner's hand was a revolver. So it might not be what it looked like.

For the other death, it seemed likely that Dominic was holding the gun; it was on the ground underneath him. Ray grabbed at it; they wrestled; it went off. Accidental. Justifiable. It could be that; it could be something else. He'd take a statement from Ray when the medics finished with him. Not something he looked forward to, walking the guy through it again. It would be best to get it over with, so he'd do it, neither of them liking it.

From the looks of things, he'd be here all goddamn night. He could see the *News* and the *Post* in the morning: "Carnage at the 42nd Street Library." They'd hound Ray once they figured out he was in the middle of it. It would make the headlines because everybody in the city, everybody everywhere—people in Iowa, for Christ's sake—knew the 42nd Street Library. What the papers might not get would be the connections.

The killings here; the death of the woman in Hell's Kitchen; her father's murder; the murder at the library a week before that; the earlier killing when everyone was young and Emily Yates a damaged child. He wasn't sure yet who killed whom. What he was sure of was that the events of that earlier time led to this. He was inclined to think it was over now. He could tell Ray the chickens had found their roosts. Everyone part of the twisted scenario was dead, except the two people he suspected early on, the ex-priest and Kay Donnelly. Things often aren't what they seem.

He wondered how long it would be before he could sit down with Ray and piece it together. Ambler wasn't a guy to think good triumphed over evil. After all this, he'd say good people sometimes did evil and evil people often did good. He was like that. You'd wonder if killing someone, accident or not, would change him.

Watching the medics examining Ray, it took a minute for

him to notice a uniformed cop coming toward him with two bedraggled citizens in tow. He recognized Kay Donnelly and Benny Barone.

"And what have we here?" he asked.

Neither of them answered. They were subdued and scared.

"They were in this dungeon when the shooting went down," the officer said.

"So, what happened?" He looked from Benny to Kay.

"What about Ray?" Benny asked. "He's hurt."

Cosgrove gestured toward Ambler and the medics. They were helping him to his feet and seemed prepared to let him go on his own.

"We don't know," Kay said. "First, someone was shot. I think Laura Lee because Max screamed her name. But we didn't see. Right after the shot, Ray Ambler came down into the stacks and called to Dominic."

Cosgrove broke with his usual practice, which was to let the suspect or witness talk without getting in the way, and interrupted. "Why were you down here?" He shifted his gaze to Benny.

"She came to warn Max Wagner. I came after her. I guess Ray came after me."

"Why would you all do that?"

Kay and Benny looked puzzled.

Cosgrove tried again. "Try to stop a guy with a gun."

They stood in front of him, arms around each other. The idea of it, budding love in the midst of murder, said something about life, how you find hope in the worst of things. Looking at it the other way, you find evil and cruelty and despair all around you that love can never overcome. However you choose to look at life, it's a wash.

"I got my daughter back," he said to Benny.

• • •

It was late when Cosgrove finished his work. He popped two Tums into his mouth and stood for a few moments on the broad landing in front of the steps leading from the massive bronze main door of the library to Fifth Avenue. That door had been closed for hours. What was left of the cruisers, ambulances, ME vans, lined the curb on 40th Street in front of a side door. Those who had business there, detectives, uniformed cops, shift supervisors, crime scene and medical examiner's office technicians and investigators, went in and out the side door there.

A couple of hours before, the president of the New York Public Library in a tuxedo, the police commissioner, the Midtown South commander, and a half-dozen others—white shirts and gold badges—stood where he was standing. Facing a battery of TV cameras, the steps lit up like Yankee Stadium, they reassured the city there had not been a terrorist attack. A shooting took place. Three people were dead, including the perpetrator. None of the victims were library employees, and there were no other suspects.

Yellow cabs streamed down Fifth Avenue despite the lateness of the hour. But the sidewalks were quiet. The small crowd, mostly tourists, that gathered for the press conference dispersed as soon as the klieg lights were turned off. A lone cruiser idled at the curb beneath the watchful lions.

Cosgrove had spent an hour or so interviewing Kay and Benny separately, and then another hour with Ambler. After all the books Ray read and after knowing murder as an abstraction, he'd taken part in one, and he couldn't get his mind around it. Going over what happened, step-by-step, more than once, he stumbled when he came to what happened with the gun. "It went off" was what he said each time. He couldn't say who was holding it, didn't know if they were wrestling for the gun, couldn't say where he was when it went off.

"You're going to suffer for this, Ray," Cosgrove told him. "I'm telling you that upfront. It wasn't your fault. It's the way it worked out. The guy brought it on himself. He deserved it. But he'll follow you. You'll see him in your dreams. You need to talk about it. Get it out of your system. Not now maybe. Soon. You can talk to me. I've been there. It's better talking to someone who's been there."

Ray nodded. He had that hollow-eyed look, already seeing his ghosts.

The DA's office would decide if there'd be charges. He thought about trying to fix it—arrange Ray's answers so there'd be no doubt it was self-defense. The problem was Ray was distracted. He might not remember and come up with a different story when the ADA interviewed him. If that happened, one of the stories would be a lie—not confusion or forgetfulness—so he'd be in trouble. The way Ray was feeling, all that guilt hanging over him, no telling what he might cop to. Tired as he was, he decided to truck over to 80 Centre Street to call in some favors.

As he walked down the steps, he recognized a burly figure coming toward him.

"Sorry I got you wrong, padre."

"It's a form of hubris to judge but difficult not to."

"You're wrong, Father. I don't judge. I gather information."

"It's Harry. You didn't judge me?"

"I tell you what, Harry. Let me take you to dinner when your life gets back to normal to make up for my error in judgment, to talk this through. Neither of us may be what the other thinks."

Chapter 30

After a fitful sleep, Ambler woke, did his tai chi exercises, and went for a walk. He kept picturing Dominic's face in the moments before he died. He didn't look angry, more like exasperated and determined, like he wanted to say something and either thought better of it or couldn't get it said before the gun went off. If the gun hadn't gone off when it did, who knows what would have happened? Dominic wanted to kill Max, and Max was dead. Dominic might have walked out of there and left him and Kay and Benny alone. Dominic might not have had to die if Ambler had done something differently, waited, thought about it more.

Walking didn't help. Working through the tai chi form didn't help either. Usually, he could stop thinking when he did the form. This time, it reminded him of what became a dance of death in the stacks of the library. He knew what he wanted to do. Cosgrove told him he should talk to someone. A couple of blocks below Astor Place and the *Alamo* cube where Third Avenue became Bowery, he took out his cell phone and called Adele.

"Where are you?"

"I don't know if I should tell you. Promise you won't tell me to turn myself in."

"You can't hide forever."

"I'll stay in hiding if I have to. I'll move somewhere and start over, start a new life."

"I won't tell you to turn yourself in."

"I'm at McNulty's apartment on the Upper West Side."

She hugged him when she opened the apartment door. "I knew it was terrible for you. I wanted to call. I knew you'd feel awful. I was afraid we'd get caught if I called."

Ambler nodded. Words wouldn't come. He'd told her he wanted to talk to her. She was the only one he wanted to talk to. Now he couldn't find any words; he wanted her back hugging him again. Johnny ran out from somewhere inside the apartment, took a flying leap from deep inside the hallway, and landed in his arms. Adele put her arm around his shoulder and led him into the apartment.

"I made you some lunch. I bet you haven't eaten in ages."

They sat together at a table in a combination living/dining room. Adele and Johnny watched while he ate pasta and meatballs.

After a few minutes, Adele sent Johnny to the bedroom to read one of the books she'd gotten for him from the library on Broadway. She understood Ambler wasn't ready to talk about what happened and didn't ask him to. She did want to talk about what would happen with Johnny.

"He does have a maternal grandmother," Ambler said.

"Who deserted her daughter and never laid eyes on him."

"I don't know how these things work. We'll get a lawyer."

"What if we lose?" Tears sprung from Adele's eyes.

He didn't answer. He thought he might persuade Lisa Young

to let Adele adopt Johnny. She seemed reasonable enough, and she hadn't shown any signs of wanting a grandchild. Ambler hadn't exposed her connection to Nelson Yates or Emily.

Adele decided that she and Johnny and Ambler should go to the Museum of Natural History since Johnny was missing school and should do something educational. Visiting the museum with Johnny was strange. The boy was quiet, taking things in. Adele would say something or read from the display cards. Johnny nodded. He was interested in everything they saw. Ambler didn't care if he didn't want to talk. The boy had lost his mother. Ambler killed a man. They had lots on their minds.

He was reminded of taking his son to the museum. John was a quiet kid, too. Their outings were forced, not fun. He never knew what to say to his son, mostly because John had a way of taking charge of the conversation by not talking. Thinking about him now, he realized he'd now killed someone, as his son had. It wasn't the kind of bond he'd wished for. Once he began thinking about John, he couldn't stop. Every few minutes, it seemed, for the rest of the day, another memory of his son popped into his head, when it wasn't an image of Dominic.

After the museum, they walked to Broadway and down to 72nd Street where they stopped at Gray's Papaya for hot dogs. Johnny was more upbeat about the food.

"These are good. The hot dogs at Yankee Stadium are better," he told Adele.

Ambler smiled. "We'll go to another game soon."

Johnny nodded, munching on his hot dog.

Ambler watched him for a minute. "I have an idea."

On the walk back to the apartment, near 99th Street on Columbus Avenue, Ambler led them into a sports store and bought two baseball gloves and a couple of balls. He played catch with Johnny in Riverside Park for almost an hour, talking about good throws and nice catches and getting your body in front of grounders. When they finished and walked the block and a half to McNulty's apartment, Ambler draped his arm over the boy's shoulder.

"There's something I was wondering," Johnny said. He looked up at Ambler. "Will there be a funeral for my mother?"

When he dropped the boy off, he spoke with Adele in the hallway for a moment, telling her he wanted to talk with Lisa Young.

"I'm scared." She clutched at him, her face close to his. "What will we do if she says no?"

As soon as he heard Lisa Young's voice on the phone, he knew he was wrong. She volunteered nothing. He could picture the condescension, the haughty stance, the lifeless expression in her eyes. He spoke quickly and nervously. He was sorry for her loss. Emily loved her son. Adele was a friend to them both. Emily would want Adele to take care of Johnny. Could they meet and talk? "It's complicated, I'm sure. We'll do whatever it takes legally. I wanted to know your thinking—"

"I don't know what you're trying to say, Mr. Ambler."

"I'm hoping . . . Johnny—"

"This is a family affair, Mr. Ambler. I don't see how it concerns you. If you can tell me how to reach that woman, my attorney will contact her and make arrangements for—"

"You don't understand—"

"You don't understand, Mr. Ambler. My family will take care of the final arrangements for Emily. We'll take charge of her son and do what's best for him."

"You're going to raise him? Can we meet and talk about this?"

"You'll hear from my attorney. Neither you nor your lady friend has any legal right to the boy. I do."

He closed his cell phone and stared at it. How would he tell Adele? This woman deserted her daughter. She never acknowledged her grandson's existence; now she had a legal right to the boy? That couldn't be right.

He called Adele and said they needed to talk

"It didn't work," she said.

"I promise we'll fight this. There's got to be a way."

"Can we meet and talk? McNulty took Johnny out for the afternoon."

"McNulty? Where?"

"He said the park. Belmont?"

"That's the race track."

Saturday morning, the third day after the incident in the library, Ambler went to a tai chi class for the first time in months. It was a corrections class, ironic because he'd received a phone message the evening before from his son asking him to visit him at the correctional facility.

The tai chi teacher, an ageless Chinese woman, who'd studied with one of the masters of tai chi chuan in China, was also a Taoist priestess. He'd studied with her for more than twenty years, first learning tai chi for exercise and later as a martial art. He came this time in search of the inner peace and harmony with life that tai chi and Taoism promised. Following the hour-long practice in the form, and the meditation that went with it, he boarded a train for Beacon and from the Beacon station took a cab to the Shawangunk Correctional Facility, a trip he'd made almost monthly since John's incarceration.

He and Adele talked for hours the afternoon before in a café near McNulty's apartment. They'd mapped out a number of possible plans, with Adele saying the best one would be for her to disappear with Johnny. She'd spoken to a lawyer, who wasn't encouraging. The court would first have to deny the grandparent rights, not at all a sure thing, and then would require Adele to go through an adoption process that had no guarantee of success.

At the prison, he went through the usual rigmarole; the interminable wait; the guards harried and irritated; the visitors frustrated and angry, as the short amount of time they had to visit with someone they cared about was frittered away. He was curious about the timing of the message from John, coming when he'd been thinking about him so much. It was as if his thinking about John had summoned his message.

John looked thinner when he walked through the door of the visitor's room ahead of the guard. His hair was close cropped, as it had been since he'd been in prison. Before prison, he'd worn his hair long and shaggy. It fit his image as he'd played the guitar and sung in quiet bars or coffeehouses. When John finally did meet his gaze, his expression, as always, was slightly mocking, slightly defensive—and embarrassed. He looked away before he spoke.

"I read about you. You shot a guy, Mr. Violence-Is-Never-the-Answer. I guess your time came when it was the answer."

"No. It wasn't."

John met his gaze again. "I've said that a few times myself."

"I never doubted you. I've always believed it was an accident."

John smirked. "Yeh. But you're out there and I'm in here. No charges against you?"

"I don't think so."

"Some guys get the breaks."

He wanted to say more. But John went back into his shell, discouraging more talk. "Is this why you wanted me to come?"

"That and something else." He hesitated.

"I've got change. Do you want something from the vending machines?"

They walked over to the machines and waited their turn. John got a canned root beer, chips, and a couple of candy bars. When they sat down again, John chewed on his candy bar and drank from his soda.

"And the something else?"

John's manner was different, more confident. "The girl who was killed, Emily Smith. I knew her."

"Her real name is Emily Yates. Are you sure it's the same girl?"

John nodded. "I knew she had a different name. Her father was a famous writer."

"Yes."

"You know anything about her kid?"

Ambler felt a thousand synapses go off. Every fiber of his body was alert. "Yes. What about him?"

"He's my son. I'm wondering what happens with him now she's dead—"

Ambler wasn't hearing. His head was spinning. "What did you say?"

"I went with Emily for a while."

"You're Johnny's father? Are you sure? How do you know?"

John smiled, not a smirk this time, a real smile. "Check the birth certificate. I gave it to Mom to keep for me. My name's on it."

Ambler felt his face light up. He was smiling at his son.

His son was smiling at him. "Just like yours on mine."

"Raymond. That's nothing to joke about."

"It's not a joke. I'm Johnny's grandfather. I found out from my son. Last night, I toured a few bars and found his mother. She has a copy of Johnny's birth certificate with some of John's stuff in a safe-deposit box."

"You're Johnny's grandfather? We can keep him. Oh my

God! It's a miracle." She was screaming and then she was crying. "What will you do? How does it work? What about Lisa Young and her lawyers?"

"I can't wait to talk to them."

"Will they let you keep him? You're a man, and you're old." She paused. "Well, not that old." She hesitated again and spoke carefully. "What about me, Raymond? You can keep him. What about me?"

"You can keep him, too. We'll work something out."

"Really?"

"Really." He heard the doubt in his voice.

"Can I tell Johnny?"

"You can tell Johnny but carefully. I'm not sure he'll understand it all."

Adele laughed. It was a pretty sound. He'd never really listened to her laugh before. "I'm not sure I understand it all. Do we have to keep hiding?"

"No. You can take him to your place, or bring him to my place."

Her tone changed. "You know he has to go to school. And he needs clothes. I bought him some things and shoes. But he needs his own things. . . ." She went on about so many things he hadn't thought of that she sounded so sure of. He couldn't keep up. "And we need to get him away from McNulty. He's a terrible influence. Johnny won a hundred dollars at the track yesterday. Now, he's talking about trifectas and five buck on the nose and sounds like Louie the Lip."